The
BREATH
BETWEEN
WAVES

The BREATH BETWEEN WAVES

~≈~

CHARLOTTE ANNE HAMILTON

Entangled Publishing, LLC
10940 S Parker Rd
Suite 327
Parker, CO 80134
rights@entangledpublishing.com

Embrace is an imprint of Entangled Publishing, LLC.

Edited by Jen Bouvier
Cover design by LJ Anderson/Mayhem Cover Creations
Cover photography by napa74/Adobe Stock
kanareva and vrvalerian/Deposit Photos
Christian Petersen and holgs/Getty Images

Manufactured in the United States of America

First Edition August 2021

embrace

At Entangled, we want our readers to be well-informed. If you would like to know if this book contains any elements that might be of concern for you, please check the book's webpage for details.

https://entangledpublishing.com/books/the-breath-between-waves

for Gran,
for never giving up on me
even when I gave up on myself

Boat Deck
LIFEBOATS
BRIDGE
SECOND CLASS ENTRANCE
FUNNELS

A-Deck
FIRST CLASS EXCLUSIVE PROMENADE DECK
GRAND STAIRCASE WITH "HONOUR AND
GLORY CROWNING TIME"

Bridge Deck
SECOND CLASS ENTRANCE
POOP DECK
SECOND CLASS SMOKING ROOM

TITANIC

C-Deck
THIRD CLASS
COMMON ROOM

D-Deck
SECOND CLASS
DINING ROOM

E-Deck
PENELOPE'S & RUBY'S
ROOM (E-56)
SCOTLAND ROAD

F-Deck
SWIMMING POOL
TURKISH BATHS
KENNELS

G-Deck
POST OFFICE

Orlop Decks/Tank Tops
CARGO
ENGINES
BOILERS

Chapter One

10TH APRIL 1912

The docks were wild.

Penelope had never seen anything like it.

She couldn't count the number of bodies; a huge variety of people from different backgrounds. She passed upper-class ladies with maids trailing behind them with their luggage. Young children ran off in front of their parents as they headed towards the steerage entrance.

Penelope tightened her hands around her bag as she stepped closer to her mother. She was so focused on ensuring that she didn't get separated, she hadn't had a chance to pay attention to the ship. It wasn't until they stepped into the line for Second Class passengers that she finally allowed herself a moment to look.

There were no words that suited the ship.

Four yellow and black funnels were spaced along the deck on top, and countless windows adorned the ship's body, together with white, black, and red horizontal stripes.

"She's magnificent," Penelope whispered.

Her father gave a soft laugh. "Isn't she just?" He slowly shook his head in wonder. "She's nearly nine hundred feet long and one hundred across, and more than that tall." There was a sparkle in his eyes that she couldn't recall ever seeing. "If all goes well with the new job, it is my dream to take a trip back here in First Class… It would be a wonder."

Penelope wasn't sure what shocked her more: that her father had planned to return to Scotland at all, or that he was actually sharing a *dream* with her. She was so bemused that she couldn't form a reply.

Her mother went through the entrance first, and Penelope followed closely, knowing that there was no way off anymore.

She was aboard, and she was leaving Scotland.

That thought didn't keep her attention for long, however—she was mesmerised by the sheer beauty of her surroundings. The walls were white-painted wood, to match the linoleum of the floor. A darker wooden rail sat along the centre of each wall panel, with elegant, electric wall scones placed intermittently to provide lighting.

A young man beckoned them to the reception desk.

"Mr. and Mrs. Samuel Fletcher, and Miss Penelope Fletcher." Her father's voice was straight to the point, not even bothering with returning the young man's "Hello." Penelope winced and offered the steward a small smile when his gaze flicked over to her, wishing that the ground would swallow her whole.

The steward merely turned his attention to the folder in front of him, glancing down the long list before ticking three times. He smiled and waved his arm out to the side.

"This way, Mr. Fletcher, and I'll show you and your wife to your room." He took off without a backwards glance. Penelope wondered if she had been forgotten about, but he added, "Miss Fletcher will be sharing a room, as you are aware. Thankfully, it is only a few doors down from where you and Mrs. Fletcher will be staying."

Penelope was just able to hold her snort of laughter in. Her parents would not care if she were two doors away or down in steerage. For the twenty years of her life, she had drifted through their house like a visitor, feeling like an afterthought. She didn't think it would change now.

"Your luggage is already in your rooms. Linens are changed daily, and you may request a bath from any of the stewards." The steward's pace was so brisk that Penelope had to trot to keep up. Her heart hammered in her chest.

He said a few more things, giving them directions to the dining hall and some of the amenities, but Penelope hardly listened. Mostly because the things she was interested in— the gymnasium, the saltwater swimming pool, the Café Parisien—were all restricted to First Class, which she was not. She vowed to take some time, after the ship had set sail, to just wander and try and create a map in her mind of the areas she was able to explore.

They were brought to a stop as the steward opened a door and ushered her mother and father inside. Penelope waited in the corridor, stepping up against the wall to let other people pass by and take a brief minute to catch her breath.

She had just gotten her breathing back under control when the steward reappeared. Penelope straightened, once again offering him a gentle smile, which he returned this time.

"Right this way, Miss Fletcher," he stated and took off again.

Licking her lips, Penelope took a deep breath and asked, "Is it too much to hope that the room has a map inside?"

The steward glanced over his shoulder. "You'll get the hang of it soon enough, Miss Fletcher." His voice had a different twang to it, an accent she was pretty certain was American, but she had no idea *where* in America he hailed from.

The things that Penelope knew about America could barely fill a thimble. It seemed utterly ironic that she would now be calling it her home. A thought that filled her with distaste. She'd been born in Scotland and had hoped to die there. Scotland meant loved ones and cherished memories. She knew no one in America. Perhaps it would be where she lived, but it would never be her home.

"I pray you're right," Penelope said to the steward. "I do hope to eat on this journey." She allowed herself a small chuckle and fell into a comfortable silence as they made their way down the corridor.

Before they reached the end, he stopped and turned to her. "And this is your room, Miss Fletcher."

He reached for the handle and pushed the door open as Penelope took a deep breath and held it in her lungs. She let it out in a long gust when she realised that the room was empty—her roommate obviously hadn't made it aboard yet.

The steward stepped aside to let her enter and closed the door behind her.

There was a small floral sofa off to the side. Dark mahogany wood extended through the entire cabin, from the bunks against the wall to two cabinets.

Penelope turned towards the beds. She couldn't remember ever sleeping on a bunk, never mind on a ship.

Placing her case on the bottom bed, Penelope sat down. She was surprised at how soft the mattress seemed as she smoothed her hands along the covers. There was a faint rumble from the engines that she hoped she would grow accustomed to, otherwise she would never get any sleep.

"No turning back now, Penelope." She took a deep breath and closed her eyes. "The New World means a new life."

A distinct click forced Penelope's eyes open, and she bolted to her feet, narrowly missing banging her head against the top bed.

Her eyes landed on the opening door, watching as another steward stepped aside and let a young woman enter.

A large hat with blue and white silk flowers was perched on her head, and she wore a light cotton and lace dress that flew elegantly around her person. Her blonde hair was pinned beneath the hat in messy curls, and her skin had a beautiful pink tinge to it. She looked like an angel.

"Oh!" The woman drew to a halt as she took in Penelope. An easy smile spread across her face. "May I assume that you're to be my roommate during this journey?" When she stepped farther into the room, the steward left and closed the door behind him.

"I am. My name is Penelope Fletcher." As Penelope held her hand out, she noticed that the stranger's hands were clad in crocheted lace gloves.

"Charmed." She had an Irish lilt to her voice that had grown more noticeable after she'd heard Penelope speak. "Ruby Cole, at your service." Her plump lips tugged into a grin, and she gently squeezed Penelope's hand.

Ruby then released her hand, looking around the room. "So this is it? I must confess, it is nicer than I dared hope." She slowly turned in a circle. "I see you've already claimed a bed." Her eyes rested on Penelope's case that she'd left on the lower bunk.

Colour flooded Penelope's cheeks. "I hope you don't mind, I was worried about being on the top..."

Ruby carelessly waved a hand. "Have no fear. I have no preference." She had a small purse looped around her wrist, and as she spoke, she slid it free and placed it by the pillow on the top bed. "And I'm rather used to sea voyages. My family makes the journey across to America quite often."

Penelope's eyes widened. "Truly?" Ruby nodded once, that easy smile still in place. "I've never been on a ship before," Penelope confessed, even though she felt a little like a fool for saying such a thing.

Ruby's thick brows puckered, and her smile grew. "Well, perhaps it is a good thing that you picked the bottom bunk. We shall also have to move a bucket nearby, just in case."

Penelope's cheeks felt like they were aflame, and she wondered what sort of a mess she looked like. Her hair was in disarray due to having had no care for more than an easy bun, and now her cheeks were red from embarrassment. Sometimes she wondered just what Caroline had ever seen in her.

At the thought of the ex-lover she'd had to leave behind, Penelope flinched, turning her back on Ruby to examine the piles of luggage that had been brought to the rooms. They mostly contained clothes, but she had managed to sneak an embroidery hoop and some threads inside with help of the maid.

"Shall we share the wardrobe, or will we live out of our suitcases?" Ruby asked.

Before Penelope could reply, a loud sound shook the ship, causing her to give a startled yelp. Her hand flew to her heart, and she felt it hammering against her ribs.

Ruby placed a hand on Penelope's shoulder, and the touch tingled Penelope's skin, even through the cotton of her dress. It did nothing to ease the rapid beating of her heart, however, especially when her grip tightened as their eyes met.

"Calm down, dear, it is just the horn to signal that we're getting ready to launch." Ruby's touch lingered for a moment longer before she clasped her hands together in front of her. "Do you wish to go up to the deck? I heard talk that there is a huge crowd here to see the ship off."

Penelope nodded and followed Ruby through the corridors towards the stairs. It seemed that other people had had similar ideas, for the entire staircase was packed, both up towards the deck and down towards the engines.

The quick journey, which should have taken no more than five minutes, ended up taking fifteen. Penelope started to worry that they would miss it all, but when they stepped onto the deck, the ship had barely moved. It was leaving at a painfully slow pace.

Penelope had believed that the crowd on the docks would have thinned out by now, but it seemed even busier. The people looked tiny from here as they cheered and waved farewell to loved ones.

"Is it always like this?" she enquired when she felt Ruby step up to her side at the railing.

Ruby answered her with a carefree laugh. "No, I'm afraid not. This"—she spread her arm out towards the cheering crowds—"is because the ship is setting a precedent, both as the largest ship afloat and the first ship to sail to America from Southampton. If it goes well, Daddy reckons all ships will soon be sailing from here."

Ruby started to wave back at the crowd. It took Penelope only a second of hesitation before she joined in.

"So…in many ways…*RMS Titanic* is making history?"

"Exactly." Ruby smiled as she continued to wave. "And everyone loves to be a part of history."

Chapter Two

Penelope still didn't want to move while the ship set sail. Even after Ruby had left to find her family, she had stayed on the deck.

She found it difficult to believe that it would be the last time she would ever see Britain—at least for a while.

It was only when the sea stretched on before her and a cool wind started to chill her bones that Penelope wrapped her arms around her midriff and made her way back below deck.

She remembered the deck—E Deck—but navigating there proved a touch more difficult, especially since every room seemed to be a cabin and she'd been so anxious when boarding that she hadn't made a note of their room number.

Penelope pursed her lips, glancing around to find something familiar to ground herself.

Her pace was slow, taking in every little detail as she walked. She could tell from all the doors that she passed that E Deck was largely cabins for all classes. She passed door numbers as high as E-200, and it made her head swim, wondering how many rooms there were in total and how many people such a mighty ship could hold.

When she turned a corner, she was thankful to see Ruby leaving a nearby room. She was pretty certain it *wasn't* their room, however, and so she called out, "Miss Cole!"

Her roommate drew to a halt, turning to face her with wide eyes and raised eyebrows. "Oh! Miss Fletcher, please, call me Ruby!" She smiled. "What can I do for you?"

"I'm...afraid I'm a little lost? I'm trying to find our room so that I can find my parents' room to see what we're doing for luncheon."

The teasing nature of Ruby's smile only served to make Penelope's face redden further. Her hands fisted the folds in her skirt that cascaded from the pleats at her waist.

"You weren't too far away. At the very least, you'll remember now that our room number is E-56."

Penelope didn't want to admit that, despite now knowing the room number, she would probably still get lost. It was such a huge ship, and she was painfully aware that there were so many different directions and so many corridors. It made her wonder how she was going to cope in Massachusetts with all its bustle.

Ruby stepped forwards, winding her arm through Penelope's.

As soon as her fingers settled in the crook of Ruby's elbow, all she could focus on—and *look* at—was the way they nestled so perfectly against her as she led her down the corridor, thankfully in the same direction she had been heading.

There were so many layers between them—Penelope's coat and dress, Ruby's gloves—but that didn't seem to matter. As Penelope stared at where they touched, she was pretty positive she could *feel* Ruby's skin against her own...feel her breath against her lips...feel her moan in her ear.

Surprised at the direction of her thoughts, Penelope cleared her throat and tried to remember what Ruby had been saying. "Then...my parents must be in Room E-62..." Penelope declared, distracting herself.

When they stopped in front of the door, she was all too aware that Ruby was still there, watching her with that damnable smile on her pink lips. "Will you knock to see if you are correct? Or just stand there, hoping it'll magically open before you?" Her Irish accent was so strong, her tease rolling off her tongue so quickly, it seemed to be one long word. And even though it was completely different from Penelope's, it made her feel a bit less homesick.

Catching herself as she bit her lower lip, Penelope rapped her knuckles against the door. Ruby smiled before moving down towards their shared bedroom.

Please let this be the right room. I shall die of embarrassment if an unfamiliar face answers, she thought as she heard the door handle click. Her breath left her in a gush as her father's clean-shaven, sharp face greeted her, his chestnut brown hair combed to one side.

From the corner of her eye, she saw Ruby grin before she stepped into their room.

Penelope turned her attention back towards her father, offering him a small smile. "I just wanted to see whether we had plans for luncheon. If a table had been booked or..." She trailed off as her father stepped aside to let her enter.

"We have a table booked in the dining room. It is rather soon, so we're getting ready to go. We had planned to see if you wished to join us," her mother answered as her father shut the door and headed to the sofa. Her parents' room was pretty much the exact same as her own, even down to the bunks, the bottom of which held her mother's nightgown.

"Of course. I didn't even realise that was the time." Penelope knew it had been around noon when the ship had finally left Southampton. They weren't crossing the Atlantic yet but heading to a place in France to pick up and drop off more passengers. "Let me go and freshen up."

Before either of them could say a word, she turned and left their room.

It was strange how they were the people to whom she owed her life, and yet, spending more time with her parents than necessary just made her uncomfortable. There was always a suffocating silence that made her feel unwelcome. It almost made her wish she were married, so she didn't have to constantly be around them.

When she entered her room, she found Ruby on the floor by her luggage, sorting through the clothes.

She had removed her hat and taken her blonde hair down, letting it cascade down her back in soft ringlets. It seemed so intimate, so improper, to see her in such a carefree, undone state, but Penelope would have to get used to it—they would be sharing a room for a week, and that meant that certain boundaries had to be lowered.

"I do hope that you got the right room." Ruby stopped her organising and turned to face Penelope, lips tugged into a smirk that made Penelope want to trace it with her tongue.

"I did, yes. I just came back to get ready for luncheon…"

Penelope hovered slightly, glancing down at Ruby for a moment. Then she stepped around her luggage to get to her own and quickly sorted through her belongings until she found a lavender cardigan and pulled a brooch out of her small jewellery box.

Once she had everything she needed, she removed her coat—a beautiful navy wool decorated with buttons and a capelet draped over the shoulders. Then she pulled the cardigan on and secured it just at the top edge of her corset with the brooch.

She had no doubt that her father wouldn't be too pleased,

but she wasn't going to sit through the meal in her coat, regardless of if she was surrounded by strangers or not.

"It's a bit of a shame we're not on the other side of the ship," Ruby announced. She still sat on the floor, sorting through her belongings. Penelope watched as she removed a large, leather-bound book from her case and carefully set it on the floor.

Penelope's gaze was focused on the book as she asked, "How so?"

"The crew have taken to calling the corridor on that side Scotland Road." Ruby's plump lips curved into a wry grin. "It seemed fitting for you."

Penelope finally turned away from the book. "Why would they call it that?" Her father had told her that the ship had been built in Ireland, was registered in Liverpool and set sail from Southampton. What did it have to do with Scotland?

Ruby cocked her head to side. "The street in Liverpool? A lot of the crew hail from there…you've never heard of it?"

Penelope felt her cheeks beginning to redden. "No. I've never been out of Scotland before now."

Ruby *hmm*ed, saying nothing more for a long moment. Penelope worried that perhaps she had proven herself an utter fool now, and Ruby would want nothing more to do with her, when she spoke again. "It's my stamp collection." Ruby reached for the book and flipped it open, revealing countless stamps placed on thick paper, with small notes written underneath.

Ruby turned it around and allowed Penelope a better look, finding that the notes contained information about where and when Ruby had gotten the stamp, as well as some small comments. "Mammy started it with me." Ruby turned the book back around and gently brushed her fingers over the pages. "Every time I go over, the family has some new ones for me."

Penelope didn't know what to say. She had known that stamp collecting was a thing that people did; she had just never met anyone who did it. Or been inclined herself.

Ruby closed her book over and set it aside, behind herself, almost as if to protect it from Penelope's gaze. She smiled at Penelope. "I must suggest you try the scalloped veal when you get to the dining room. I've heard it is rather delicious on the White Star Line ships."

"Oh!" She tried to hide her surprise at the sudden change in conversation. She swallowed and offered Ruby a smile. "Thank you. I shall give it a try."

Not wanting to linger awkwardly, Penelope hurried off to head to luncheon with her parents.

It seemed that they both had a better sense of direction than she did, for they found it without any sort of trouble. She wished that it had rubbed off on her.

On Ruby's recommendation, she ordered the scalloped veal, along with a lemon tart. She wasn't really *surprised* that Ruby had been right about the meat being utterly delicious, she just hadn't expected to enjoy it as much as she had.

Once they had finished their luncheon, she joined her mother and father on a walk around the Bridge Deck.

On more than one occasion, Penelope felt her gaze flicker to the Promenade Deck above them. It was mostly concealed from view thanks to the low walls, but each end of the ship was open to allow the First Class passengers some variety in their walking area. It also meant that, if the weather was bad, they would still be able to walk and enjoy the view without getting wet, thanks to most of it being covered by the Boat Deck.

The women she saw up there wore the most stunning dresses, paired with large hats that were decorated with fruit or flowers or birds.

Every time she caught herself staring, she would quickly

avert her gaze and try to focus on what her father was saying as he explained the ship's engineering and design elements that Penelope didn't particularly care about.

Penelope clasped her hands in front of her body as she looked up. From where she stood, she could see not only the Promenade Deck, but the Boat Deck at the very top, those huge funnels giving off a light-grey smoke as the coal-powered engines pushed the ship through the waves.

"There...seems to be very few lifeboats up there," she said, raising her finger to briefly point. Her father followed her gaze with his brows furrowed. "Are there more on the other side or somewhere else?"

Her father was silent for a second before he let out a low laugh as he shook his head. "Oh, my dear Penelope. This ship is *unsinkable*. The lifeboats are purely a precaution." He reached out and pinched her cheek with more force than he probably realised, and she flinched away from the touch. "You are a woman, Penelope, you shouldn't worry your pretty head about such a thing. This ship was built by some of the finest men."

Penelope gritted her teeth, taking a deep breath in through her nose. Before she could say something she'd regret, she made her excuses and quickly retreated to her cabin.

Thankfully, this time she didn't get lost.

Still, she was relieved when she entered and found Ruby stretched out across the sofa, reading a small book—*The Wind in the Willows* by Kenneth Grahame, Penelope saw—for she could use the distraction.

Ruby's hair was braided down her back. Penelope could only assume that she had pinned it up when she had left for luncheon and had then promptly taken it down when she'd returned.

At Penelope's sudden entrance, Ruby looked up from her

book before folding it over, keeping her place with her fingers still trapped between the pages. "Goodness, you look riled up about something."

"I..." She shook her head and leaned heavily against the door, pressing her hand against her stomach and feeling the stiffness of her corset underneath. "What is it with men believing that, just because we're women, we know nothing? That we can form no opinions of our own?"

She promptly regretted her words when she realised that Ruby might really be a traditionalist. She didn't know her. And maybe she'd just made things awkward with the woman she'd be sharing a room with for an entire week.

Ruby raised her brows high. "That is because men are birdbrained fools," she said flippantly, and returned to her reading.

It seemed to take her a long moment before she realised that Penelope was still just standing there, leaning heavily against the door and staring at her, eyes wide with wonder.

When she did, she cocked her head to the side and grinned. "I do hope I didn't shock you." Her blue gaze was teasing, and she spoke quickly, which made the *H*s in certain words disappear completely. "But I meant what I said. There was this one lad back home who *refused* to believe me when I said I wasn't interested in him. It took me being on the arm of another man for the message to finally sink in." Ruby finished with a loud sigh and a roll of her eyes. When Penelope didn't say a word in reply, she asked, "Everything all right over there?"

Penelope pushed away from the door with a shake of her head. She swallowed, trying to hide her disappointment. Of course, it seemed only plausible that Ruby would be interested in men—hadn't Caroline always said that what Penelope felt wasn't common?

"It is. Thank you for understanding." She ducked down

to sit on the edge of her bed.

"Not a problem." Ruby turned her wrist, glancing at her watch. She tucked a small bookmark between the pages of her book and set it aside on a rather large pile of books that hadn't been there earlier. It contained many familiar titles that Penelope had read at a young age. "I must go, I'm afraid. If I don't see you at dinner, I'll see you before bed."

She was gone before Penelope could reply or even enquire about the children's novels Ruby had brought aboard. Her hands covered her burning cheeks, and she allowed herself to fall backwards, lying down on her bed with a groan.

She did not mean it like that, Penelope hissed at herself, closing her eyes with a sigh. She readjusted herself to get a bit more comfortable, keeping her feet dangling over the edge. She didn't want to let her boots touch the clean linens.

Penelope forced her mind to quiet, trying to ignore the thoughts of Ruby, of Caroline, of her parents. She focused on nothing more than her breathing until, without really meaning to, she drifted off to sleep.

Chapter Three

Penelope was awoken by a gentle shake of her shoulder. She groaned and turned towards the source, frowning when the face before her wasn't her mother's.

Instead, it was a blonde beauty with large blue eyes and plump lips pulled into a dazzling smile. It took her a long moment to even remember that she knew Ruby.

"What time is it?" Penelope reached up to wipe the sleep from her eyes.

Ruby stepped back from her. "Just after six on the ship's time. You've not been sleeping *too* long, but I thought you'd like to see Cherbourg now that we've docked."

Penelope pushed herself from the bed, dusting down her clothes and tutting at how dishevelled she looked. There was a large crease down the side of her skirt.

"Cherbourg?" she repeated. France had always been one of those places she wished she could have visited. Everything seemed so forwards, so fashionable, so beautiful…

Pushing such thoughts to the back of her mind, Penelope focused on Ruby. Her hair was fully pinned up, and she still wore the gorgeous lace dress that made Penelope wonder why she was in Second Class when she looked like she belonged with those ladies on the Promenade Deck. She would have fitted in easily.

"We won't be here for long, an hour or so at most as I understand it. There aren't as many people to pick up here as there were in Southampton. It will probably be the same with Queenstown tomorrow."

"Queenstown?" At Ruby's nod, Penelope frowned. "In Ireland?" Penelope's mind rarely worked quickly on the best of days, never mind when she had just been woken up from a nap. She pinched the bridge of her nose. "I'm sorry. I just... If we're stopping in Ireland, why were you and your family in Southampton?"

Ruby's thick brows pulled down, almost until her eyelashes touched them. "I was born in Ireland, but my family moved to England when my father got a job as a valet to a duke about ten years ago."

"Is that the reason you're going to America now?"

"Sort of? My father is up in First Class, sleeping in a small room in the duke's suite, for valets and ladies' maids. We have family in New York. They emigrated a few years back. When the duke visits America, we stay with the relatives, and Daddy visits whenever he can." Ruby then smoothed her hand down over her dress. She seemed to notice Penelope take in the splendour of it, for her lips twisted into a grin. "It's a hand-me-down from the duke's daughter. She doesn't have a maid to give her old clothes to, so because Daddy has been with them for so long, they give him her clothes for me."

"I bet it suits you better than it did the duke's daughter." The words were out of her mouth before she could stop them. Already, she could feel her cheeks begin to warm, and she cleared her throat in a desperate attempt to distract herself, which only made the flushing worse. "So... Does that mean you'll be returning to England? You're not *moving* to America?" Penelope tried her hardest not to feel disheartened at that thought.

There was a twinkle in Ruby's blue eyes that spoke of mischief as her grin shifted slightly, turning to something a bit more...self-deprecating. "Unless I find a stunning husband in the couple of months that we're there, then yes. I shall be returning to England at the end of it all."

Of course. Penelope wanted to smack herself—first Caroline, going off and getting married without a word to her, and now Ruby, her latest crush, had plans to marry as well.

Would she ever find someone who felt like she did?

Then again, she knew that her parents would be desperate to see her married as well. And she wouldn't be able to convince them otherwise.

"I understand that feeling all too well," she said instead of voicing any of her thoughts. "I know that as soon as we're settled, I'll be expected to do whatever I can to secure a husband." Penelope gnawed on her lower lip. Ruby hadn't shied away from her outburst over her father earlier, so Penelope knew that she wasn't a *traditionalist,* but whether she believed in women's rights was another thing. Still, there was something in her gut that told her to take the risk.

"I asked Mother if she'd let me attend university, get an education—nothing too extreme, I was thinking English or History—before I settle down, but I doubt that'll happen. She'll have to talk it over with my father, and he will say no. I know it."

Ruby shook her head. "Do you ever get tired of listening to men? Of having to run every little thing you do by one?" She pushed a stray curl behind her ear. Her lips curved into a wry grin. "Though, I must confess, I don't know what's worse—a lifetime in America or a lifetime in England."

Her words startled a laugh from Penelope. That had been half the reason she had fought so hard to stay behind.

Ruby offered her a smile. "Come. We can continue this conversation on deck as we take in the wonders of France."

Penelope dusted herself off before thinking better of it and pulling her coat from the wardrobe. At the very least, it would cover the wrinkles that her nap had pressed into her clothes.

Ruby reached for an embroidered navy shawl and wrapped it around her shoulders. It offered a stunning contrast to the white of her dress. It was so delicate, and from the way Ruby's hand smoothed over it, Penelope could tell it had a special meaning to her.

Penelope caught Ruby's gaze and said, "It's braw."

Ruby's hands once more caressed the fabric. "It was Mammy's." Ruby cleared her throat and straightened. "We'd best get a move on. Don't want to miss it."

Ruby took off and Penelope followed, fastening her coat buttons.

When they stepped onto the deck, Penelope felt her heart leap to her throat.

The docks were just as busy as Southampton's had been, with people cheering as *Titanic* lowered its anchor ready for the smaller boats that would bring passengers to the ship and take those wanting to disembark ashore.

Penelope stumbled towards the railing so that she could get a better look at the city. There were many dock buildings around her, warehouses and offices—shops making the most of such a busy area. It was still light enough that the gaslights didn't need to be lit, but the sun was slowly setting, casting the area in a beautiful orange hue.

"It is beautiful, isn't it? People always say that, after a while, seeing new sights becomes boring. But I don't see how that's possible." Ruby's hands tightened around the railing. They were so close to Penelope's that all she had to do was reach out with her pinkie finger and they'd be touching. Instead, she kept her fingers to herself, tightening them further around the metal lest they betray her. "Even if you had to visit the same place," Ruby continued. "Each time there'd be something different because the people there would be different—the world is always shifting, changing. And it's always stunning to see."

Penelope *hmm*ed and settled her elbows onto the railing, watching children run about the docks excitedly as their parents shouted after them. Her attention then moved towards the odd-looking boats that were bringing new passengers aboard.

One held those in First Class and Second Class, if their general appearance was anything to go by. She saw a middle-aged man with short hair and a long, slightly chubby face, who was with a woman dressed in the latest fashion, wearing a large ostrich feather on her hat and several strings of pearls around her neck.

It was a sharp contrast to the other boat, which seemed to be carrying Third Class passengers. Most of them were thin, their clothes basic and functional rather than decorative.

She knew that so many in Third Class were joining relatives across the ocean and no doubt were excited to begin this new chapter with their loved ones.

But Penelope just wanted to return to Scotland. It was her home, where her friends, Millicent, Deborah, and Emma were. Everything about it was familiar, from the green hills and the dreich weather to the words people said and the way they said them.

Nothing about America was going to give the same feeling of safety and security that Scotland gave her. And, most importantly, America didn't have her granny.

Her right hand moved from the railing to clasp her

granny's locket around her neck. She let her fingers trail over the engraving as she watched the people board from the smaller ship.

"That is pretty," Ruby said after a long moment. Honestly, Penelope had forgotten she was still there.

Penelope readjusted her grip so that it was cradled in her palm, allowing Ruby a better look. "Granny gave it to me. There's a pressed thistle inside, so I can remember her and Scotland whenever I feel homesick." She flicked it open to show Ruby. "There used to be a photograph of my grandfather in there, but she must have taken it out when she gave it to me."

"That was sweet of her. It is good to have reminders of home."

"It's her I miss more than anything, truthfully. She's always been there for me, always sticking up for me. I remember once when I was a young girl, this other girl was teasing me—we shared a nanny, so we were often watched together. I had no idea that Granny had noticed until the girl's mother showed up. I have never seen anyone threaten and insult someone as gracefully and tactfully as Granny. The girl never bothered me again." Penelope lowered the locket and turned towards Ruby. "What about you? Do you have any reminders of home? Of Ireland?"

Ruby's hands smoothed over her shawl. "Not really. Mammy was still alive when we moved... Another reason for the move was because we had no family left in Ireland. Gran, Mhamó, Papa, and Dhaideo were all gone... I was twelve when we moved to England, fifteen when my mother died. Too old to forget what I'd had before, but too young to think of keeping a memento. All I have is my stamp book, which Mammy started when she was a girl, and this." She tugged the navy shawl further around her body until the ends were tucked firmly under her arms.

Penelope's throat was tight. She'd only ever had Granny. Her father's parents had died before she'd been born, and her mother's father had died not long after.

And even though she and her parents never seemed to get on, the three of them acutely aware that Penelope was an accident they weren't too pleased about, they were still there. They looked after her and raised her right, and she'd be devastated should anything happen to them.

"I'm sorry," she whispered.

"It is what it is," Ruby replied. Silence washed over them as they both turned their gazes back to France, watching the passengers continue to board.

By the time the ship moved again, the sky had started to darken, and Penelope was glad that she had put her coat on. The wind was picking up, and she noticed Ruby wrapping her arms around herself.

Pushing away from the railing, Penelope smiled at her. "You look like you're going to drop. Let's get you back below deck for some warmth."

Ruby laughed as she followed Penelope. "I wish it were as simple as that. Dinner will be soon—I believe we have a table booked at half-past-eight."

They went down the staircase, and when they reached E Deck and started their way down the corridor to their rooms, they passed a clock that made both of them stop.

There were only twenty minutes until Ruby's dinner booking, and Penelope was running late, too. "Oh."

"I have never been more glad that you never change the first night of a voyage," Ruby said.

"You don't? Why?"

"Mostly because the luggage is rarely organised in time. We have been rather lucky, and I assume that's due to our room number, but I am willing to bet most other passengers don't have theirs."

"I'm a little relieved to hear that, then. My parents have ours booked in five minutes." Penelope laughed as she rubbed her forehead and tried her best to smooth her hair. She had been in such a rush to see Cherbourg that she'd forgotten to put on her hat.

She hoped that her father hadn't seen her. She remembered coming back from an outing with Emma and Millicent one day—they had been walking through some hidden fields and, in a moment of childish glee, had started a game of tag. Their hats had been cumbersome in the wind, so they had removed them. When it had been time to return home, Penelope couldn't find her hatpin, and the wind had been too brisk to keep her hat atop her head without it. Her father had caught her and given a long spiel about how a young woman had to be modest and virtuous, and how no daughter of his would ever be considered clatty.

It had been rather difficult keeping a straight face as her friends had stood a few feet away, making funny faces at her and her father.

"I cannot believe we stood up there for that long..." Penelope trailed off, her eyes darting to Ruby's, and tried to ignore the way her heart leapt to her throat at the soft smile on her face. It was so strange how similar she was in appearance to Caroline—the same blonde hair and blue eyes and soft features. But that was where the similarities ended.

Caroline was always trying to appear grander than she was. Everything Caroline did was thought over meticulously. Ruby held herself with the sort of carefree, beautiful abandon that Caroline could never hope to achieve, even though it seemed to be her life's goal.

Yet the most terrifying part wasn't that Penelope was attracted to her. What terrified her was just how *easy* it was to spend time around this perfect stranger.

There was something in Ruby's eyes now that Penelope

couldn't decipher.

She swallowed, wanting nothing more than to ask what she was thinking, but decided against it. She had to attend her dinner. She didn't want her parents taking away the freedom she had on this ship because she couldn't be trusted to keep simple appointments.

"I don't think I'll have time to freshen up after all," Penelope said as she drew to a halt. "I'd best hurry to the dining room now, before my parents send the stewards searching for me."

With an awkward laugh and a wave of her hand, Penelope started to retrace her steps back towards the stairs to go to the dining room on D Deck. She didn't even give Ruby a chance to reply, and by the time Penelope reached the end of the corridor and turned back, she was nowhere to be seen.

Penelope stopped and leaned against the wall.

She ground her knuckles in her eyes, cursing herself. *You are not doing this. You are not developing a crush on someone else so soon after Caroline. I forbid it!*

Penelope took a deep breath and pushed away from the wall, ready to join her parents in the dining room.

And yet, as she walked, she was pretty sure she felt her heart laughing at her foolish belief that she had any say in what it did or did not do.

Chapter Four

When Penelope returned to their room after dinner, it was empty.

She was more than grateful for that. She wasn't sure she could deal with having to speak to Ruby right now. Not after the realisation that a silly crush had already started to develop after a day.

Not even a day! Less than a day! Honestly!

Scoffing, Penelope moved towards her luggage.

After changing into her nightgown and placing her clothes back in her cases, she sat on her bed and started to untangle her hair from the wild mess it had turned into over the course of the day.

Her lips curled in distaste as it fell over her shoulder, reaching just under her rib cage. Grabbing her brush, she divided her hair into sections and started brushing it into something more manageable.

She had just finished, and was in the process of braiding it, when the door opened and Ruby entered. Her eyes were heavy with sleep. "I cannot tell you how jealous I am that you're in your nightclothes already," she said with a soft laugh as she let her braid fall down her back. She then moved over to her suitcases and pulled out her nightgown. "Do you mind if I dress in here, or would you rather I go to one of the bathrooms?"

The very thought of having Ruby undress in front of her made Penelope's mind go blank—as if someone had poured cold water over burning coal inside her head. She distracted herself by looking for her ribbon to tie her hair. "No, no, it's fine." She tied off her braid and tried to smile at Ruby. "It hardly seems fair to make you change somewhere else and then have to walk back here, especially when you look so tired."

I'll just have to face the wall and pretend I'm not thinking about what you look like.

Some colour started to spread across Ruby's face. For once, it wasn't Penelope who was blushing like a fool. Though she had to wonder what she had said—she *really* hoped she hadn't said that last thought aloud.

"Thank you, I am shattered. My brother and niece were playing hide-and-seek across the *whole* of the Boat Deck. You wouldn't think there'd be so many places for a child to hide there, but trust me, there are." Ruby rolled her eyes and stifled a yawn before she started to remove her clothes.

Penelope grinned. "That explains the books on the table," she said before she shuffled under her covers, turning away from Ruby to give her some privacy as she undressed. She pulled her knees up to her chest and folded her hands under her head.

"Yes. If the book is present, they force themselves awake to read more and more. I realised quickly that, if I read ahead and recite what I can remember, they fall asleep after a chapter or so."

Penelope made a sound in acknowledgment as she

focused her gaze on the wall— it was metal, and she was near a joint. She wanted to reply, but she was afraid of what would come out should she try. Instead, she distracted herself by counting the rivets that joined the two pieces together. Yet no matter how hard she tried, she couldn't get past five, because by the time she got to that, her resolve had weakened, and she was trying to picture what Ruby was doing—what she would look like.

An image of her in nothing but white stockings tied with silk garters came to her mind, and she swallowed hard.

It seemed to take forever and yet no time at all before the room was encompassed in darkness as Ruby turned off the lights before pulling herself onto the top bunk and shuffling underneath the covers. "So, how was your first day aboard a ship?" Ruby asked, in a voice soft as a whisper.

"Not as devastating as I believed it would be," Penelope answered, her voice just as soft as Ruby's. "And this motion isn't quite as bad either... You get used to it quite quickly."

"Most people do. It's only a very few that find it too much and spend their journey locked in their cabin." Penelope could hear the smile in her voice. She wished that she could see Ruby's face. "So... What brings you aboard?"

"Father accepted a new job." Penelope stared at the wood that made up the slats of Ruby's bed, noticing how the mattress dipped from her weight. "He's a mathematics teacher. He's...terribly clever. But he wasn't happy with his old position and so he started applying for new jobs at more prestigious universities. He told Mother and me that there was a good chance it would mean moving to England... Then he announced that he'd been offered a position at some college in Massachusetts and had accepted, without even talking it over with Mother." She rolled her eyes in the darkness. "But that's a man's prerogative, though, isn't it?" An inelegant scoff broke free from her lips.

Ruby was silent for a moment before she made a sympathetic noise. "So you had to leave everyone you knew and loved without any warning?"

Penelope's heart tightened as images of Caroline and her friends were conjured in her head. She could see Caroline staring at her in shock as she had given the news of her imminent move, and watched as it changed to chagrin as she'd said that Penelope didn't need to do what her parents wished her to. Millicent and Deborah had been more excited than she, seeing the opportunities rather than what it would mean leaving behind.

Penelope had been unable to match their excitement.

Her breath lodged in her throat. "Yes. You could say that. He told us maybe a month ago? I fought it every step—believed I would be able to stay with Granny and it would be enough... Obviously, that plan did not succeed." Her hand snaked up her torso and tightened around her locket, the press of the stones into her skin a rather reassuring pain.

"I'm sorry you had to deal with that."

Sighing, Penelope shuffled a little, turning her head farther into her pillow. Despite herself, her eyes were starting to feel heavy with sleep. "Don't be. There's nothing more to be done now, is there?" Taking a deep breath, Penelope pulled the covers tighter around her body. She somehow knew that Ruby was mulling over the right words to say, and so she took the decision away from her.

She wasn't in the mood to discuss it further, anyway.

Already, images of Caroline were cycling through her mind, and pain and worry were starting to grip at her throat. They hadn't parted on the best of terms, but nearly two years of her life had been consumed by Caroline—she had believed they would spend the rest of their lives together. Right up until Caroline had announced her engagement to a man, and Penelope had stopped fighting the move to America.

Now, her thoughts of the future weren't as pure or as sweet. She knew that she would be expected to marry some well-off man and give him countless children, even though men had never interested her and never would.

The carefree, blissful, almost childish hopes she'd had for a life with Caroline had disappeared into nothing, and there would be no way to get them back. She would merely be a pawn in the game of society.

"Goodnight, Ruby."

A small sigh escaped Ruby's lips before she replied with, "Goodnight, Penelope. I'm sure tomorrow will bring you a brighter day."

Those last words caused a smile to spread across Penelope's lips, which remained on her face even after she fell asleep.

Chapter Five

11TH APRIL 1912

Ruby was already gone when Penelope woke up the next morning.

While she got dressed, the memories of the dream she'd had last night came back to her.

Her mind had conjured up an alternate ending, where, as Ruby had undressed, she had watched and then moved to assist her, touching all the skin that was made visible with each article she'd removed. She'd followed her fingertips with her lips and tongue before pushing Ruby down onto her bed and continuing her exploration.

Her mouth had just reached the apex of her thighs when she had woken up.

How was she supposed to look Ruby in the eye again after she had thought about touching her so intimately? After she'd dreamt of so many ways to make her moan?

Stepping from her room, Penelope made her way towards her parents' cabin, hoping that they hadn't decided to leave for breakfast without her.

Her father greeted her as he opened the door, dressed and with his hat already in place. "Ah. Good. We were just about to come and fetch you."

The three of them walked in silence towards the dining room, and Penelope tried her hardest to ignore the way her eyes kept darting around, expecting Ruby to appear out of thin air. She wasn't sure she *wanted* that...not with her parents still with her.

They would no doubt take one look at her and disapprove—they usually did whenever they met someone Penelope liked. Not even her friend Emma, with all her social graces, had been able to impress them. They had never said as much to Penelope, but she had overheard them talking one night when they had thought her retired to her room. They had been concerned about Emma's eagerness to better herself. It had almost made her laugh. People were judged for not working hard enough to better their lot in life, and then Emma was also being judged for trying too hard to do just that.

Then again, looking back, Penelope realised that they hadn't been too wrong about Emma. After she had married a coal owner, she had drifted away from her old friends, as if they were no longer good enough for her. Especially since her husband was on the rise, and, if things continued on their way, would be looking at a peerage. And that had always been Emma's goal.

After they had ordered their food, Penelope felt as though the silence had gone on long enough.

She politely cleared her throat and offered them both a smile. "How was your first night aboard?"

"Not as bad as I expected," her mother said, returning her smile. "It was rather easy to fall asleep."

"Yes. She handles the sea remarkably well. It may be a

different story once we get out into the Atlantic, however," Father declared.

Why thank you for that reassuring note, Father. Penelope drew a deep breath and fell silent once more. Her gaze dropped to the table at first, as she wondered how long it would take before they reached Queenstown today and how many people would be boarding.

But she'd need to *ask* about that in order to get an answer, and considering how awkward the little conversation she'd had with her parents had been, she'd rather not. So she lifted her gaze and started to survey the dining room instead. There were several long rows of tables, causing people to mingle as they ate. Many were at different stages of their breakfast—some finishing up and readying to leave, others just being seated in their mahogany chairs, which swivelled to allow access since they were bolted to the floor. Her gaze briefly landed on the piano, a small upright one, by which a man sat playing "The Merry Widow."

Every person she looked at made her wonder what their story was. What was bringing them from Britain—or even France—to America? Were they holidaymakers, visiting family like Ruby, or were they making a permanent move like she was? She wished that she were able to ask.

As her gaze moved from table to table, she caught sight of a familiar face.

The second she saw Ruby seated two tables away, her gaze flitted back to the table, staring at the white cotton tablecloth. She gnawed on her lower lip until her mother gently nudged her with her foot to make her stop.

After offering her mother an apologetic glance, Penelope looked back towards Ruby's table.

Her hair was braided again, down both sides of her head, and secured at the nape of her neck in a long, loose ponytail. Instead of the intricate lacy dress she had worn yesterday, she wore something simpler with a shirtwaist, a fitted waistcoat in a gorgeous brown wool, and a tan skirt. And once again she wore her mother's shawl, though it had fallen from her shoulders and was pooled in the crooks of her elbows.

She looked stunning, like a proper lady, her back straight and not touching the back of the chair. One arm held the saucer whilst the other held her teacup—her pinkie raised daintily—as she took a long sip. It was only when she lowered it back to the table and resumed talking that Penelope realised Ruby had company.

The young man she sat with couldn't be much older than Penelope, maybe early twenties. He had the beginnings of a dark-brown moustache, one that would no doubt grow into something impressive like those she had seen on the men in First Class.

He wore a decent suit. It was perhaps a little bit tight, but she had no doubt that, at some point, it had fitted him perfectly. He smiled at Ruby, laughing at whatever she'd said and earning a giggle from her in response. Their interactions were so simple, so easy, that Penelope wondered if they had known each other before, or if they had just met at breakfast and things had clicked. She knew that happened to people, after all.

And who was to say that a chaperone wasn't sitting a few tables away, watching them like a hawk so that nothing untoward happened? Almost on instinct, Penelope's gaze scanned the room to see if someone was watching them, but she found no one.

If there was a chaperone, they were doing a terrible job.

She turned away from the sight and stared at her plate, wondering how she was supposed to eat when her stomach was roiling with a strange, unfamiliar jealousy. She poured herself some tea instead, willing her hands not to shake so that they wouldn't give her away to her parents.

It was at that very moment that she found herself missing Millicent. Mostly because she missed having someone to talk to. Even though she had never shared the truth about her and Caroline, she had shared everything else. She had sat quietly and allowed Penelope to rant about the little things that troubled her, like the times when her parents had been particularly harsh concerning her appearance or behaviour, or when one of the local lads had tried to court her and she had to work out a way to put him off without it reflecting poorly on her. Millicent had often given her ideas or playfully insulted her parents to make her feel better.

And throughout it all, the one who knew her every secret was Granny, her constant pillar of support.

Penelope's hand reached for her locket as her gaze moved back towards Ruby.

Her vision started to blur with tears, but she refused to let them fall. She considered running away, yet she knew that her parents wouldn't allow it. Once she had stormed off in the middle of dinner after defending the actions of the Women's Social and Political Union. They hadn't let her leave the house for a week after that, and she hadn't been allowed to join them for dinner until she had apologised profusely for her behaviour.

So, in order to avoid a repeat, she ate in silence, blinking long and hard to avoid any stray tears.

When a server came to take their plates away, Penelope made her excuses to her parents and left the dining room. She considered going back to her room, but decided against it. It was also Ruby's room, and she didn't want to run the risk of seeing her now.

So she took the elevator up to the deck, allowing the harsh wind to knock some sense into her.

She was thankful that despite the breeze, it was a warm day, and she didn't need to do much more than wrap her arms around herself to keep warm.

She rested her elbows against the metal of the railing and looked down at the water below her. It was a dark blue that appeared never-ending.

It sparkled as the sun beat down upon it, yet she was willing to bet that it was well below freezing.

Then, suddenly, she felt someone come up beside her.

"I wasn't sure whether to wake you or just let you sleep in this morning," Ruby said by way of greeting. She was so close to Penelope that every time she shuffled, their shoulders brushed, causing Penelope's heart to leap and soar. Ruby stood tall, looking out over the water, and Penelope wondered if she was searching for any sign of her homeland.

"I had been a little concerned that I had slept in, but thankfully, my body still has its own alarm clock." Penelope chanced a look at Ruby from the corner of her eye. The sun gave her a beautiful glow, making her look nearly angelic as it haloed out around her.

"I would have come back to awaken you, had I not noticed you in the dining room…"

She raised her eyebrows and turned to face Ruby. "You had company…" It hadn't been what she had planned to say—she hadn't wanted to make it so obvious that she had been watching them. And that she felt jealous over a man she didn't know.

Then again, after what Caroline had put her through, she couldn't blame herself.

Ruby's brows furrowed for a second before they shot upwards as her lips spread into a grin. "Oh, no." She carelessly waved her hand as she turned back towards the sea. "Frank wouldn't have cared if I had slipped away—he was waiting on my sister getting their daughter ready so they could have breakfast together. He had merely gone on ahead to secure their table."

Penelope's head perked up.

He wasn't a suitor or a lover. He was her brother-in-law.

The thought made her so utterly giddy that she couldn't control the smile that spread across her face. She tried to hide it by turning away, pretending to survey the ship and the people strolling on the decks.

"I hope you do not think it too bold of me to inform you that you have a beautiful smile," Ruby announced, just as Penelope was certain she had gotten away with concealing her joy.

All the blood in her body seemed to rush towards her face, and she licked her lips as she attempted to calm her leaping heart. "Not too bold at all," she croaked, clearing her throat when the sound of her voice reached her ears. "You're sweet to say so."

Feeling brave, Penelope looked at Ruby, who was already staring at her, eyes hooded and smile soft. Penelope's heart thudded out a rapid rhythm against her chest.

She knew she was staring for far too long—she should now be averting her gaze lest someone start to suspect her. Yet she couldn't bring herself to do so.

Looking into those beautiful blues, so like the water they sailed on, Penelope was mesmerised.

"Auntie Ruby!" a young voice cried out.

Penelope turned just in time to avoid a collision with a young girl of about five or six, who barrelled straight into Ruby's body with such force that they nearly went overboard.

"Julia!" another voice admonished.

After removing her hands from Ruby's arm, where they had shot to stop her from losing her balance, Penelope saw a woman striding towards them.

She had sandy blonde hair pulled into a messy bun, and she wore a Gainsborough hat. Her face was soft and round, and her skin, while pale, was accented with a healthy pink glow.

She wore a looser cut that reminded Penelope of the styles that had been in fashion a couple of years ago. The man from earlier—Frank—was at her side, in a boater hat and looking slimmer and taller now that he was upright. Their arms were linked.

Ruby steadied herself, her hand resting atop the young girl's head, fingers combing through her long, dark-brown ringlets. "I've got your back, my girl," Ruby whispered just before the couple arrived, their eyes narrowed at the girl, who was quite obviously their daughter.

"How was breakfast?" Ruby questioned, easily drawing their attention away from Julia, who had a toothy smile on her face as she looked up to her auntie.

"Don't you try and distract me. I've told her time and again to *stop running*," Ruby's sister replied, eyes flitting briefly towards Ruby before focusing entirely on her daughter, free hand resting on her hip.

Julia's smile faltered and she lowered her head. "Sorry, Mammy."

Ruby's sister only *hmm*ed; then she finally seemed to realise that Penelope was there. Her cheeks started to colour, and her chin lowered a little. "Oh! Sorry...I..."

Ruby stepped forwards, easing the awkwardness as she linked her arm with her sister's. "Ah, yes, allow me to introduce you to Miss Penelope Fletcher, the woman I am sharing my room with." Her eyes landed on Penelope. "Penelope, allow me to introduce my sister, Mrs. Victoria Cameron, my brother-in-law, Mr. Frank Cameron, and my wonderful niece, Miss Julia."

At the mention of her name, Julia fisted her hands in the skirts of her dress and bobbed in a dainty curtsey. It was the cutest thing Penelope had ever witnessed, and she found herself returning the action. "Charmed to meet you, Miss

Julia."

Victoria gave Ruby a rather strange look, which caused Ruby to shake her head once, a discreet movement that she was obviously trying to hide.

"Where is Liam?" Ruby asked when she noticed that Penelope was watching. "My younger brother," she explained.

"He's already made his way to the Boat Deck. You know he loves it up there." Victoria sighed and rubbed her forehead. "Would you mind taking Julia and watching over them for me? I know it's a lot to ask, but I..."

Ruby raised her hand, stopping Victoria's words short. Her accent seemed to grow stronger the more she was around her sister, Penelope noticed. Her words were shorter, her speech faster, and if Penelope hadn't spent her life around a similar-sounding accent, she was certain she'd never have understood it. "Vicky, it's fine. Whatever it is you need to do, go and do it. I'll manage."

Penelope had no idea what came over her. The next thing she knew, she was taking a small step forwards and saying, "And I'll be there to help, should anything go wrong."

Four sets of eyes turned to her, all of them wide with shock, though they didn't stay that way for long. Julia's expression quickly turned to excitement, Frank looked relieved, and both Victoria and Ruby shared another ominous look.

"You don't need to..." Ruby started.

"Don't worry about it... I adore children." It wasn't a lie. Penelope often resented that she was an only child. Especially because most of her friends had a never-ending stream of siblings. Millicent had two older sisters, one younger, and twin brothers who were fifteen years her juniors. Deborah had three sisters, two of whom were older and one younger.

Due to a lack of children in her immediate life, Penelope had often volunteered to assist whenever they were responsible for their siblings. And after a time, they started to invite her first, taking advantage of her love of children, but Penelope never complained. She enjoyed it far too much.

"If you're sure…" Ruby trailed off after Penelope nodded. Her face transformed as she realised Penelope was serious and not simply saying it out of duty. Her smile was stunning, but unlike the previous ones Penelope had been graced with, it lit up her eyes, brightening her features.

"Then I must thank you, Miss Fletcher," Victoria announced as she stepped forwards and reached for Penelope's hands, distracting her from Ruby's smile.

She looked so much like Ruby, but there were subtle differences that marked them apart—her hair was a little bit darker, her eyes a little bit lighter, and her features rounder. She was also a couple of inches taller, and she seemed plumper, though that could just be the cut of the dress she wore. Victoria studied Penelope for a moment longer before dropping her hands and turning back to her husband, entwining their arms. "I shall say goodbye. And thank you."

Victoria and Frank walked away, leaving Penelope with Ruby and Julia, the latter staring up at Penelope with wide eyes and a huge smile.

"Do you know how to play hopscotch?" she asked, tugging on her skirt to get her attention.

Penelope smiled down at her. "I do…though I must confess to being surprised there's a hopscotch court aboard."

Julia beckoned her closer with a conspiratorial wave of her hand, not speaking until Penelope was doubled over, her ear at the young girl's lips. "I heard that someone drew one down on a deck below…"

"Well, then, what are we waiting for?" Penelope's grin stretched wider as Julia slipped her hand into her own and then led her off towards the stairs.

Chapter Six

They hadn't been able to find the fabled hopscotch, so instead they returned to the Boat Deck at the top, where Liam and Julia played tag with the other children.

One young girl, Miss Bertha, heard Penelope's voice and rushed over, overjoyed to hear an accent like her own, although hers was a little thicker, a little more guttural, due to being from Aberdeen. She joined in with Julia and Liam's games—and the three didn't allow Ruby and Penelope to remain idle.

It had been years since she had run around like that. Penelope shrieked like a child and desperately tried to catch Ruby—she only felt it fair that she focus mainly on the other adult. At least, that was what she told herself.

It had nothing to do with the way Ruby's eyes lit up whenever she spotted Penelope coming closer, or the way she laughed when she nearly caught her. Nor how her entire body jolted as if electrocuted whenever her fingers were able to caress her waist, or her arm, or even brush her shoulder.

It was almost a disappointment when Victoria and Frank

reappeared and pointed out that the ship had been *still* the whole time they had been playing.

Penelope hadn't even realised that they had docked and were preparing to weigh anchor. She was a little disappointed, for she had wanted to look upon Queenstown and see the last of the United Kingdom of Great Britain and Ireland one final time.

"Can we play tomorrow, Penelope?" Julia asked. She took her mother's hand, but dug her heels in to prevent herself from being hauled away just yet. Her mother started to berate her for the familiarity until Penelope informed her that she had given the children permission to address her by her first name.

Ruby's brother Liam stood by Frank's elbow. He was such a cute little boy, tall and lanky, with the same sandy blond hair as his sisters. He seemed a little shy, a little hesitant, but he had been as much a part of the game as the others. "Please," he added for his niece.

Penelope's eyes flickered between Julia and Liam before she nodded once. "If you'd like." Her smile was warm, genuine. And she couldn't help herself as she turned to Ruby to see what her reaction was.

Her blue eyes weren't focused on Penelope, however, but on her sister, the two of them having some sort of silent conversation. She was a little bit jealous of such a thing. She didn't think there was anyone who knew her that well...not even Caroline nor Millicent or Deborah.

Suddenly feeling as though she were intruding, Penelope cleared her throat and dusted down her skirt.

"Forgive me, but I really must take my leave," she announced with a gentle smile on her face, watching as Frank tugged on the rim of his hat and Ruby and Victoria snapped their attention away from each other and back to her.

"Truly?" Ruby asked.

She ignored the way her heart leapt at that. "Look at me. If I show up to luncheon like this, my parents will never forgive me." She saw Ruby's mouth open as if she were going to say something, before she clamped it firmly shut.

That made it just that little bit more difficult to leave her. Penelope wanted to stay and ask what had been about to leave her lips. She was pretty certain that, had the others not been there, she would have... But they *were* there, and Penelope couldn't stand going through the pain of another crush going horribly wrong.

So she turned away and headed back to her room.

It was a rather quiet affair, as most of their meals usually were, and she was quick to part ways with her parents. She had considered wandering the ship aimlessly to process her thoughts, but every time she spotted something interesting, her first thought was to make a note of it to ask Ruby about later. Her roommate certainly seemed to know an awful lot about boats and *Titanic*.

So, instead, she retreated to her room, thankful when Ruby wasn't inside. She pulled her hoop free, careful of the long train of excess fabric. She had always enjoyed needlework, finding the repetition allowed her to settle her mind.

With a sigh, Penelope settled onto the sofa, the small wooden box that she kept all her threads and needles in open beside her. She had decided, after she had given in to the idea of moving to America and leaving Granny behind, that she would do something to send home to her. It had taken her a while to settle on a threadpainting of her grandmother's old dog, Poppy. She had been a Scottie and her gran's first—and only—dog, and she had loved her more than anything.

It seemed only fitting to create a portrait of the dog to send home, so that her grandmother could look at it and remember both her only grandchild and her dog whenever she felt lonely.

Penelope worked on the outline with a pencil, letting her mind still as she lost herself to the movements of her hand against the strong canvas fabric.

She was so lost in the process—having moved from the initial sketch to outlining it with long stitches—that she didn't hear the door open and close. She was only aware of her company when Ruby said, "I don't have the patience for needlework."

Penelope gave a startled yelp, letting go of her hoop. It fell into her lap as she placed her hands over her rapidly beating heart.

Ruby grinned down at her. "I didn't mean to startle you."

Waving her hand, Penelope picked up her hoop to ensure that nothing had been damaged in its hasty drop. She then carefully wound the fabric around it and set it aside.

"I never used to have the patience either," Penelope said. "But it was the only acceptable hobby that I *did* enjoy, so it grew on me. When I started at five, I couldn't do more than a few stitches before I grew bored. Now I could miss my meals, I'm so involved."

"That much is obvious," Ruby said, that familiar twinkle in her eyes as she moved to the wardrobe. "Because I saw your parents retreat to their cabin, no doubt to get ready for their dinner." Ruby removed the same beautiful dress she had worn yesterday, turning back to Penelope with a frown. "Have you been here since luncheon?"

Penelope flushed as she nodded. "I told you, it enraptures me." Her fingers reached to stroke the fabric, to distract herself from saying that the real reason she had started was to avoid thinking about Ruby. "It helped that it's a piece for Granny, to send back to her. It's of her old dog, Poppy. She loved her. And I have so many happy memories with that dog as well. Granny got her on my eighth birthday, so I always felt like she was *mine*." Penelope moved as she spoke, slipping into something a touch more fancy for dinner. It had a simple underdress with an A-line skirt made from lavender silk. The skirts of the overdress were gathered up to the knee and secured with lavender silk flowers, showing a small triangle of the underdress.

"We stayed close by, so I was always there, seeing how she was doing and accompanying Granny on walks," she continued. "And when I was old enough, I started taking her myself to the nearby loch because she loved to swim. Goodness, I remember once, Caroline and I weren't watching her, and she started chasing some swans. Next thing I know, there's this loud commotion as she tried to scramble back to land while the swan started chasing her back. I rushed into the loch up to my calves in an attempt to scare the swan so that Poppy could get to safety, and all the while Caroline was on the bank, crying tears of laughter."

She stopped talking just as she finished getting dressed, and she turned to face Ruby, surprised that she hadn't said anything.

Just as she was about to prompt Ruby, there was a soft knock at the door. Penelope's mother stood on the threshold, a smile on her face. "Oh, good, you're ready. I was a little worried since I hadn't heard hide nor hair of you since luncheon." Her eyes landed on Ruby, giving her a courteous nod, before turning to Penelope once more. "Shall we go?"

Knowing better than to ask for some extra time when she already looked presentable, Penelope nodded and followed her mother from the cabin, stopping only to give Ruby a confused glance before the door shut.

Chapter Seven

Penelope was the first to return to the room.

Tucking her feet under herself as she settled on the sofa after changing into her nightgown, Penelope continued her work on the outline of Poppy's face. It was a tad more difficult getting things accurate when she only had her memory to go off, but as she stopped to rethread her needle, she realised she was making good progress.

And at least it looked like a *dog*.

This time, when the door opened and clicked shut, Penelope was acutely aware of it, so didn't startle when Ruby said, "I've never had a dog."

"Poppy is the only one I've had. Father would never allow one in the house—too messy, he says." She rolled her eyes as she started to work on Poppy's beard, which was always unruly, no matter how much she was groomed.

"No worse than a baby, *believe* me," Ruby laughed as she pulled her nightgown off the bed and started to peel her clothes off.

Penelope focused on her work, concentrating on each

push and pull of her needle, and the pinging sound the fabric made as it was tugged through. Anything that would stop her from raising her gaze and watching Ruby undress and change into her nightgown, which looked to be a sheer cotton that would *definitely* leave nothing to the imagination.

She only knew that Ruby was changed when she joined her on the sofa. She had pulled on a dressing gown for which Penelope was thankful. She didn't need her mind being clogged with lascivious thoughts as she tried to have a simple conversation.

Ruby said nothing, sitting upright as if she hadn't removed her corset, but a quick glance told Penelope she had. Her eyes dove back to her hoop. *No indecent thoughts.*

"Earlier, you mentioned a girl...Caroline..." Ruby began.

Penelope's hands froze first, then started to tremble. So much so that she had to lower the hoop to her lap so that its movement didn't give her nerves away. She swallowed once, twice, raising her gaze up to Ruby.

She wanted to deny it. Caroline was a sensitive subject, and bringing her up around this woman who was already making her feel things seemed like a recipe for disaster. But she *couldn't* deny it, for she had mentioned Caroline when she had been sharing her story about Poppy. She tried to recall what she had said, to see if there had been anything incriminating, but she couldn't remember.

Penelope swallowed again. "Yes. My friend."

Ruby gnawed on her lower lip for a moment, her hands clasped firmly in her lap. Her voice was soft as she asked, "Just a friend?"

With those three words, Penelope's mind silenced.

Her heart beat an erratic rhythm against her chest. She swayed where she sat, and she was thankful she had already let go of her hoop, for it would have slipped from her hands.

"What?" The word scratched her throat as it came out.

The pain was enough of a sensation to bring her back to herself. Her instincts kicked in. She had known for a long time that she was more of a fighter than someone who would flee. She shot to her feet, her hoop falling to the ground in her haste. *"What?"* she repeated, her fear and panic turning into anger and venom as she spat the word at Ruby. "How *dare* you imply such a thing!"

Ruby recoiled, looking as though Penelope had struck her. Her fists tightened in her nightgown until her knuckles matched the white of the fabric. She looked so small, so meek, that it tempered Penelope's spirit a little.

Ruby let loose a long breath and raised her eyes to Penelope's. There was a thin film of tears over them, and yet they were still sure and strong. Her jaw was tight as she said, "You talk in your sleep, Penelope. And you spoke of her then."

Penelope knew that. It had been something Caroline had teased her about, since most of her dreams *were* about her. And the worrying part was, she *had* dreamt of Caroline last night. It hadn't been one of the lust-filled dreams that she'd had at the beginning of their relationship—she hadn't had one of those in a long time, if she was being honest.

It had been about the day she had told Caroline that she wasn't going to fight the move any longer. That not being informed of her engagement by Caroline herself proved that she had never cared for Penelope as Penelope had cared for her.

But even then, that argument couldn't be mistaken for anything else. If she had whispered just one sentence aloud, there would be no other plausible interpretation. Her secret would be known.

Her mouth gaped open for a moment before she started to sputter. She could do nothing but stare, feeling like a foolish fish out of water, knowing that her reaction was all the confirmation that Ruby needed.

Ruby pushed onto her feet, causing Penelope to take a stumbling step backwards. Was she asking this so that she could go running to an officer and report Penelope? Did she plan to spew hurtful words at her? Would she be alienated from her one companion for the rest of the voyage?

"Penelope," Ruby whispered. "I… I only say these things because…because I…never expected to meet someone aboard who feels the same way I do." Her tone had trailed off to almost nothing as she spoke, each word growing quieter and quieter.

Penelope's mouth continued to flutter open and shut like that of a suffocating fish. Ruby shuffled on her feet, her fingers twisting around each other nervously as her gaze darted all around the room.

Of all the things Penelope had expected, that had never even crossed her mind.

She tried to think back to their previous interactions, to see if there had been signs that she had missed, but she came up with nothing.

After all, they were still pretty much strangers. There was no way she could expect Ruby to reveal such a secret to someone she had *just* met and would never meet again once this journey was over.

Which made Penelope wonder why she had chosen *now* to do so.

Too afraid to let down the guard she had put up since Caroline had revealed her true colours, Penelope raised her chin and threw her shoulders back. "I'm afraid I don't know what you're talking about."

After having her heart broken by Caroline, she hadn't really expected to find anyone interesting for a long time.

Whatever the reason, she couldn't deny that attraction for Miss Ruby Cole had sprung up from the moment she'd seen her.

"Penelope, I know this isn't the most *normal* of conversations, but I'm no fool. I can read between the lines. The way you spoke of her, the look on your face, and the things you said in your sleep..." Ruby's cheeks were flushed a brilliant red. "I don't know what you've convinced yourself of, but trust me, I'm not going to tell anyone! No matter how this conversation ends."

Trust. How many people had Penelope trusted in her life who had ultimately let her down? Caroline had been one. Emma another. Even her parents with their constant nitpicking over her personality and appearance. And yet this utter stranger was expecting to gain her trust because, what? She had made some observations and come to some sort of conclusion?

Penelope folded her arms over her chest. "Trust you? How can I trust you? We barely know each other!"

Ruby's eyes narrowed, and she took another step forwards. "By realising that *I'm the vulnerable one here*! I asked the question, I'm the one fishing to see if my instincts are right!"

Penelope tilted her head to the side. "And why did you?"

Ruby gnawed on her plump lower lip, and her gaze fell to her feet. Her fingers fiddled with the lace cuff of her nightgown. She took a long, steady breath as a million different emotions flickered across her face.

It was a little strange to see her look so bashful. In the moments Penelope had spent with her, she had always been so sure, so bold.

After a long moment, she sighed and finally raised her head. Ruby's features were no longer nervous, but bold, certain. She pulled her shoulders back and raised her chin as her eyes met Penelope's.

"Because I *wanted* you to know," Ruby admitted, her

voice strong. She took a step forwards. "There's something about you I *like*." She shook her head, pressing on. "All I care about is that *you* drive me wild, and I can't stop thinking about you. And if there's a *chance* that you feel something similar, I'm going to take it, because God knows, my life isn't going to be this exciting again!"

Penelope stared at Ruby, trying to figure out whether she was dreaming, hallucinating, or if all of this was really happening. She watched as resignation appeared on Ruby's face, as she lowered her head to the side, her lip still trapped between her teeth.

It didn't seem *real*.

And yet, as she discreetly pinched herself, she realised it was.

Before Penelope's mind could catch up with her heart, she surged forwards, her hands cupping either side of Ruby's face and bringing their lips together in a fierce kiss.

It felt like all the air had been knocked out of her lungs when their lips met, a little awkwardly at first, the movement so sudden and unexpected by both of them.

It didn't take them long to readjust, for Penelope's fingers to push further into Ruby's blonde locks. Ruby's hands settled on Penelope's waist as her hands slid back down to Penelope's waist.

The touch brought forth a new fervour in Penelope as she used her tongue to part Ruby's mouth, and she couldn't help her grin as Ruby met her halfway.

Penelope didn't even notice that she was walking them backwards until they came to an abrupt halt, Ruby's back meeting the solid wood of the door.

Not that she seemed to care.

Her touch grew bolder as her hands wandered, slipping from her waist upwards until they brushed the undersides of Penelope's breasts. It was enough to make Penelope pull back, her breath leaving her in sharp pants as Ruby slowly opened her eyes.

"I...was that too much?" Ruby asked, as her hands slid down to Penelope's waist.

Licking her swollen lips, Penelope shook her head. "Not at all. I just...wanted to talk...first...make sure that we're on the same page."

Ruby nodded slowly, even as her hands tightened further on Penelope's waist. "Well, I am on the page where my father will probably ensure that I find someone to marry when we land in New York, and so I would really like to enjoy the company of a woman in my bed during this voyage." She then cocked her head to the side as she regarded Penelope. At the same time, her hands slowly bundled up the fabric of Penelope's nightgown, so that the hem was around her knees. "What page are you on?"

Warmth flooded through Penelope's veins, settling deep in the pit of her stomach. Her breath came out in a ragged laugh as she leaned forwards to press a brief kiss to Ruby's jaw, unable to help herself. "A rather similar page, if I'm being honest... Just, may we wait before taking it further? I've rushed in once before, and it caused me nothing but pain."

She didn't want to mention Caroline again tonight, but the thoughts were already there. Caroline had caused Penelope to experience so many firsts within such a short time. She had been so swept up by Caroline that it had taken two years and their falling out for Penelope to even realise how much she had controlled and smothered her. How her time with Millicent and Deborah had dwindled until she'd been consumed only by Caroline.

Ruby's smile turned gentle, as if she had heard Penelope's thoughts and wanted to comfort her. She released her hold on Penelope's nightgown to brush her thumbs over Penelope's cheeks. "Of course, darling," she whispered softly. "Why don't we share the bed and kiss until we fall asleep?"

Penelope's smile returned as her nerves eased. She smoothed her hand from Ruby's neck down over her shoulders until she entwined their hands.

Then, with a grin, she led them towards the bed.

Chapter Eight

The first thing Penelope registered as she woke up the next morning was that there was a heavy weight splayed across her midriff.

A soft groan reached her ears as she felt Ruby stir in her arms, her nose brushing along Penelope's jaw as she adjusted herself. Penelope allowed her fingers to trail along the bare skin of Ruby's shoulder, where her nightgown had slipped, and then down over her cotton-clad arm.

Ruby stilled for just a second, and then Penelope felt a smile stretch against her neck. "I was almost certain it had been a rather vivid dream." Her beautiful blue eyes were still a little hooded from sleep, but there was no denying the happiness hidden in their depths.

"Not a dream, no. It was something much better than that," Penelope said. It seemed so natural to adjust her position and press her lips against Ruby's in a soft, fleeting kiss. She pulled back so that she could brush Ruby's hair away from her face, tucking it behind her ear.

"I daresay it is something we should talk about." Ruby rolled onto her back, pillowing her head on Penelope's arm. "But I want to enjoy this moment a little bit longer."

Penelope turned her head to the side, watching Ruby's profile as she stared up at the slats that made up the bottom of the top bunk.

She had always considered Ruby beautiful, from the second she had set eyes upon her.

But now, her beauty had only grown.

Her nose was a cute little button thing, her lips were full and soft to the touch, and her eyes were like oceans, bottomless and mysterious and downright mystical. She had the odd freckle spattered across her milky white skin, a pattern that continued all over her body.

After spending hours exploring her as much as she could without removing their clothes, Penelope had discovered that Ruby was soft and supple, her thighs and stomach patterned with silver lines.

She was so beautiful, that honestly, Penelope could have spent hours just *staring* at her.

"I don't even know what time it is." Penelope stifled a yawn with her free hand. "I'm a little worried that my mother is going to walk in to tell me to get ready for breakfast and catch us like this."

That would most likely cause the early demise of all involved. Her mother's from shock, Penelope's from embarrassment. Then again, perhaps her mother would consider it innocent, that Ruby had fallen ill and they had decided to share the bunk. Penelope had used that excuse several times when Caroline had slept over and had been caught in her room at inappropriate hours.

Ruby was silent for a moment as her gaze flickered towards the door. "...You're probably right." She pushed herself into as much of a sitting position as she was able to, thanks to the top bunk. "We should get up and get dressed. Eat breakfast. We can meet back here afterwards, to talk. If that's okay with you, of course. If you would rather talk now, we can..."

"I..." Penelope swallowed, trying her best not to let Ruby know that this was really the first time in...well...all her life that someone had cared about her opinion. "No. After breakfast is good with me. I'd much rather deal with it on a full stomach, if I'm being honest."

Rolling out of bed, Penelope stretched out her limbs, her arms reaching towards the ceiling as she rocked onto the balls of her feet. She looked over her shoulder, feeling pride swell in her chest when she saw Ruby openly appraising her. She knew her nightgown was sheer and left little to the imagination.

Perhaps it was the hunger in her gaze and the memories from last night that made her add, "I don't know how, but I have worked up an awful appetite."

Ruby snorted and pushed herself up from the bed. She lifted Penelope's combinations from the chair and threw them at her. "Oh shush, you, and get dressed before your mother or my sister comes knocking."

Getting dressed seemed to take double the time. Penelope couldn't stop herself from constantly glancing over her shoulder. Especially when, most of the time, she knew Ruby was already staring at her. And every time their eyes met, Penelope smiled and reached out to touch her, whether it was a fleeting kiss or a gentle caress.

By the time they were decent, Penelope had to fight the urge to remove it all again and lead Ruby back to the bed.

Her throat tightened when she realised that only her bed was rumpled. Not wanting to start any rumours, she quickly disturbed the sheets on Ruby's bed so that they looked slept in.

"Oh," Ruby said. Her cheeks flooded with a hint of red. "Yes. That's probably a good idea." She looked at her reflection in the mirror above the cabinet with the stowaway basin. Ruby fiddled with the hairs that she had left out to frame her face, pushing and pulling strands away until she got an arrangement that she liked.

Penelope watched her with hooded eyes. She couldn't help daydreaming about how her hair would look haloed around her, or as she stifled moans with a hand clamped over her lips.

Blinking furiously, Penelope pushed those thoughts away before she stepped towards the door. "Perhaps we should set a time? Just in case we get pulled into something by our families and we can't send word?"

Ruby nodded. "Good idea. Eleven?"

"Eleven is fine with me." Penelope almost couldn't look at her; her mind was still burning with her fantasies. She had a better idea of what Ruby looked and felt like now, which made them all the more vivid.

And it didn't help how Ruby looked at her as if she *knew* and was beckoning her to make them come true.

Penelope cleared her throat and pulled the door open, stepping out into the corridor, thankful when Ruby took off in the opposite direction after giving a low chuckle in her ear.

Her parents were already dressed and didn't look too happy about her tardy arrival, but Penelope found she didn't care quite as much. Not with her thoughts still running rampant. She apologised because it was what they expected, then followed them towards the dining room.

Thankfully, neither of them was particularly interested in keeping her in their company, so the moment she was finished, she retreated to her bedroom, not really surprised when it was still empty.

Collapsing into the sofa, Penelope buried her face in her hands, bending over as much as she could with her corset. She noticed the embroidery hoop still sitting on the floor, and picked it up, her fingers brushing over the outline of Poppy as she let her mind wander.

What did she want? What did this even mean? Out of all the things she'd expected on this journey, never in her wildest dreams had this come up.

She rather liked Ruby's idea of creating some fond memories before life caught up with them and they were forced to find husbands.

Times were changing, that much she knew, but she feared it wouldn't come about fast enough to convince her father to let her remain unwed for the rest of her life. Or to put courting aside for some time whilst she went to college. Despite being a learned man himself and coming from a background that wouldn't have allowed him an education not that long ago, he held the opinion that women were homemakers and nothing more.

So, perhaps it'd be good to have memories that weren't tied to Caroline and bitterness. Now, when she had to lie with her future husband, she could think instead of Ruby.

When Ruby finally arrived, Penelope stood, her body thrumming with excitement.

Ruby licked her lips and then nodded her head, wasting no time. "Right. Well. Last night was rather good." Her cheeks started to darken. "More than good, even. And I do believe I already told you that it is my father's intention to see me settled this year…" She trailed off with a frown. "He is worried about me, should we lose his income."

"I'm sorry," Penelope said, because she didn't know what else to say.

"It is what it is." Ruby gently shrugged her shoulders. "So I did mean what I said about seeing no harm in creating some memories aboard before that becomes a reality."

"Perhaps I won't be married quite as soon as you, yet I know my parents well enough to know that it won't be too long." Penelope reached for the locket still fastened around her neck and hidden in the high collar of her blouse.

"So… We both are in agreement that our futures aren't going to be that brilliant," Ruby started. "That still leaves the decision on what we *do* now. Do we consider last night a onetime thing, or do we continue for the rest of the journey and hope we don't raise any suspicions?"

A million different thoughts ran through Penelope's mind.

She couldn't deny that their night together had been amazing.

Perhaps this was what she needed. Something careless; a passionate fling that meant nothing.

Of course, such a confined area could lead to problems—but most people would look at them and see friends, sisters even, before they saw lovers.

Penelope cleared her throat.

"I…I still don't see much harm in having fun before we grow serious. Lord knows I haven't had much of that in my life," she announced in a soft voice.

Ruby's lips quirked up at the corners. "Now that I relate to." They shared a laugh before Ruby took a deep breath and added, "I'm glad we're in agreement, then."

She offered Penelope a bashful smile as her hand moved from her lap to settle over Penelope's, who threaded their fingers together.

Penelope raised her gaze from their entwined hands and licked her lips, feeling a thrum shoot through her when she noticed Ruby tracking the movement with hungry eyes.

So she leaned forwards, moving slowly.

When their lips met, it felt as though she had been struck

by lightning. Every nerve in her body came alive and she pulled Ruby closer, her free hand cupping the nape of Ruby's neck.

She removed the metal pins from Ruby's hair, letting it cascade over her shoulders and back. The second it was free, her fingers tangled through it to pull Ruby's face closer.

Eventually, her lips landed on the long column of Ruby's neck, and heavy gasps fell from her mouth.

"I'd love nothing more than to keep this going," Ruby breathed, as Penelope's teeth and lips worked their way down her neck.

Penelope brushed Ruby's hair away from her shoulder and wished that their clothes were looser so that she could slide the sleeve down and get access to her bare skin.

"But I'm afraid I told my sister I'd watch Liam and Julia." Ruby's hand came up and rested on the back of Penelope's head, the touch enough to pull her from the spell she was under.

Penelope straightened, her cheeks aflame as she stared at Ruby, finding her equally flushed. She looked beautiful like that, and Penelope had to bite her tongue to stop herself from leaning forwards again, from trying to see just how far she could make that blush spread.

Nodding slowly, she watched Ruby stand up and start to fix her hair, casting disapproving looks at Penelope whenever she slid a pin back into its previous place.

Penelope merely shrugged in response.

Once Ruby was decent again, she made her way to the door, but she stopped with her hand on the handle. She seemed to be thinking about something, if that small crease between her brows was anything to go by. "Do you... Do you wish to join me? If you're not busy, of course."

Penelope was on her feet almost instantly, wincing when she realised she must look like an abandoned puppy. She distracted herself by smoothing her skirt. "I'd like that."

Ruby's beaming smile was all Penelope needed to convince herself that she wasn't alone in her excitement. "Wonderful! Let's go! I don't want to keep Victoria waiting."

The urge to take Ruby's hand or arm was almost too strong, so to stop herself, Penelope bundled her hoop and sewing box into her hands. Then she followed Ruby towards C Deck.

Chapter Nine

This time, there were more than enough children for Julia and Liam to play tag with, so Ruby and Penelope sat off to the side to watch.

Even though Penelope's hands were occupied with her work, they kept itching to touch Ruby, whether to take her hand or caress her face or stroke her hair. Penelope only ever did a stitch every few minutes.

As she pulled her needle through, she said, "It's lovely to see you so involved with your niece and brother."

Ruby turned towards her. "What do you mean?"

"I mean, here you are, looking after them. I'd say that it also speaks to your closeness with your sister that you're minding her daughter whilst she's around and able to do it herself."

"She can't."

"Beg pardon?"

"She can't look after Julia herself. Well, she can, but she gets tired a lot. And it doesn't help that she's also pregnant again." Penelope's shocked expression caused her to laugh.

"You honestly didn't notice?"

Penelope turned her gaze back to the children and watched them run around. She shrugged with one shoulder. "I don't really go around looking at people's bellies all the time." She shot a grin at Ruby. "But no, I did not notice that at all."

"I often think it is so obvious. Though I suppose that's because I know."

Penelope pressed her fingertips into her stomach, feeling the edge of her corset. She lost herself to the sensation, tracing out the contours of the thick fabric. She took a deep breath in. "When is she due?"

"Not for another couple of months. They hope to make it back over before she gives birth. I don't think either of them would be pleased with him being born in America." Ruby's lips quirked up at the corner, and she laughed gently. "And Daddy wouldn't like that at all. He'd probably yell at Victoria to keep him in, should she go into labour."

Penelope giggled, and for a brief moment, she wondered how her father would react to becoming a grandparent. Or her mother, for that matter. She almost felt as though they wouldn't care. She knew that they hadn't exactly wanted Penelope herself, so it seemed only natural that a grandchild would face the same indifference. It was just another thing that would take time away from them being husband and wife.

Not that they would ever have to worry about such a thing from her. Penelope loved children, but the act required to produce one was *not* something she wished to experience.

She turned her attention back to the matter at hand as she continued to work on her grandmother's present. "So you help your sister out a lot, then? With Julia?"

Ruby nodded. "Yes. There's not much else for me to do. And it seems like the decent thing to do, since they give me a home."

Penelope cocked an eyebrow. "You live with them? Not with your father?"

"Daddy used to rent a little cottage by the estate where he serves. However, after Mother died from tuberculosis... Well, the last thing he wanted to do was be around such familiar trappings. He asked Victoria and Frank to take me and Liam in, and he moved back into a room at the house where His Grace stays." Ruby fiddled with her fingers, nervously twisting them together, interlocking them only to release them a moment later. All Penelope wanted to do was entwine her hands with Ruby's, just to settle her a little. But she knew it was too risky.

"That must be difficult," Penelope whispered. She wondered how different her life would be if she didn't always have to see her parents; if they weren't there, constantly nagging at her, trying to get her to become someone she was not—to carry herself better, stop being so interested in education and politics, to be a good little woman to attract a rich little husband.

Don't eat so much, sit up straight, a woman should never speak out of term. They tried to chip away everything that made her who she was, and mould her into something they thought acceptable.

"It is. I miss him so much." Ruby drew a deep breath. "But I love being with my sister and my niece all the time. As does Liam. I think he's the one who suffers most. He lost his mother at such a young age, and then his father just withdrew from his life. It's like he's an orphan." Ruby's eyes were locked on her younger brother, watching as he dove around the deck, giggling and screaming whenever another child got too close to him.

He was adept at moving out of the way, and in the hour or so that Penelope had been watching him, she didn't think she had ever seen him get caught.

"He has you and Victoria. That's something."

Ruby only *hmm*ed, so Penelope said no more, not wanting to pull her away from her thoughts. Whatever she was thinking and feeling didn't last long, however, for a smile appeared on her face. "Enough about me, casting a gloom on the day." She waved her hand. "Have you heard about First Class? How utterly over-the-top it is?"

Penelope shook her head. "No... What do you mean?"

"Well, the plan with *Titanic* has always been luxury. And they've gone overboard for First Class. There's *everything* you could imagine—a gymnasium, fancy restaurants, a swimming pool! Turkish baths!"

"What on earth is a Turkish bath? And how do you even know all of this?"

Ruby laughed. "Well, a Turkish bath is a public area where people sit in a really hot room which makes them sweat, then they bathe in cold water, receive a massage, and sit in a cool room to relax." Her smile turned wry as she noticed Penelope's nose wrinkle. "As for how I know, Daddy told me. His Grace likes to boast a little, and so he was telling Daddy all of the things he was looking forwards to aboard the ship."

"It must be really useful to be close to someone who knows a duke. I don't think I would have ever learned about such a scandalous thing." Penelope let out a laugh, feeling her heart soar when Ruby joined in.

"The best thing about the ship, however, is supposed to be the Grand Staircase," Ruby said.

Penelope raised an eyebrow. "Wait. All of those amazing amenities, and yet the best thing is...a staircase?"

Ruby shuffled so close that the hems of their skirts brushed. Penelope was pretty sure she felt Ruby's foot stroke her ankle. Her heart stammered, and her hold on her hoop loosened just a little. She cleared her throat as she set it in her lap so that it wouldn't happen again and give her away.

"I know it sounds silly, but it's an amazing piece of architecture, according to Daddy. It's built from solid English oak, there's a glass dome above it, and it has a chandelier in the centre. On the A Deck there's supposed to be a stunning clock. It's framed by angels...and they're supposed to be..." Ruby trailed off again. Just when Penelope worried that she was never going to speak again, she snapped her fingers and exclaimed, "Glory and Honour! They're supposed to be Glory and Honour placing a crown atop the clock, so they're crowning Time! That's what it's supposed to be!"

"You seem to know an awful lot about this. Are you sure those are just things you've heard from your father?"

A pretty blush spread across Ruby's cheeks, and she brought her chin down to her chest. "Well, perhaps I did a bit more reading in the library. I find it fascinating how something so utterly huge and heavy and so ornately lavish can float. How she is forty-six-thousand tons and cannot sink. That's a wonder, is it not?"

"I can't say I have ever thought about it much. However"— Penelope's gaze shifted, and she watched the children run around—"That is...rather Father's area of expertise. Mathematics and suchlike. I...tend to avoid such things when I can."

Penelope rather loathed herself for that, because it was something that interested her.

How a ship like *Titanic* remained afloat. How they built the engines that powered her through the waves. But because she was a woman, she would never learn the answers. Any time she tried to ask her father, he would wave her off and tell her it didn't concern her.

Once, when she'd tried to read one of his books, she'd been caught and had had to listen to a whole lecture about how mathematics and engineering weren't suitable subjects for a woman.

She sighed, turning her gaze back to Ruby. "I would love to see that clock, however. Art is the one thing that my family don't think out of place for a woman to know about. And the concept is rather interesting. 'Tis a shame that it's always the upper class who receive such benefits, as if anyone lower than a baron doesn't deserve the arts." She cringed. "I can only imagine what Third Class facilities must be like."

"I hear they're adequate. White Star are trying to focus on luxury, so they've made Third Class rather comparable to Second Class on other liners." Ruby leaned in and lowered her voice to a whisper. "Trust me. I fear you've been rather spoiled by your first trip. You won't know what hit you if you set foot on a ship that isn't part of the *Olympic* class."

"Well, I'm certain this is the only ship I shall be on." She took a deep breath to summon the courage to lift her gaze and meet Ruby's head-on. "Thankfully, I'm sharing it with such wonderful company."

Ruby's eyelashes fluttered.

"Auntie Ruby!" Julia's voice cut through the tension, and Penelope turned away as Ruby cleared her throat.

Julia blinked owlishly up at them. Her brown hair was in long ringlets, pulled out of her face with a pale-pink satin bow that was nearly the same size as her head. Her face was round and soft, and she wore an adorable dress of pink cotton trimmed with a great deal of frills and lace under her dark-green coat.

"What is it, dear?" Ruby asked as she straightened the lapels of Julia's coat.

"Me and Liam are hungry," she announced.

Penelope looked at the small watch that adorned her wrist and immediately darted to her feet. "Oh my, that can't be right!" She turned her wrist so that Ruby could read the time, and watched as her pale, thick brows darted upwards.

"Well, my dear, you're in luck because it's luncheon," Ruby said to Julia before she looked at Penelope.

Whilst Penelope had never been the best at understanding subtle social cues, she instinctively knew Ruby was asking her to dine with them. She nodded, watching as Ruby's plump lips spread into a wide smile.

"Excellent! Then let's go and find your mammy, and we'll get you and your uncle fed."

Just as they turned to walk away, a trio of young men came towards them.

The other two pushed one of them into Penelope and Ruby's path. He had short, dark-blond hair that was slicked to the side, and a youthful face, making Penelope guess that he wasn't much older than she. Judging from his clothes—plain, a little bit ill-fitting—and the calluses and scars on his hands, he was from Third Class.

Ruby immediately pushed Julia and Liam behind her back as her eyes warily danced over the man and then regarded his two friends off to the side. Penelope rather resented that her hands were occupied with her sewing box. Then again, if they tried anything, it was made of solid wood and would do some damage if knocked over their heads.

The man raised both his hands in a placating manner. "I'm sorry, I didn't mean to startle you." He smiled, his teeth crooked and yellow, but it lit up his face and made him look friendlier. "My friends and I just wanted to let you know there's a little celebration in the Third Class common room tonight, on C Deck. A lot of us are heading to America for a new life, and anyway, we"—he glanced over his shoulder at his friends—"wanted to invite you both."

One of his friends laughed. "Aye, you can't have too many pretty ladies at a party."

It was on the tip of Penelope's tongue to immediately shut the idea down. She didn't even want to *think* about the fallout with her parents if she went, but she noticed the way Ruby's lips curved and stopped herself.

"That is sweet of you, gentlemen, thank you," Ruby said. She then took hold of Julia's and Liam's hands and stepped around the first man. He frowned deeply, turning to watch her as she walked away.

Penelope swallowed as she followed Ruby.

"Are you going to marry that man?" Julia asked as soon as they were inside the lift and heading down to D Deck.

Her words startled a laugh from Ruby. "Why do you ask that?"

"He asked you to a ball! It's like a fairy tale!" Her sweet, innocent words brought a smile to Penelope's face.

"He hardly looked like a prince," Liam announced, rolling his eyes at Julia, who in turn stuck her tongue out at him.

Ruby's blue eyes met Penelope's briefly before they flickered back down to her niece and brother. "Liam, be kinder, looks do not mean everything. And Julia, fairy tales are sweet and all, but that man was *not* my Prince Charming, for I won't even be attending this ball. Now, come! Your mother is probably worried sick because we're so late."

Penelope tried her hardest to ignore the way her heart soared at hearing those words as they made their way to the dining room.

Chapter Ten

Back in their cabin after dinner, Penelope locked the door
and moved towards Ruby, settling her hands on her hips.

With a seductive smile, she tilted her head towards Ruby's
and kissed her.

She released a soft whimper as her hands circled Ruby's
waist, adjusting the position of her head to deepen the kiss.
Her hands travelled upwards, seeking out the small pearl
buttons at the back of Ruby's dress, but when they found
them, Ruby pulled away.

"Wait, wait, wait." Ruby took a ragged breath, resting her
forehead against Penelope's. The strands of hair she had left
loose to frame her face tickled Penelope's nose. "If we start
that, we won't stop."

Penelope laughed breathlessly. "And why should we
stop?" She pulled her head back and lifted her hand to cup
Ruby's cheek.

Ruby's lips grew into that sure smile that Penelope had
come to adore. "Because we have a party to attend."

Penelope lowered her hand from Ruby's cheek, cocking

her head to the side as Ruby continued to grin at her. "Away and boil your head," she said with a nervous laugh, almost expecting Ruby to declare it a joke. When that didn't come, she pulled herself free from Ruby's hold, stepping back to stare incredulously.

Ruby shrugged elegantly with one shoulder as she fiddled with the black lace around the neckline of her underdress. The emerald-green silk chiffon of her overdress clung stunningly to her figure, draping her like some Greek goddess.

"Why shouldn't we go?" Ruby smoothed her hair, twirling those strands that had just been tickling Penelope's nose around her finger.

Penelope had no real answer to that. It just seemed so risky.

Not only because her parents would be upset if they found out, but because they didn't know anyone in Third Class. Whilst they weren't wealthy duchesses decked out in diamonds and pearls, they were still better-off than those they'd be celebrating with.

You sound just like Father, her mind hissed at her, and she was just able to hold back a grimace. She hated that she was judging these people before she even knew them based purely on their societal status.

Ruby reached up and smoothed the wrinkles on Penelope's forehead with her gloved hand. The action made Penelope smile and she relaxed, casting away her worries.

She took Ruby's hand in hers, pressing a gentle kiss to her knuckles. "All right. But if you cast me aside for your Prince Charming, I will not be pleased."

Ruby laughed loudly, closing the distance between them. "The chances of that happening are as likely as *Titanic* sinking." Ruby placed a fleeting kiss on Penelope's lips, just enough for her to want more, to *crave* Ruby's fingers on her skin, before she pulled away and made her way back to the door.

Penelope watched as Ruby unlocked it and opened it just a little, looking from left to right to ensure that no one was around to see them. "Why do I feel you've done this before?"

Ruby turned back around with a wide grin. "Maybe because I have. Not a *lot,* but once or twice I've sneaked out to attend a party thrown by the duke's servants. And the odd time I wanted to meet a pretty girl without the risk of getting caught." Ruby winked before turning to face the front once more. "The corridor is clear—I can't see your parents or my family, so I think we're fine."

Her expression softened when she seemed to notice how nervous Penelope was. She closed the door and came close to her again. "If you *really* don't want to go, I won't pressure you. I just didn't want you saying no because of some misguided sense of propriety or honour or whatever other reason they use to prevent women from enjoying our lives."

Penelope shook her head. "No. I do wish to go..." She closed her eyes and took a deep breath. "Come on. Before Father comes back from the smoking room."

Ruby's smile was dazzling as she giggled, took Penelope's hand, and led them out of the room.

Penelope refused to release her hold on Ruby, even as they weaved their way towards the stairs instead of the lift so that not even the staff saw them. They passed one or two people, but no one looked their way. For all intents and purposes, they looked like they were making their way back to their cabin after dinner.

Music started to filter down the corridor when they stepped through the barrier that kept Third Class separate from Second Class.

It was a melody that reminded her of home, of those rare nights she had attended dinners and she had been allowed to reel, with its lively fiddle, steady drumbeat, and tinkle of a piano. The only sound missing to make her truly feel at home was the wail of bagpipes.

When they finally reached the Third Class General Room, Penelope and Ruby drew to a halt outside, their eyes wide as they took in the sight before them.

The room was modest. Wooden benches covered the length of the walls with some in the centre. No one sat on those, though, instead moving around them as if they were some sort of centrepiece. A piano sat off to the side, and several people holding their own instruments stood beside it. There was a haze of smoke, a hum of constant chatter, and an alluring aroma of cigars, alcohol, and food. And every inch was filled with people expertly moving to avoid colliding with others.

It was so bizarre to see—the lively dancing, the utter chaos of it all.

"Wow," Ruby whispered.

Two young women stumbled towards the door, pushing past Ruby and Penelope with a muttered apology before resuming the conversation they'd been having.

Penelope's mind was torn. On one hand, she wanted nothing more than to step inside, to join in the revelry. The reckless abandon called to her soul. And yet, the other part of her wanted to run as far away from it as possible.

The amount of trouble she could get into if she stepped over the threshold was terrifying.

"Shall we go in?" Ruby asked in a soft voice.

Penelope swallowed, her heart thudding out a rapid rhythm against her chest. "Don't you think we stand out a little?" She took in the people around her, all of them wearing casual clothes, whilst she and Ruby were still wearing their nice gowns from dinner. And goodness, how would she explain any marks on her dress when they landed in New York and her clothing had to be washed?

Ruby sharply exhaled. "Judging by how drunk they are, I don't think they're going to care."

"That is *not* reassuring," Penelope replied sharply, before taking a deep breath in to try and calm herself. She closed her eyes as she placed her hand over her heart, feeling the relentless thud greet her fingertips. The hard outline of her grandmother's locket was hidden under her dress, and she trailed her fingers over it, trying to draw strength from the touch.

When she reopened her eyes, she nodded. Her fingers were still trembling, and her legs felt ready to crumble, but still she said, "Let's go."

She was rewarded by Ruby's stunning smile and a tight squeeze of her hand. Ruby expertly weaved them through the crowds until they were able to find a spot where they could stand.

Three familiar figures appeared by their side.

"You made it!" one exclaimed, a huge smile on his face. It was the same man who had invited them. "We just realised we didn't properly introduce ourselves. I'm Mr. Daniel Lee, and these are my friends, Mr. Albert Wright and Mr. Joshua Wilkinson." The three of them touched the brim of their caps in order, and despite her nerves being aflame, Penelope managed a smile in return.

"Pleasure," Ruby replied, easily taking the lead. "I'm Miss Ruby Cole, and this is my friend, Miss Penelope Fletcher." Ruby glanced around. "This is rather lively."

"I bet it's nothing like the parties you're used to," Mr. Wright said. He had a strong Welsh accent and a thick, blond moustache. Despite his warm smile, the bags under his eyes gave him a rather sickly appearance.

"Not at all," Penelope said, voice soft, almost drowned out by the music and cheers. She only hoped that the whisper of her tone hid the disdain that had crept in.

"So... What do we do?" Ruby enquired, giving Penelope's hand another soft squeeze.

"Dance!" "Drink!" "Have fun!" the three men answered at the same time, then dissolved into laughter.

Penelope glanced at Ruby and saw her lips curl just a little.

"Dance wherever there's a space, no fancy routine needed. There's beer on a table in that corner there, you're welcome to it. And, as we said, just have fun. Mingle. It's up to you, ladies," Mr. Lee said. "We'll be here, so, if you need any help, or if someone is giving you a hard time, just come and find us."

"You're...not going to stay with us?" Both Ruby and the men looked at her, so she clarified, "I meant... I almost expected you to *assume* that we were interested. I..."

"I understand, Miss Penelope. But no. We invited you because you seemed like you needed a way to blow off some steam, so to speak. We've noticed you've been running around after kids for a bit now. I have a younger brother myself. However, if you'd feel safer having us around, we can form some sort of group...?"

"No, that won't be necessary," Ruby said with a kind smile. "Thank you so much, gentlemen."

They tugged at the brims of their caps again and said their farewells.

Ruby turned to Penelope with wide, rather shocked eyes. "That was...unexpected. I almost believed we would have to fight them off." She tilted her head, watching them retreat and embrace their loved ones. "Now, shall we go and visit that table with the beer?"

Chapter Eleven

Penelope's head was spinning.

Even as she stood still, her head resting against the metal wall, everything in front of her moved in a slow, orderly fashion to the right. It was so disorientating that she had to close her eyes.

But then a hand landed on her shoulder. Ruby's face came into view, yet there was a second Ruby standing beside her, which was a little confusing. Not that Penelope minded; if there was anything better than one Ruby, it would be two.

"I think...we should go now," Ruby announced with a tiny hiccup, her hand immediately flying to cover her mouth. The sound was so high-pitched and sudden that it pulled a giggle from Penelope's mouth, even as her hand sought out Ruby's so they could entwine their fingers.

"You are adorable," Penelope said as she stumbled forwards into Ruby's arms.

"Are you two going to be okay?" a man asked and even though Penelope was looking right at him, she couldn't tell whether it was Mr. Lee, Mr. Wilkinson, or Mr. Wright. They all looked very much the same to Penelope in that moment.

It wasn't until a pretty, ginger-haired woman came up beside him, wrapping her arm through his, that she realised it was Mr. Albert Wright. His fiancée, Betsy, gave them a concerned look.

"Are you sure you can manage her?" she asked, her accent rather similar to Ruby's, but just that little bit deeper. She had spent the night dancing with Mr. Wright and had periodically checked in on Ruby and Penelope when she'd discovered that her fiancé had invited them, making sure that they were well and still felt safe.

"Aye, have no fear! Thank you for the invite! It was grand!" Ruby wrapped her arm around Penelope's waist and led her towards the door.

"Well, there'll be another tomorrow night, you're more than welcome to come then as well!" Albert called out after them. "In fact, there'll be a party every night until we arrive in New York! We're going to celebrate this voyage for what it is!"

Penelope let out an undignified whoop, waving at him with a silly grin on her face.

Ruby shook her head. "I should have known you'd never had a drink."

"I get a glass of wine at dinner!" Penelope replied indignantly, before dissolving into giggles. "The beer was disgusting, though. I don't know why people drink that."

"Then why did *you* keep drinking it?" There was a deep frown on Ruby's face as her hands tightened their hold on Penelope, no doubt in response to the way Penelope kept stumbling over her own feet.

Penelope didn't have an answer. Every drink she had taken had been horrible—but she had just mirrored Ruby, who had drunk it with no problem. And, after a while, the taste had faded a bit anyway.

Of course, that was when the room had started to sway and her body had started to feel like a live wire.

"You are half-cut. We need to get you to bed," Ruby said as they stepped into the stairwell. She led them towards the descending stairs, but something stirred within Penelope. She had no idea if it was all the alcohol and the dancing that had made her feel so utterly carefree, all she knew was that the last place she wanted to go was room E-56.

She ripped herself free from Ruby's embrace—a feat more difficult than she cared to admit—and stumbled over to the ascending stairs.

"Penelope! What are you doing?" Ruby whispered sternly, her eyes darting around.

Penelope grinned over her shoulder at Ruby, then extended her hand. "I do believe you said something about wanting a keek at the Grand Staircase." Her smile stretched wider as she watched Ruby's mouth fall open. She stood like that for several seconds as she surveyed the stairwell.

Ruby licked her lips and took a small step towards Penelope. "Are you certain about this?"

Penelope giggled, the sound echoing around the empty stairwell. "When else are we going to get the *chance*? And besides, it's not fair, all those snooty toffs getting to enjoy all the fun." Penelope swayed just a little as she spoke. She knew it was definitely the alcohol talking now—she would never have dared say such a thing aloud before.

It took only another second of contemplation before Ruby skipped forwards and entwined her fingers with Penelope's. A careless laugh bubbled free from her lips, and all Penelope wanted to do was capture it.

So she did.

She leaned forwards and pressed her lips to Ruby's, swallowing the laugh and enjoying the taste of Ruby's lips. She wasn't too drunk to know that this was still a dangerous game they were playing, however, so she pulled away before she lost herself completely in the kiss.

Then she turned and ran up the stairs, hoisting her evening gown in her free hand as she dragged Ruby along behind her. Their laughter stopped as they reached the Bridge Deck and continued to the next level.

"Last chance to back out," Ruby announced, even though she had overtaken Penelope and was now leading the way.

Penelope just scoffed. "No chance, my dear."

So they continued to climb the stairs up to A Deck.

Ruby had told her that the staircase actually began on the Boat Deck, and to get the true effect of stepping inside and then descending the Grand Staircase, it would be best to approach it from that direction.

The two slowed, creeping up the stairs, and as soon as they were able, peeked around the corner onto the exclusively First Class Promenade Deck.

It was adequately lit for the time of night, and as far as Penelope could tell, no one was around. She heard the faint sound of ragtime music and chatter, no doubt coming from the smoking room the gentlemen retreated to. And perhaps even from the reading and writing room the ladies would be in.

"I think we're clear," Ruby whispered, her hand tightening around Penelope's just a little.

The courage that the beer had given her had faded a little. The last thing she wanted was to get caught—she knew it wouldn't be a criminal offence, but God above, her father would see it as such. And punish her accordingly.

When they stopped at the foot of the stairs, the pair drew to a halt.

The Grand Staircase was huge, spreading out wide and taking up most of the open area. It was made from solid oak with wrought-iron grilles decorating the bannisters. The floor was made up of cream tiles interspersed with occasional decorative tiles with a black-and-white cross pattern.

A cherub holding an illuminated torch graced the central newel post at the bottom of the staircase, while overhead, at the very top, was a large glass dome that would have allowed natural sunlight to enter the room. Now, as the sun had long since set, countless chandeliers illuminated the area.

Penelope turned slowly on the spot, seeing large and comfortable-looking sofas and chairs, all upholstered in a plush blue velvet. There were even potted palms in raised containers in each corner of the open waiting area.

"This is…" she started, only to stop because she could think of no words that would adequately describe the splendour.

Ruby was looking up at the clock with wide eyes. Penelope recalled what she had told her about it—"Honour and Glory crowning Time."

Two angels stood, one on either side of the main clock face, which was set within a carved pedestal. One of the angels had her foot resting upon a small globe as she wrote upon a tablet. The other angel held a palm branch over the clock, and near her feet was a laurel wreath. The frame of the main clock was plain, but it was supported at the bottom by two griffins, and a variety of fruit and flowers filled the area between the frame and arch.

"Daddy was right," Ruby whispered as she reached out to graze the wood with a fingertip. "It is breathtaking. It's been carved so perfectly…" She lowered her hand and took a step back.

"Do you think the people of First Class even give it a second glance?" Penelope asked with derision. "Or do you think they just see a *clock*, rather than a work of art?"

Ruby looked at Penelope with a wry twist of her lips. "I think that they don't even bother to know the time. I'd bet that most of them haven't even noticed this is here." She shook her head, waving her arm at all the grandeur. "That *any* of this is here!"

Penelope felt an anger at these people grow inside her, stirred further by the alcohol in her veins. She resented them and the wealth they hoarded, flaunting it in front of others only to make them feel inadequate. And she loathed that her father and mother wanted to *be* them, because that's what was expected of everyone—to further their station and improve their lot.

They wanted to get to a point where *this* was their life.

But what good was a life when the money around you meant you could no longer see the beauty?

Before she could start letting out her anger, a voice cut through the silence. "May I help you?"

The pair whirled around. A steward, dressed in fine livery with his hair smoothed to the side and his arms folded behind his back, stood at the base of the staircase.

As soon as they turned, the realisation that they didn't belong there seemed to slowly dawn on his face—whether due to their clothes, their flushed cheeks, their guilty looks, or even because he simply didn't recognise them, Penelope had no idea.

Penelope grabbed Ruby's hand and shrieked, "Leg it!" Then she promptly took off up the staircase towards the Boat Deck above.

She heard the steward call out after them, but neither paid any attention to him as they hoisted their skirts up to an improper height and dashed up the stairs, stepping out into the frigid night air.

Penelope's breath created puffs of smoke as she panted. She didn't dare to stop in case the man was following them. They just kept moving, their hands locked firmly around each other's, uncaring as to how it looked.

No doubt they were in utter disarray, hair falling loose from their messy chignons, their stockings visible to the world as they weaved around the obstacles on the Boat Deck until they got to the stairs at the rear of the ship. They passed the four funnels—only three of which were functional if the steam was anything to go by—and the First Class-exclusive gymnasium. They made their way past room numbers as high as E-100 and the Second Class barbers before they finally reached their own cabin.

Ruby giggled as Penelope shut the door and pushed her up against it, then fell silent as Penelope rocked forwards and pressed their lips together.

Her fingers tightened against the soft chiffon of Ruby's dress, bunching it up so much that it raised the hem several inches from the ground.

Penelope pressed her body further into Ruby's as her fingers trailed from Ruby's waist, following her curves up to cup her breasts. The loose cut of her dress made it easy for Penelope to guide the fabric over Ruby's shoulders and down her arms, revealing the soft cotton and lace of her chemise.

Her tongue teased at Ruby's lips, but just as she went to part them, her stomach started to churn, causing her to freeze. She pulled away, clenching her jaw, and was just able to see Ruby's puzzled expression before she threw herself across the room.

Her hands fumbled for the handle to the foldaway basin, yanking it down just in time for the beer in her stomach to come rushing back up.

She vaguely heard Ruby call her name and felt her hands rubbing soothing circles on her back. Tears flooded her eyes as her throat started to burn, and when she had finally finished vomiting, she wiped her mouth and groaned, resting her head against the porcelain of the basin.

Ruby murmured soothing sounds, her hands wrapping

around Penelope's arms, guiding her upwards. The movement was almost too much for Penelope, who had to close her eyes.

The world was still swaying, but it no longer felt fun—it was as if she were trapped on some awful carnival ride, and she wanted *off.*

"Shh, let's get you out of these and into bed, you silly cookie." Ruby's voice dropped to a whisper. Penelope grunted in response, continuing to stand still with her eyes shut, raising her arms when bid. She only knew that Ruby was undressing her as the fabric brushed her skin before exposing it to the colder air.

When Ruby slid her stockings from her legs and guided her down onto the bed, Penelope knew that she must be down to her chemise. She felt the covers being draped over her body and, as she settled into the pillow, she was already descending into the depths of sleep.

Chapter Twelve

As Penelope awoke the next morning, it was to a dull, constant thudding in her head.

Everything hurt, even places she didn't know she had. She groaned and rolled herself over, burying her face into the soft pillow.

When she stilled, she realised that the pillow was moving, slowly rising up and down. It wasn't a pillow—she was resting upon Ruby's bosom.

She knew that she should move, yet no matter how hard she tried, she remained in place, her arms winding around Ruby's waist. Then she registered short nails scraping against her scalp and long fingers trailing down between the long strands of her hair.

The touch was so soothing, so mesmerising, that Penelope relaxed further, as if ready to fall asleep once more. "I don't even want to ask what time it is," she murmured into the soft cotton of Ruby's nightgown.

"Luckily it's not too late. We've not even missed breakfast yet."

The mere suggestion of scran made Penelope groan. Her stomach churned at the thought.

She pressed her face farther into Ruby's chest, allowing her eyes to fall shut.

She soon regretted that decision, however, when Ruby's body started to shake as she laughed softly at Penelope's reaction.

It reminded her too much of the spinning sensations she had felt last night, just before the contents of her stomach had made a reappearance, and she quickly rolled off Ruby's chest and onto her back. One hand landed on her stomach whilst the other landed on her forehead.

Ruby shuffled over to her side, her hands snaking down Penelope's arms so that they rested atop her hands, and Ruby threaded their fingers together.

When Penelope felt lips against her exposed shoulder, she finally reopened her eyes.

Ruby grinned back at her, a smile so enticing that, despite the effort it took, Penelope mirrored it.

Penelope leaned forwards, and Ruby readjusted her position so she could meet Penelope halfway. Her smile caused her cheeks to ache when their lips finally met in a soft, gentle kiss.

Ruby's hand moved to thread into Penelope's hair, wrapping it around her long, elegant fingers until there was just a faint sting of pain. It shocked a moan out of her mouth and she rocked her hips forwards, adjusting herself so that Ruby's leg was now between her own.

Just as she began to enjoy it, as if the kiss had cured the pain and dizziness, Ruby pulled away.

"You are so adorable when you pout." Ruby pressed her finger against the centre of her lower lip, just as she had done last night. She laughed quietly to herself when her words made Penelope pout more.

"I only pout when I have reason to," Penelope admitted. Her hand moved to Ruby's hip and started a slow trail up to her waist. "Why did you have to stop?"

"Because we need to get up and have breakfast with our families. If we don't, they'll come looking." She glanced over Penelope's shoulder. "I'm actually surprised they haven't come knocking already."

Penelope groaned and threw her free hand back over her face. Ruby laughed, a beautiful song sung directly into her ear. It was followed by a light kiss to the knuckles of the hand covering her face.

"Come, we must get up." Ruby gave the side of Penelope's thigh a soft pat. She started to climb over Penelope, who removed her hand just as Ruby was straddling her waist, her hands planted on either side of Penelope's head.

"I'm now expected to get *out* of bed when you're doing *this*?" Penelope asked incredulously.

Ruby rolled her eyes. "Oh shush, and get your mind out of the gutter." She leaned down and pressed the briefest of kisses to Penelope's lips, then slipped from the bed in one elegant move.

She danced easily out of the way of Penelope's hands as they tried to grab at her to keep her where she was. Penelope's fingertips were only able to graze Ruby's nightgown.

"You, miss, are *evil*." Penelope sighed and threw off the thin cotton covers. It took her another minute to find the strength to roll to the edge of the bed and into a sitting position.

She surveyed the room, finding no evidence of her embarrassing situation last night, and when her gaze returned to Ruby—who was getting their clothes sorted—she felt her heart stutter and swell.

She moved over to Ruby, wrapping her arms around her waist from behind. Her chin perched on Ruby's bare, freckled shoulder. She couldn't resist pressing a kiss to the constellations on her pale skin. "You are wonderful."

Ruby snorted and continued to sort through their clothes. "I thought I was *evil* for being some sort of temptress?"

Penelope tightened her arms around Ruby's waist. "You're not evil. You are wonderful. You've been so sweet to me, not just last night, making me have fun and then looking after me when I had *too much fun*. But this entire journey so far... It feels like we've known each other longer than three days." Penelope cleared her throat, realising she was being overly sentimental and no doubt embarrassing Ruby. She stepped out of the embrace and hastily gathered her clothes over her arm. "I'm going to go and have a bath drawn."

It was suddenly impossible to meet Ruby's gaze, so she focused on the adorable spattering of freckles on her shoulder. "Don't feel like you have to wait on me. I'll meet you at the dining room before breakfast."

"Penelope—" Ruby started, but Penelope didn't wait to hear what she had to say and rushed to the bathroom.

She took her time as she bathed and dressed herself. Anything to stop her from looking so peely-wally. When she gingerly made her way back to her room to retrieve the boots she had forgotten in her haste, she stopped and stared at the door for a solid minute, wishing she could see through the wood to find out whether Ruby was still inside.

After taking a deep breath and pushing the door open, she let it out in a long gust when she was greeted with an empty chamber. Her fingers combed through her loose ponytail as she stepped farther into the room and shut the door behind her.

The bath had helped with the ache in her bones, but the throbbing in her head was still there, as was the roiling in her stomach. She *knew* that she would probably vomit all over her parents' plates if she had to look at food.

Even though she knew it would raise questions, Penelope lowered herself back onto her bunk and closed her eyes.

• • •

She was awoken by a gentle shake of her shoulder.

When she opened her eyes, Ruby was staring down at her, her blonde hair piled atop her head in messy curls with several hanging loose around her face and the nape of her neck. Her blue eyes were soft, gentle, filled with concern.

Penelope rolled onto her side, holding her weight up on one of her arms as the other reached up to cup her grandmother's locket. She had rather hoped to get her thoughts in order before she had to see Ruby again.

Ruby cleared her throat and moved from her perch on the edge of the bed. Her fingers were tangled together in front of her body, drumming nervously against each other.

"I just wanted to make sure you were all right. I managed to keep your parents away by telling them it was just a small sick spell. They seemed to believe it and didn't ask any further questions." She gestured towards the small table by the sofa. "I snuck some scones and water out for you, should you feel up to them. You must drink, at the very least, if you do not feel up to eating. And I'm rambling…sorry…"

Penelope rose from the bed, reaching for the glass of water on the table and taking a sip. "I'm sorry I didn't show up for breakfast," she said as she lowered the glass. Her nap had helped ease the pain, and she was pretty certain the rumbling in her stomach was from hunger rather than sickness. "And that I just…ran away this morning."

Her nerves were on fire, as she thought about what she had said. She had wanted to tell Ruby that she was wonderful and had planned to stop there, but perhaps the alcohol had still been in her system and had caused more words to come spilling out instead.

Ruby's soft lips stretched into an easy smile. "You did dash off rather quickly. You didn't even give me a chance to agree with your sentiment."

Penelope's eyebrows darted upwards. "What?" she croaked out, her mouth dry.

"It does feel like we've known each other longer than we have. Perhaps we can't explain it, or people would think we're fools, but they obviously haven't experienced anything like this." She shrugged one shoulder, taking a step towards Penelope and, after a brief moment, wrapping her arms around her waist. "And if you hadn't run away earlier, *I could have told you that.*"

Penelope ducked her head against the curve of Ruby's neck. "Sorry," she mumbled, her arms snaking around Ruby's hips. It was rather strange how perfect it felt to hold her like this.

Ruby's tinkling laughter sang in her ear, and she felt her fingertips dance up and down her spine. "It's all right. You can make it up to me later."

Penelope leaned back in Ruby's arms. Her brows furrowed as she asked, "Whatever do you mean?"

Ruby let out a low laugh and said, "Why, at the party in Third Class. That's happening again tonight. It seems only fitting we attend it again, since it was such fun last night."

Penelope's brows furrowed further until they almost caused her pain. "Yes, it was fun, but there's no way we can go again. Not after what happened last night."

Ruby giggled. "No one is asking you to drink as much as you did then, Penelope. We can share one bottle between us and enjoy the music and the dancing! It'll be delightful!"

Penelope wanted to agree—she wanted to be that

carefree person—but she had already done that. And look where it had got her. Utterly drunk, feeling horrible the next day, and admitting some embarrassing things to her lover.

It wasn't really a situation she was eager to repeat.

Penelope shook her head. "Sorry, Ruby... I just can't risk it. Mother or Father might catch us. Or someone from Third Class could turn us in or even try something untoward. And what if that steward comes looking for us? It was a nice party, but the sort of thing that should be experienced just once in a life."

By the time she had finished speaking, the smile had fallen off Ruby's face and she had removed herself from Penelope's arm, taking several steps backwards. She looked more upset than angry.

"Ruby—" Penelope tried.

"I thought we were supposed to be having fun?" Ruby shook her head slowly before she turned and left the room, the door clicking softly behind her.

Chapter Thirteen

It took Penelope only a second to move towards the door, pulling it open with more force than necessary. Her heart raced in her chest as she scanned the corridor.

Instead of Ruby, she found several other people strolling aimlessly. No one looked, or even glanced her way as they meandered past.

Her gaze darted back and forth as she tried desperately to work out which way Ruby would have gone. Her heart thudded out a rapid rhythm as she stepped over the threshold, closing the door behind her.

Her feet were moving before her mind had caught up to her. She only realised that it was in the direction of her parents' room when their door opened and both her mother and father stepped outside.

Penelope froze, staring at them as she hoped and prayed that they wouldn't turn to face her. However, her luck had never been good, and so, after linking arms, that was exactly the direction that her parents turned in.

For a brief moment, they didn't notice their daughter

standing there like a startled deer, and it gave Penelope a chance to study them. She almost couldn't believe that the man and woman in front of her were, in fact, her parents.

Their eyes were locked as they talked softly to themselves, and they had gentle, almost *loving* smiles on their faces. It made Penelope wonder if all they had ever needed was some time without her to remind them of how their lives had changed.

Or maybe it was that they were stuck aboard a ship where they knew no one else and so they were finally able to *talk* and rediscover each other. It was better than thinking that her parents would do better without her around.

Her parents glanced away from each other, then spotted Penelope standing in the middle of the hall. Their smiles remained in place as they drew to a halt in front of her.

"Are you feeling better, dear?" Her mother asked. She pressed her free hand against Penelope's forehead. The leather of her gloves was so soft and cool, and as her mother moved her hand from Penelope's forehead to cup her cheek, Penelope couldn't stop herself from leaning heavily in, desperately craving the soft touch.

"I am." It felt like a lie, even though she did feel better. Her heart was still racing from the altercation with Ruby, and whilst she wanted nothing more than to continue her search, she also knew that the damn ship was too large for her to find Ruby now. She could be anywhere.

"We were just going for a walk along the promenade on the Bridge Deck," her father announced, sending his wife a teasing smile as he added, "Your mother is rather adamant about trying to spot a whale."

Penelope stared, trying to wrap her head around this change in her parents. She'd never seen them so affectionate. She cleared her throat when she noticed that they expected her to say something. "A whale? Wouldn't *Titanic*'s size scare them off? And the sound of her engines?"

"Rightly so!" Her father turned back to his wife and added, "Really, dear, whales are intelligent creatures. They are going to *avoid* the forty-six-thousand-ton lump of metal slicing through the water."

Penelope's mother's lower lip jutted out in a small pout, which made Penelope swallow thickly. Her mind immediately replayed her earlier conversation with Ruby. And, judging by the way her father's eyes softened and he reached up to stroke the backs of his fingers down his wife's cheek, he also found the action adorable.

"Well, even if that is the case, I am still adamant about *trying*. You get rather foolish people, perhaps you get rather foolish whales as well." Her eyes met Penelope's and her pout retreated into a smile. "Would you care to join us? Or do you have other plans? I know you've become close with your roommate... We spoke to her earlier. She seems rather nice."

Penelope cleared her throat and gave a jerky nod of her head. "Yes. Yes, she is." Her eyes darted over her mother's shoulder, hoping that Ruby would miraculously appear there. She had to hide her disappointment when she was greeted with strangers. "Shall we head up to the promenade? We don't want to miss these whales."

Her mother frowned at her for only a moment before her father gave a low laugh, diverting her attention. Penelope stepped aside, allowing her parents to overtake her. It was only then that the full import of her mother's words dawned on her, and her steps faltered just a little. Her parents *never* liked her friends. They normally considered them too bad an influence on Penelope, or unworthy of her time. And yet they had deemed Ruby to be "rather nice," which was probably the highest praise her parents could give.

Penelope allowed herself one last glance over her shoulder, almost willing Ruby to appear. It made her wonder if her parents had known things about her old friends back in Scotland, or if they were just willing to say nice things since Ruby was only a temporary companion.

Penelope heaved a sigh as she realised that Ruby wasn't going to appear. She had no idea what had gotten into the other girl, why everything seemed to be getting her so wound up, but she *wanted* to know and help her figure it out.

And she couldn't do that if she didn't *talk* to her.

Folding her arms around her midriff, she followed her parents from E Deck to the promenade on the Bridge Deck.

She and her parents stayed out on the deck right up until dinner, eagerly looking for whales and other sea creatures. They had lost track of time so much that they didn't even bother changing or freshening up.

They went straight from the promenade to the dining room, and Penelope's heart dropped to her stomach when she found Ruby dining with her sister and brother-in-law.

Their eyes locked, but before Penelope could smile at her, Ruby looked away.

And didn't look back again.

She left before Penelope, and then Penelope's parents mentioned continuing their whale-spotting adventure. Penelope happily joined them, since she knew she wouldn't find Ruby anytime soon.

After the fifth involuntary convulsion that her body gave in a desperate attempt to warm herself up, her father tutted and turned to her. "Darling, why don't you skedaddle down to your room before you catch your death?" He shook his head. "I still don't know why you didn't go back for your coat. You know it gets chilly in the evenings."

Penelope had a perfectly valid reason. She hadn't wanted to run the risk of meeting Ruby—not after seeing her dismissive look in the dining room. The courage and determination she had felt earlier had left with that fleeting glance.

But all of that wasn't exactly something she could admit to her father, so she merely forced a smile. "Very well. But I will *not* be happy if I leave and a whale appears."

Her father laughed softly and pressed a gentle kiss to her forehead. The touch made Penelope frown as she pulled away.

She couldn't remember the last time her father had kissed her forehead like that.

"I—" she started, almost ready to just blurt out and ask what had changed before thinking better of it. It wasn't as though it was a bad change, so she wasn't going to say something and risk her parents going back to how they had been before.

"Goodbye," she said instead, then turned and left.

She walked to the stairwell, but before she crossed the threshold, she stopped and turned back to see what her parents were doing. She wanted to know if it was some elaborate show they were putting on, whether they had finally noticed how their relationship had warned Penelope off marriage and so were trying to pretend to be happy in order to inspire her.

As if such an act would wipe away the years of sitting in the same room and never saying a word, creating an atmosphere so tense Penelope always felt as if she were suffocating.

But her parents still stood talking animatedly arm in arm, so it obviously wasn't just for Penelope's benefit.

She suddenly realised that she had been so busy fighting this move that she hadn't considered that perhaps it was best for her parents. That maybe this change was causing them to re-evaluate where they stood and to talk openly—to remember why they had fallen in love and gotten married.

With a soft smile on her lips, Penelope headed towards her room.

With every step she took, her heart leapt further and further into her throat. And when her door was finally visible, she felt as if it were going to burst from her mouth and choke her. Her hand trembled as she reached for the handle, and she had to take a deep breath before she pushed the door open.

The second she stepped through the doorway, her heart plummeted to the pit of her stomach.

The room was empty.

Judging by the clothes neatly folded over one of the chairs, Ruby had returned and then had left again. Whether she had decided to attend the party alone or if she had retreated to her sister's room for some privacy, Penelope couldn't say.

With a huff, Penelope started to undress, finally slipping into her nightgown and crawling into the bottom bunk.

She tried to ignore how big the bed seemed without Ruby's body pressed up against her, but she couldn't settle.

Everything just seemed wrong.

She was too hot with the covers over her, but too cold when she pushed them off. She tried lying on her back, side, and stomach, to no avail. Every position just brought its own discomfort.

It felt as though it took an eternity for every minute to crawl by.

When she heard the click of the door, her breath lodged in her throat.

Her eyes closed—feigning sleep was the better choice when the alternative was confronting Ruby when they were both tired.

"Penelope?" Ruby whispered as the door shut behind her.

Penelope remained on her side, facing away from the door, eyes shut. Her hands were tucked under her pillow, and she allowed herself to rub her fingertips along the mattress, the gentle motion enough to ground her.

Ruby sighed and, as the sound of fabric rustling filled the silence, Penelope assumed she was getting changed. Then she felt the bunk shake as Ruby hauled herself from the ground up the ladders to the top.

Another sigh filled the room.

"The party was even busier tonight," Ruby said as she finally fell still. "I think word is starting to spread. I can't imagine what it will be like on the night before we dock." She huffed out a small laugh. "The musicians changed a little, but they were still good. At one point, everyone was showing off their special talents. This one man was juggling with knives! And do you remember Betsy? Albert's girl? She can bend in ways I never thought possible!"

Ruby fell silent for a moment, the seconds stretching on so that Penelope wondered if she had fallen asleep. She gnawed on her lower lip to stop herself from asking Ruby to continue and instead focused on the back and forth of her finger on the mattress.

"And all throughout it," Ruby finally continued after she took a deep inhale, "I kept turning my head to the side, wanting to see your reaction."

The mattress above Penelope moved as Ruby adjusted her position once more.

"My father is dying. Cancer. And his last wish is to walk me down the aisle. Because he's already done it with Victoria. He wants me safe and secure before he dies. And it terrifies me—the thought of losing my father and the idea of marriage to a man. So I vowed to have fun on this voyage because it would be the last time I'd get it. Because a world without my father in it would be so empty for me.

"I never expected to meet someone like you, though. Nor to *feel* what I do. And so I just wanted to build some more memories—not just fun ones, but meaningful ones. Which is why I wanted to attend that blasted party every night until we reached New York. But it wasn't until I got there that I realised that spending time with you would be more fun, even if we just sat in this room and cuddled." Ruby let out a long sigh as she shuffled once again. "Goodnight, Penelope."

Penelope's heart had returned to her throat. Her tears trailed cold, wet lines over her nose and down her cheek onto the pillow. Her hand no longer stroked the mattress but fisted into the pillow, clutching at it as though it were a lifeline.

Her lungs ached as she tried to stay quiet and keep her breathing even.

The tears on her face were uncomfortable, yet she didn't move to wipe them away. She knew that, if she moved even an inch, she would leave her bed and climb up to Ruby's. And she couldn't do that. Not now.

So she remained wound up tight, her jaw clenched, her lungs aching, and her fist clutching her pillow until her body couldn't take it anymore and she allowed sleep to claim her.

Chapter Fourteen

Penelope stared out at the ocean, amazed at how clear it was.

Only the odd lump of ice floated by. It felt surreal as she stood by the back of the ship and watched the propeller cut through the waves at an incredible speed.

Especially when she didn't really *feel* as if the ship was moving that fast.

She closed her eyes and smiled, feeling the wind caress her face as if it were a lover. She had only known two in her life, and the gentleness of this touch reminded her more of Ruby than of Caroline.

Ruby with her easy smile and easier attitude, who seemed to take everything in her stride.

Who, even though she had lost her mother and was losing her father, hadn't once seemed in pain. Being in her presence was like a breath of fresh air after being held underwater for so long.

Penelope had never quite been that carefree, but she had

been able to *feel* before. And it hadn't been until she'd met Ruby that she'd realised how long she had gone without doing so.

Penelope drew her shoulders back and pushed away from the railing.

She walked past the few couples who had risen as early as she, though most of the people she did pass were members of the crew—stewards and sailors.

When she made it back to their room, Ruby was still asleep, her long, blonde hair in disarray, casting a golden halo around her head. She had bundled the pillow up underneath her cheek, and had both arms wrapped tightly around it.

Penelope gnawed on her lower lip as she reached up and brushed away a strand of hair that had fallen over Ruby's face. The contact was enough to make Ruby twitch, and she rubbed her head into the pillow with a groan.

She hated waking her, but it was getting close to breakfast-time, and she didn't want Ruby getting into trouble with her family.

"Ruby?" Penelope called softly, brushing at another strand of hair and tucking it behind her ear. Ruby's blonde brows furrowed as she stirred, her legs shuffling under the covers and her arms tightening their hold around the pillow. "Ruby."

Her lips spread into a sleepy smile as she stared at Penelope with half-lidded eyes. "Morning," she whispered. "I'm surprised you're talking to me after I stormed away like a child last night."

Penelope chuckled. "I wasn't much better myself." Her fingers wound through Ruby's hair, gently rubbing circles on her scalp. "Alas, we don't have much time to talk about this. Breakfast won't be long, and then there's the church service afterwards." Ruby's nose wrinkled, causing Penelope to laugh. "Not a fan of church?"

"Not a fan of the preachers of church. I've read the Bible, and nowhere does it say half the things they claim it does." She moved a little so that her chin was propped on her hands. "Are you a fan of church?"

"Not at all. I have my faith in God, but I don't believe half the things in the Bible." Penelope rolled her eyes. "Nor the way that they constantly bicker amongst themselves, trying to decide which interpretation of a *book* is more correct."

Penelope pulled away after a final brush over Ruby's cheeks, but Ruby's hand grabbed hers, stopping her in her tracks. She entwined their fingers, and Penelope felt her heart throb.

"But... We will talk?" Ruby's voice sounded so small that Penelope felt her chest constrict in response.

Penelope leaned forwards until her chin was resting on their hands and her face was only an inch away from Ruby's. "As soon as church is over, we will come back here and talk."

She couldn't stop herself from pressing her lips to Ruby's in a soft, gentle kiss. Ruby was like a magnet, and she was too weak to try and fight it.

Once Ruby was dressed in a simple blouse with a cotton lace cardigan and a tan A-line skirt, she started to brush her hair. Penelope stood aside and watched for a moment as Ruby winced with every comb of the bristles through the knotted strands. Then she stepped up behind Ruby and gently pulled the brush from her hand.

Ruby stared back at her through the small mirror, eyes wide as Penelope parted her hair down the centre.

Starting at the bottom, Penelope started to untangle the mess Ruby's hair had gotten into from sleeping with it down and unbraided. It was soft to the touch, like silk, and Penelope adored combing her fingers through it as she worked.

Ruby grabbed Penelope's hand, stopping it from reaching for a pin to fix a curl in place.

She opened her mouth, but Penelope felt something rise in her chest, and she blurted out, "I heard what you said last night."

Ruby's hand tensed over Penelope's, and Penelope clasped her other one tightly over Ruby's. She gave it a tight squeeze, hoping to God that she was being reassuring.

She licked her lips and pressed on. "And I just want to say I'm sorry. I've been thinking about the things you said, and I realised that I let my former lover, Caroline, take away parts of me. And one of those is trusting in happiness. She's had me believing that I couldn't trust happiness, that it would always go wrong, and so I learnt to push it away before that could happen."

Penelope took a deep breath, biting at her lower lip and using that pain to centre herself. Ruby's hand shifted underneath hers, allowing Penelope to thread their fingers.

"But by drawing away, I'm denying myself happiness, I'm letting her win. And that's the last thing I want." Her lips twisted. "I'm too spiteful and petty for that."

Her words startled a short laugh from Ruby, and the sound was so beautiful that Penelope pulled her other hand free so she could brush her fingers along Ruby's lips.

"So, I'm sorry," she said as she cupped Ruby's jaw. "I'm sorry for pushing you away when you're suffering and just looking for some happy memories before things turn dark. And I'm sorry for denying myself exactly the same thing."

Penelope knew that, in a year's time, she and Ruby would be married to men that they didn't love, and that they would be expected to be obedient and dutiful wives. And neither of them was in a position to fight it.

This voyage was their chance of happiness. And Penelope hated herself a little for trying to take that away from them.

Her lips spread into a wide smile. "But what I *do* know is that we have another three days left on this voyage, and, if you're up for it, we can make them the most wonderful days we'll ever experience in our lives."

Ruby was silent as she stared back at Penelope through the mirror. Her lips had tugged into a small hint of a smile, which eased Penelope's nerves—at least it meant she wasn't so furious she had decided to hate her rather than forgive her.

As worry started to rise in Penelope's chest, working its way up from her stomach like bile, Ruby's lips finally caved and a full smile lit up her entire face.

"I rather like the sound of that," she declared, voice soft as she stood, hair still unfinished, and turned to face Penelope.

They moved slowly as they inched closer and closer until their lips were pressed together.

Penelope's hand slid from Ruby's jaw to cup the back of her neck, fingers winding through the hair she had yet to pin up. She used the touch to bring Ruby's face closer and to tilt it to just the right angle so that she could part her lips with her tongue.

When they broke apart, both were panting, their cheeks flushed a pretty pink.

"So much for the talk happening after church." Ruby snorted.

Penelope grinned. "Then why don't we come back here after and find something else to pass the time?" Her brows rose as her hands inched down over Ruby's shoulders and chest.

Ruby gnawed on her lower lip as her expression turned bashful. She turned her gaze away and cleared her throat. "I'm afraid I told my sister that I'd help her with Julia and Liam after breakfast."

Penelope pouted. As much as she loved spending time with the younger members of the Cole family, she would much prefer having Ruby to herself, locked in their room, so that she could show her just how much fun she had planned for the next three days.

Ruby giggled, bopping her finger off Penelope's nose before pressing a fleeting kiss there. "Still adorable." She then turned and sat back down, and Penelope distracted herself from her lustful thoughts by finishing Ruby's hair.

Chapter Fifteen

When Penelope and Ruby stepped into the dining room that night, both of them immediately drew to a halt as they found their respective families.

Sitting *together*.

The dining room was always bright, whether from the natural light that came in through the portholes during the day or the beautiful lighting fixtures during the evening.

Everything was panelled with oak, and the Second Class dining room had rows of long, rectangular tables with mahogany chairs upholstered in red leather bolted to the floor. It meant that, depending on what time you dined, you would usually be surrounded by strangers.

Thankfully for Penelope, no one had tried talking to her, and she had managed to make it through the four days aboard without many problems. Until now.

Frank and Victoria, dressed in fine clothing, sat on one side of the table, whilst Penelope's mother and father were seated directly across from them. The children were no doubt already abed, and the lack of responsibility enlivened both

Frank and Victoria more than Penelope had ever seen. Their smiles were wide, their gestures jovial. Penelope could almost *feel* the ease and relaxation rolling off them.

"Why are my parents sitting with your sister and brother-in-law?" Penelope asked.

"I have no idea," Ruby said, making Penelope groan. "It can't be that bad, can it?"

"You do not know my parents."

Penelope heaved a sigh, which quickly turned to a groan as Ruby declared, "Well, after tonight I will." Ruby took off first, Penelope trailing behind her as she tried to steel her nerves. She hoped her parents wouldn't say anything that would cause issues with Ruby's family.

Just as they approached the table, their small group burst into laughter. Penelope and Ruby shared a look.

"This is new," Ruby said by way of greeting, leaning down to press kisses to Victoria's and Frank's cheeks.

Penelope mirrored the greeting with her parents, taking the vacant seat beside her mother as Ruby slid into the one beside her sister. They were diagonally across from each other, still close enough that Penelope could shoot worried looks at Ruby.

"After Miss Cole spoke to us last night about your sick spell, Penelope, I met Mr. Cameron—" Penelope's father began.

"Call me Frank, please."

Penelope's father nodded. "I met Frank in the smoking room after dinner. We struck up a conversation, during which he mentioned a Miss Fletcher and then informed me that he had already met you, Penelope."

"And when we arrived at the dining room around the same time, we decided that we might as well sit and get to know each other," Frank finished as he took a sip of his wine.

"We can't have you two being the only ones who made

friends during the voyage," Victoria added with a twinkle in her eyes as she turned her head slightly to shoot her sister a look.

Ruby bowed her head as some colour started to flood her cheeks. Penelope looked at the sisters, her head cocked to the side in curiosity.

Does she know? she wanted to ask, even though she knew she couldn't. Not now, anyway. She would have to file that away for later.

"Shall we order?" her father asked, pulling her from her thoughts. She offered him a smile and nodded as she accepted the menu for a quick glance-over.

"So, where in Ireland are you from?" her father asked. Penelope closed her eyes and let out a long sigh. Politics was always a tricky subject, and she knew that things were tense between Ireland and Britain. To some it could be seen as an innocent question, and perhaps it was, but Penelope didn't want Frank to think that her father was trying to see where he stood on Home Rule in Ireland.

"Londonderry," Frank replied easily. "Victoria and her family hail from Belfast, though."

As her father opened his mouth to reply, Penelope cut in, "Mr. Cole is valet to a duke. I believe he joins his family later, after getting His Grace settled."

Her eyes met Ruby's across the table, imploring her to help steer the conversation away from the dangerous territory it had sailed into. Penelope didn't want a single whiff of politics getting near their table.

"Yes. He shouldn't be long." Ruby turned her smile on Penelope's father. "I daresay you shall get along swimmingly, Mr. Fletcher."

Penelope held her breath, worrying that her father would make some comment about not having anything in common with someone in service. She was pleasantly surprised when he merely laughed and said, "Knowing that he has raised such fine daughters as you and your sister and chosen such a stable husband for Victoria, I daresay we will."

Penelope's breath gushed out in a long, steady stream. She reached for her recently filled glass of wine and took a sip. *Perhaps this won't be as painful as I originally thought.*

"Not only that, but my father was born in Glasgow and moved to Belfast when he was three," Ruby said.

"You don't say! Such a small world, isn't it? Have you ever been to Scotland?"

"Sadly not. The family we had there are gone, and Daddy's job makes it difficult to find time to go. I do hope to go one day." Ruby's eyes darted briefly to Penelope before they danced away.

"Are the children asleep?" Penelope asked Victoria.

"Yes. They had their dinner earlier and were out cold before we left." Victoria's hand moved to her stomach, which was much more obvious now that she was sitting down. "If only this little one would do the same."

Penelope was aware of Frank and her father continuing to talk, but at the mention of the "little one," her mother's head spun around to face Victoria. "When are you due?"

"Not for another two months yet. He doesn't stop kicking, and I had forgotten what the back pain was like." Victoria snorted as Penelope hid her grimace by taking a drink of her wine. As much as she loved children, pregnancy seemed to be a whole can of worms she didn't want to deal with.

Her mother leaned a little over the table, dropping her voice to a whisper as she said, "Have you had Frank lift your bump? Samuel did that for me all the time when I was pregnant with Penelope. Just taking that weight off you is a *huge* help."

Victoria's eyes brightened at the suggestion, her gaze flickering to her husband, who was still talking to Penelope's father—and now to Ruby as well, it seemed. She nodded. "I'll give it a try. Thank you, Mrs. Fletcher."

Penelope's mother waved her hand. "Oh, please, call me Rosina."

Penelope's eyes widened. She had never once witnessed her mother give someone around her own age permission to be so familiar. She was thankfully saved from anyone noticing her look when another gentleman came over to them.

He wore a black suit, fitting for a valet, and his hair was grey, parted to one side and starting to thin at the crown. He had a cheerful smile and a sparkle in his eyes as he leaned down to kiss both Victoria's and Ruby's cheeks, and Penelope could only assume that this was their father.

"Ah, we have company for a change! This is what I like to see," he said as he took the seat beside Frank which had obviously been left empty for him. His eyes flickered over the Fletcher family before settling on Penelope's father. "Mr. Lewis Cole, at your service. Please, call me Lewis."

"Mr. Samuel Fletcher, this is my wife, Rosina and my daughter, Penelope, who is sharing a room with your daughter."

As her father spoke, Penelope watched as Mr. Cole's face lit up, a slow, steady smile appearing on his face. "By God, how I've missed that sound. Reminds me of my father."

Then two waiters arrived, carrying several bowls for their starters. Someone must have ordered for Mr. Cole as well, since he, too, had a bowl placed in front of him.

The conversation seemed to dim just a little, with everyone too focused on their food to do more than chat idly. Yet Penelope continued to watch in amazement as her father joked and laughed with Mr. Cole as the night went on and their glasses were refilled.

Mr. Cole's work as a valet to a duke inevitably arose, and they learned that while the title was English, the duke himself was Irish. He was a distance relative of the previous duke who had left no issue when he died. Mr. Cole was certain it was his Irishness that landed him the job.

"Working in the house of a duke must be…incredible. Does he have any particular interests?" Penelope's father asked.

"Oh, a great many! His Grace can be a little eccentric at times. You'd never believe the things I've had to organise for him. Sometimes I swear the butler thinks I'm making it up until something arrives. I think he's just learnt to accept whatever I say as truth now! Once, His Grace ordered a painting. All he told me was that it was a big one, so to let the butler know. I did that, and we made arrangements for its arrival… We were expecting something perhaps this size—" Mr. Cole held his arm up until it hovered above his head. "Then the blasted thing arrived, and it was so big, it wouldn't even fit through the door! In the end, His Grace built an outbuilding specifically for the piece." He snorted as he took a small sip from his wine. "He was the first in the area to get his house fitted with electricity, and the first to buy an automobile, even though he rarely uses it. His favourite thing, however, is *animals*."

"Animals? Like dogs and cats?" Penelope enquired, finding herself just that little bit confused that, having so much money and ability, the duke's greatest interest lay in pets. Not that she could blame him—she had rather loved having Poppy around and missed the dog every day—she had just expected something more extravagant.

"I wish that were the case," Ruby replied with a discreet roll of her eyes.

"No, no, nothing like that. His Grace prefers exotic animals. He has his own little menagerie on his estate, something he takes great pride in." Mr. Cole's brows furrowed. "What is there, again?"

"Daddy never goes there; the animals scare him," Ruby offered in explanation as she sent her father a teasing grin.

"Well, can you blame me? I've heard too many stories of maulings. I'm not running the risk of that happening to me."

"His Grace's animals have never mauled anyone," Ruby clarified, seeing the shock on the Fletcher family's faces. "From what I remember, he has a cheetah, two parrots, an eagle..."

"Don't forget the wallabies, the three small monkeys, and the venomous snake that he boasts about," Victoria added.

"And that zebra he insists he will race in the Derby one day," Frank concluded with a snort as he drained his whiskey.

Silence washed over them as Penelope blinked at the Coles, almost hoping they'd declare it a joke. "*Why?*" was all she was able to say, and Ruby shrugged a shoulder with a wry grin on her lips.

Her father cleared his throat once before he dissolved into a fit of giggles, raising his fist to his mouth in a futile attempt to smother them. It didn't work, however, and instead his mirth seemed to infect the lot of them until they were all laughing away, no doubt imagining the duke surrounded by his bizarre "pets".

"The next thing he wants," Mr. Cole stated in between his giggles, "is a *giraffe!*"

Hearing that just renewed their humour, and Penelope felt her ribs begin to ache, growing sore from the non-stop laughter. She dabbed the tears of mirth with her fingers, and her eyes met Ruby's across the table, feeling her heart leap. Their families were not only being civil to each other, they were laughing loudly and freely together.

Penelope was almost a little saddened when the men then made their excuses and retreated to the smoking room, followed quickly by both Victoria and Penelope's mother, who retreated to their cabins for they were both feeling tired.

It took Penelope several moments to replay the events in her mind, and when she had, she couldn't seem to help herself. She started to laugh once again. Slowly at first, the odd giggle broke free until she was choking down air and people were staring at her.

But all that mattered was that Ruby was laughing with her, until a steward came up to make sure they were all right, and they quickly vacated the dining room.

"I can't believe that went well," Ruby said between giggles as they made their way towards the stairs.

"I can't believe the duke is a havering fool!" Penelope retorted, just as Ruby headed for the staircase to E Deck. She reached for her hand, drawing her to a halt. "Where are you going?"

Ruby raised an eyebrow. "Our room?"

"What about our party?" Penelope's eyes flickered to the staircase that led upwards, where the Third Class General Room was located, and where the party was no doubt already in full swing.

Ruby bit her lower lip, no doubt in an attempt to smother her desire to grin. She reached for Penelope's hand, squeezing it tightly. "Are you certain?" Her eyes, despite brimming with excitement, bored into Penelope's with determination. "Don't do this just to make me happy. If you're not comfortable with it—"

"I mean it." Penelope squeezed her hands in return. "I... I won't pretend I'm not still a little terrified at being caught, but I also know that it was great fun, and I want to experience that with you again. Not only did I promise you happy memories, I promised myself."

She tugged at Ruby's hand, drawing her closer to the stairs to the upper level. "Now, come on!"

Ruby needed no further encouragement, and the two hastily scrambled up the steps, hands still firmly joined.

As they walked, Penelope remembered an earlier thought. "So… Does Victoria know…?" Even though there was no one else in the corridor, she didn't want to say anything incriminating aloud just in case.

"Yes," Ruby replied with no hesitation. "She's my best friend, even though we fight like enemies sometimes. But whenever I need to talk things over, she's who I turn to, and that was no different. I told her about my feelings—mostly to see if she felt something similar. She admitted she had, but she also felt the same way for men, whereas I didn't have that. Never once did she try and talk me out of it or act like it was some great sin. She just accepted me and always listens whenever I start to fancy someone new."

Penelope's eyes narrowed a little. "Did you talk to her about me? Before you asked about Caroline?"

A pretty flush spread across Ruby's cheeks. "I did. I went to her with all my evidence, and she told me to stop being a coward and just ask you, since my instincts are pretty good."

Everything suddenly made sense then; all those odd little looks Victoria had sent Penelope's way, and the silent conversations that seemed to have passed between the sisters. "So, I should really be thanking Victoria for bringing us together?" She laughed as Ruby nodded her head, looking just a little bit bashful. "I'll bear that in mind."

Ruby rolled her eyes, and she and Penelope fell into silence, allowing the familiar upbeat ragtime music to filter down the hallway as they moved towards the room. The closer they got, the more Penelope felt dizzy with the onslaught of feelings that coursed through her.

Her heart raced from the excitement of spending such a time with Ruby, getting to drink and dance with her once more; her legs trembled with each step from fear that someone would find her there.

She wanted more occasions like this—three more days

didn't seem enough.

By the time they reached the room, she felt ready to pass out, and her first instinct was to run. But she buried that deep down, instead reaching for one of the bottles of beer on the table, opening it, and taking a long swig.

She then handed it to Ruby as she swallowed, wincing. She really hated the taste of the damn stuff. Ruby took a drink as well, only her face remained neutral as she handed the bottle back to Penelope.

The music was loud and lively, and as Penelope looked over to the musicians, she found that they were different from those who had been there the previous night.

So many couples were already dancing around the wooden benches, and Penelope felt her heart soar when she noticed that the couples weren't just men and women, but women dancing with women and men dancing with men. She even saw Mr. Daniel Lee dancing with another man, which made her heart soar.

Whether they were lovers or not Penelope had no idea, but no one was looking twice at them, which was all that mattered.

After taking another drink, Penelope sat the now empty bottle back on the table and then turned to Ruby. She extended her hand out towards her, already feeling her excitement mix with the alcohol, and she couldn't stop smiling.

She bowed as she asked, "May I have this dance, m'lady?" Even to her own ears, her Scottish accent sounded more pronounced.

Ruby giggled as she slid her hand into Penelope's. "You may, m'lady."

Penelope drew Ruby close—perhaps a little too close—but she didn't care. No one was looking at them. Everyone was much too focused on having their own fun.

She then started to lead Ruby into a rather lively Turkey

Trot, laughter falling freely from her mouth with every hop and bounce.

Her heart hammered out a wild beat as they danced, moving from dance style to dance style, whether it was the Grizzly Bear, Bunny Hug, or a simple one-step, only stopping to pick up another bottle of beer to share when they needed a break.

The room swam around Penelope as they started a quadrille with three other couples—Daniel and his partner, Albert and Betsy, and two women they had just met that night.

As she and Daniel joined in the centre, he grinned at her. "I knew you and Ruby were together," he announced as they turned in a circle.

Too drunk and overjoyed to think clearly, Penelope laughed. "I wish I could say the same for you and your partner. I have no instinct for this."

They parted ways for a moment, returning to their original positions. It took only a few minutes before the dance brought them together again. "Have no fear, when I get to New York, I plan on opening a club just for the likes of us. A safe haven where no one will feel judged or fear repercussions for being themselves."

Penelope beamed at him. "I can't wait to visit such a fine establishment, Mr. Lee."

As she once more returned to Ruby's arms, she allowed the music to wash over her. The heat pressed in on her, causing sweat to slide down her back. Her body started to ache from the constant movement. She focused only on dancing, filled completely and utterly with joy every time she and Ruby rejoined after parting to perform the steps.

I never want to leave this room, this moment, she thought as she spun with Ruby, one arm draped around her back and the other across her front, their fingers entwined and sure, even as the slippery satin of their gloves threatened to tear them apart.

When they finally finished their latest quadrille and said farewell to the other couples—Daniel reminding her of their plans—Penelope and Ruby collapsed into the first free seats on one of the benches. Their chests heaved, and their bodies were flushed and covered in a thin sheen of sweat.

Penelope looked at Ruby as she fanned herself with her hand.

She was the most beautiful person in the room. Penelope wanted nothing more than to touch her, to caress her face and kiss her lips—to make her way down her body and worship her, to know that the reason for the salt on her skin was what Penelope was doing to her.

But she couldn't do any of that here.

She couldn't *touch* her in any way that would raise suspicions.

Dancing together was one thing; they didn't know anyone else here. They had no chaperone, so it was natural. She refused to push their luck and believe that everyone packed into this small room would be understanding—this wasn't Daniel's safe haven.

Swallowing, Penelope reached out and placed her hand on Ruby's knee for just a moment. She heard Ruby's breath catch in her throat as she leaned over, bringing her lips to her ear so that she could whisper, "Do you want to go back to our room? Now?"

When Penelope pulled away, she watched as Ruby swallowed heavily, her breath coming in short, sharp pants—and she knew it wasn't due to the exertion from the dancing.

Ruby nodded. "Yes," she whispered softly, barely audible.

With a giddy smile, Penelope stood, reaching for Ruby's hand. She then dragged Ruby through the crowd, pushing the two of them onwards towards the door and bursting through it with a loud laugh that echoed down the corridor.

Ruby raised her finger to her own lips, shushing Penelope, even as she giggled along with her.

Trying her hardest to swallow the passion and happiness in her veins, Penelope bit her lip and led Ruby back to their room.

Chapter Sixteen

The moment they crossed the threshold, Ruby pushed Penelope up against the door, her lips on Penelope's hot and insistent. Her hands fumbled with the lock as she made sure that no one would walk in on them.

Penelope pushed herself forwards as she kissed her back with renewed fervour. Her hands found Ruby's waist, clawing at the delicate fabric of her blouse.

Ruby's hands couldn't seem to decide where to settle—one moment they were roaming Penelope's back and down her hips, the next they were at the nape of her neck, loosening the pins in her hair. Most of the strands fell over Penelope's shoulders and down her back, but several found their way into her face and tickled her nose.

She pulled away from Ruby and combed her hair back with her fingers as she laughed breathlessly. Ruby watched her intently as she cast the remaining pins and the hair rat from her, uncaring where they landed.

Ruby's golden hair lay in soft curls over her shoulders, and her face was flushed with the prettiest of pinks, almost drowning the freckles spattered over her nose and cheeks.

"God, but you are beautiful." Penelope sighed as she cupped Ruby's jaw, her thumbs pressing into the hollows of her cheek before stroking along her stunning cheekbones. Ruby smiled softly as she tilted her head into Penelope's right hand and wrapped her own around Penelope's wrist.

"You're one to talk, my dear." Ruby smiled, a glorious thing. It was so soft and gentle and full of adoration that Penelope couldn't help but lean forwards and taste it.

She started to move them, walking away from the door and towards the bed. When Ruby's back met the wood of the bunks, her hands reached for the fine buttons on the back of Penelope's blouse. Penelope focused on the buttons at the side of Ruby's skirt, smiling to herself when she felt the fabric slide down Ruby's body and pool at her feet.

It took no time at all for them to shed their many layers. The room probably looked like a war zone, with petticoats and corsets thrown aside and lacy and frilly garments scattered everywhere, but she didn't care.

Not right now, as her skin pressed against Ruby's, sparking flames deep in her stomach.

Her mouth eagerly sought out Ruby's and when she had to break away to draw in ragged breaths, she latched on to her neck, nibbling with her teeth, alternating pressure from soft and teasing to hard and claiming. She moved her lips along her shoulder, to the soft curve as it moulded from shoulder to arm, before she moved a little lower, tracing the solid line of Ruby's collarbone with her tongue.

"My God," Ruby groaned as her head fell backwards, landing against the solid wood of the upper bunk with a thud that resonated through the room. Penelope glanced up, ensuring that she was well, before she continued.

Her lips, tongue, and teeth followed the natural curves of Ruby's skin, working her way to her breasts. She took a nipple into her mouth as her hands moved up Ruby's sides until they cupped her breasts.

Her hands squeezed and rolled the flesh as her lips continued to tease the hardened nipple, feeling Ruby shiver in response to the spasms that rocketed through her body. She groaned as she pulled away for a moment, blowing over the wet skin and earning a surprised moan from Ruby.

Ruby's hand found its way into Penelope's hair, and she tugged her head upwards, bringing their lips together once more. Penelope enjoyed the taste of Ruby on her tongue and the way their bodies slid against each other. She was on fire everywhere they touched, from their lips to her hands on Ruby's hips, to her breasts caressing Ruby's, to the way Ruby's thigh kept brushing against the crease of her legs, determined to slide between them.

"Get into bed," Ruby growled when she pulled back, the words followed by a gentle slap to the side of Penelope's thigh. Though the initial sting made her yelp breathlessly, the sensation sent pleasure through Penelope's body, settling in the pit of her stomach.

Penelope stepped around Ruby to crawl into the bottom bunk. She lay on her back, resting herself on her elbows, legs bent. When she had Ruby's attention, she relaxed, inviting her into the space between her legs.

With a low, guttural groan, Ruby eagerly pushed herself forwards.

Her hands settled on Penelope's knees, and their lips met. As they kissed, Penelope felt Ruby's hands move up her thigh towards her hip and then veer sharply to the side.

At the first touch of Ruby's fingers against her centre, Penelope felt as though she were going to burst. She closed her eyes, throwing her head back in an attempt to focus on her breathing and settle herself down.

Ruby's initial touch had been gentle, teasing, but her

second was anything but. She slipped two fingers inside, her thumb focusing on rubbing teasing circles on her clit.

Penelope's eyes flew open as her lungs ached, desperate to get more air. Her breath was ripped from her mouth and swallowed by Ruby, who pressed her lips back to Penelope's with a groan of her own.

"God, you are beautiful like this."

"You keep…taking the Lord's name in vain…" Penelope breathed, words escaping through teeth clamped tightly on her lower lip. "You should be…ashamed."

Ruby laughed, her breath mingling with Penelope's as her fingers continued to work in and out of her. Penelope felt the knowing tightening in her abdomen, felt flames flooding her veins as her lungs contracted and everything grew taut— until it suddenly snapped.

Her legs clamped shut, stopping Ruby's motions as her hips bucked and her back arched. She felt weightless, as though she had been flying and she couldn't recall what it was like to be bound by gravity. There was a pleasant hum spreading through her body, setting nerves and veins alight and numbing her until it was all she could focus on.

Just as she felt like her back was going to break, the tension broke.

Her eyes were still clenched firmly shut, and her sensations came back in bits and pieces. At first it was the hammering of her heart against her ribcage and in her ears, followed quickly by the harsh gasps ripped from her lungs as the odd moan continued to fall from her lips. After that, it was the heaviness of her limbs, how impossible it seemed to move them even though she still felt utterly weightless.

When Ruby's lips pressed soft kisses against her shoulder and across her collarbone, she fully came back to herself and realised that Ruby's hand was still trapped between her thighs.

Penelope let her legs fall open, and Ruby pulled her hand back, moving her wrist in slow circles. With a snort, Penelope cupped the back of Ruby's neck, grabbing a fistful of hair to tug Ruby forwards for a rough kiss.

When she was certain Ruby was engrossed in the kiss, Penelope manoeuvred them so that she was on top of her with Ruby lying on her back.

With a sly grin, Penelope began to press kisses to every inch of skin she could reach. She moved from her neck and cleavage across her shoulder and down her arm, noticing the way Ruby's breath hitched whenever she got close to her neck, the inner crease of her elbow, or her wrist.

She then worked her way back up, giving the other side the same attention before she started to work her way down Ruby's body.

Ruby's skin was flushed a beautiful red, and knowing that she was the reason she looked so dishevelled filled Penelope with a primal sort of pride.

Then Penelope decided to finish what she had started. She lowered her lips to Ruby's chest again, letting her breath tease her skin, causing her hairs to stand on end in anticipation.

Penelope lingered longer than she wanted to, mostly because she enjoyed the way Ruby squirmed, her body wiggling against the mattress and her hands fisting in the sheets as her hips kept bucking infinitesimally.

It was only when Ruby ground out in an almost-whine, "Penelope! For the love of all that is *holy*—" that Penelope caved and sealed her lips over Ruby's clit, causing her pleas to trail off into a deep moan. Her hips bucked, and Penelope wrapped her arms around her thighs to anchor her down and stop her from breaking her nose with her pubic bone.

That wouldn't be easily explained.

With her hips firmly under control, Penelope focused on

Ruby's pleasure.

Three times she felt the telltale signs of Ruby's peak approaching, felt the way her thighs trembled and her entire body went taut, and each time Penelope pulled away, pressing her lips into her thighs or hip bone until her breathing eased.

When it happened again, Penelope felt a hand wind in the hair at her crown. She smiled to herself as the grip tightened, holding her firm, not allowing her to lift her head or move even an inch.

"If you...even *think*..." Ruby growled, but Penelope had no intention of stringing her along for a fourth time.

She paired tongue and fingers, friction and suction, until Ruby was a whining mess, her hand still wound in Penelope's hair.

She had to remove one arm from around Ruby's leg to bring her fingers into play, and Ruby's free thigh clamped against Penelope's face and refused to move. Penelope gave it a small slap, which didn't seem to do anything but make Ruby moan again.

When Ruby reached her peak—the muscles tightening to an almost unbearable level for Penelope before relaxing altogether— Penelope was finally able to move from between the tight embrace of Ruby's thighs.

She kissed her way back up Ruby's body, capturing her lips and snorting when Ruby only responded after a delayed moment. She then flopped down beside her, throwing her arm across Ruby's midriff as she pressed herself as close to her body as she could.

"Wasn't so horrible in the end, was it?" Penelope teased, when Ruby finally opened her eyes after five or so minutes had passed.

Her words startled a laugh from Ruby, who rolled onto her side so she could face her, her arm draped around Penelope's shoulders, hand pressed between her shoulder blades.

"Don't go getting cocky on me," Ruby drawled, her voice sleepy as she shuffled down the bed to tuck her head under Penelope's chin. She pressed a kiss to the hollow of Penelope's throat before she snorted. "Who am I kidding? That was glorious—get as cocky as you want."

Penelope giggled as her fingers combed through the tangled mess of Ruby's hair. She would no doubt have to spend another ten or fifteen minutes brushing it tomorrow morning.

She didn't want to think about how much she wanted that—not just tomorrow, but for the next few weeks, months... even years, if Ruby would have her. She knew better than to call it love—it had only been a few days—but so often people didn't marry for love; they married for position or wealth. And it was usually after the marriage that the love came.

Who was to say something similar couldn't happen for them? That they were both women didn't make a difference to her, but she knew it wasn't only about what she wanted.

Penelope took a deep breath and pressed her lips to Ruby's forehead. Her breathing had already evened out. Maybe they wouldn't get a life together, but they had another three days together, and Penelope wasn't going to waste them.

After pulling the thin sheets up and over their bodies, she wrapped her arms tighter around Ruby's body and snuggled further into her, entangling their limbs until she wasn't sure where she ended and Ruby began.

And with Ruby's breath even against her chest and her heart beating a solid rhythm, Penelope allowed herself to drift off to sleep.

Chapter Seventeen

Penelope was awoken by Ruby moving in her arms.

Her grip was so tight that really it was no surprise Ruby was struggling to roll over in her sleep. Penelope groaned and opened her eyes, letting her arms loosen.

"What time is it?" Ruby asked and stifled a yawn with her hand. She then brought her wrist up close to her face, trying to read the time on her delicate wristwatch. "I *think* it says eleven thirty...or after it." She frowned, an adorable pucker appearing between her brows. "It's hard to tell for sure. Judging by how utterly exhausted I feel, it definitely hasn't been that long since I fell asleep."

"I think an hour at most." Penelope brushed her nose against Ruby's and asked, "How tired are you?"

Ruby laughed. "Is that your way of asking if I'd be up for another round?" Ruby laughed again, louder, when Penelope nodded in answer. Her hand landed on Penelope's waist, and she shook her head. "You are adorable."

Ruby surged forwards and sealed her lips over hers. No longer caring about having a witty retort, Penelope lost herself to the kiss. She opened her mouth and grazed Ruby's tongue with her own as her hands pawed and grabbed her skin, eagerly pulling her closer and closer.

The hunger in her veins was so insatiable that Penelope was certain they could spend all night doing this and it still wouldn't be enough. Though, if their stamina kept up, she was more than willing to see if there was such a thing as being sated in her lust for Ruby.

Ruby's hand moved its way into her hair, nails scraping her scalp and tugging her forwards.

There was no way they could get any closer. Their bodies were already pressed together in a long line, thighs wedged between each other's, ankles tangled, hands gripping, lips never breaking apart for more than a brief inhale of air.

Penelope grinned and trailed her fingers in a featherlight caress over Ruby's side, hip and thigh as they made their way to the apex of her legs.

Just when Ruby's thighs had fallen open, she and Penelope sprang apart with startled squeals as the ship shuddered, propelling Ruby forwards and into Penelope's arms.

Penelope just managed to brace herself to stop them both from falling out of bed. A grating sound, like long nails being drawn down a blackboard, screamed into the silence of the night, and it made her blood run cold.

Then it was suddenly over, and the silence was all-encompassing. The only sound was their ragged breathing as they lay frozen in each other's embrace.

Penelope's grip was like iron around Ruby's shoulders, her knuckles white from holding her close. Her foot was pressed into the mattress, her hip aching from the force she'd had to put behind it to stop them from tumbling from the bunk to the floor.

"Penelope...?" Ruby's voice was weak, small, and Penelope tightened her hold even further at the sound.

Her lips found purchase on Ruby's forehead. "I'm here."

"What… What was that?" Ruby was trembling, and it wasn't until Penelope loosened her grip to rub Ruby's arm in an attempt to soothe her that she realised she was too. She kept her hand on Ruby's arm, the motion probably comforting her more than it was comforting Ruby.

"I… I'm not sure," Penelope answered, after a long moment. She finally felt brave enough to move, just a little, tilting her head to the side and glancing over at the door.

A few of their belongings had fallen to the floor with the shudder, but that was it. Everything still seemed to be going fine…but one sensation was missing.

She frowned, closing her eyes as she concentrated, her mind muttering a mantra of *please, please, please* as she hoped that she was mistaken.

She didn't know much about ships—this was her first time aboard one—yet she had quickly adjusted to the constant motion. Even as she stood still, even though the sailing was generally smooth, there was always a *hum* of sorts to let her know that they were speeding through the waves.

But as she lay there, eyes closed and whispering to herself, she realised that hum had faded to almost nothing.

Ruby pushed herself upright, supporting herself on her hands even as her arms trembled with the effort. The covers fell down to her lap, and Penelope hoped that no one would walk into their room at that moment because there would be no mistaking what they had been doing.

"She's not moving as fast," Ruby whispered into the twilight, her gaze frantically darting around the room before returning to Penelope. Her eyes were wide with worry.

Penelope had no doubt that that panic was mirrored in her own face.

"Let's… We'll shove on our clothes and go and investigate. Surely we weren't the only people who felt that? The stewards must have answers," Penelope offered as she entwined her fingers with Ruby's, then brought their joined hands up to her lips to press a kiss to Ruby's knuckles.

"All right. That sounds…" Ruby trailed off with several nods, so Penelope took the initiative to slide from the bed.

Penelope gave Ruby's hand a reassuring squeeze before dropping it so that she could fish through the disarray they had caused earlier. She found her combinations and corset with no issue. But finding her stockings proved difficult, and in the end, she decided to go without. Her skirt would cover her, and she had no doubt that they'd be told everything was fine and they could return to their rooms soon anyway.

She was quick to shove on her boots, skirt, and blouse, and then pulled her coat on over the top, just in case they had to go to the deck to find someone to get answers from.

When she was ready, Penelope turned to find Ruby shakily attempting to button her blouse, so she stepped up and took over. Her own fingers were only slightly better, and it took several fumbles before the delicate buttons were completely fastened.

Ruby then reached for her hand, her grip like iron. Penelope placed her own atop it and drew Ruby close until there was only an inch between them. "We are going to be fine. I know it."

Ruby took a deep breath in, then released it in a long gush. "I know. It was maybe just some silly little iceberg and everything is fine."

Penelope laughed. She cupped Ruby's cheek with her free hand and brushed her thumb over her lips. "That's the spirit." She shook her head. "How am I the optimistic one? Shouldn't I be a curled-up mess on the floor and you the one talking me down?"

Her joke worked to soothe Ruby, and her grip on Penelope's hand started to lessen. She shrugged with one shoulder. "Sneaking aboard First Class has done you good— you're a brand-new woman."

Penelope snorted. "I wouldn't go that far. Now come on. I'm already cold, and I want to get back to bed to finish what we had started." Her smile grew seductive as she leaned forwards and pressed her lips against Ruby's.

It was a brief yet passionate kiss, and it held the promise of more in the way she teased her tongue along Ruby's lower lip before slowly pulling away. She grinned when Ruby trailed after her, as if she didn't want to part.

"Then we'd best get a move on," Ruby announced breathlessly. She tugged at Penelope's hand, leading them both from their room and out into the corridor.

Chapter Eighteen

When they stepped outside, they found several other passengers already lining the hall.

They were all still dressed for bed, only a few were in coats like Penelope and Ruby.

All of them, however, blinked blearily up and down the corridor, talking to each other and asking questions, their eyes still laden with sleep.

Most of the doors that lined their section of E Deck were still shut. And those people who were awake seemed more annoyed about being awoken than anything else.

Only a handful seemed to be concerned, including Penelope and Ruby.

"I am telling you it was nothing," one man declared loudly, folding his arms over his chest. He wore a cotton housecoat over his silk pyjamas, and Penelope could see his wife standing behind him, peeking over his shoulder.

"Didn't sound like nothing to me," another man in his sleepwear retorted.

"If it were something serious, then the stewards would

be waking us." The first man gestured wildly with his hands, causing everyone to look around. "Do you *see* any stewards?"

Reluctantly, the second man pursed his lips. "No." He turned, starting to retreat back into his room, when his eyes widened, and he gave a wordless exclamation. He raised his hand, pointing towards the staircase that another man was rushing down.

The other man had a leather folder in his hand and, whilst he turned his head at the sound of the man's shout, he didn't stop. He merely continued down the corridor and slipped through a door that led to the engine room.

"Who was that?" Penelope whispered as the two Second Class passengers started to bicker again. She tightened her hold on Ruby's hand and craned her head, feeling dread sink into her stomach at the white, worried expression on her lover's face.

"Thomas Andrews. He was the shipbuilder in charge of *Titanic*'s plans." Ruby swallowed, her gaze locked on the door where Andrews had disappeared moments ago. "I doubt anyone knows this ship better than he."

Penelope's mind raced, trying to think of reasons why the lead shipbuilder would need to be stirred if it were nothing serious.

He could merely be heading down to inform the workers in the engine room what to do. If he needed to consult on whatever was happening down below, surely that meant it was serious?

Just as she was about to voice that to Ruby, another door opened, and she was greeted by her father's face. He was rubbing his eyes with his knuckles, and judging from his expression, he had been awoken by the two men arguing outside his door, rather than by the sound.

Before he could snap at the men, Penelope darted towards him. "Father, is everything all right? Did you *feel* that?"

He seemed to take a long moment before he registered

who was talking to him and what she was saying. He cleared his throat, but his voice was still weak with sleep as he replied, "Feel what? Darling, what is going on?"

Penelope swallowed. Her parents were on the other side, away from the wall of the ship. Perhaps it had just seemed so severe to her and Ruby because they had been so close to it?

"There was this loud, scraping noise, as if something struck the ship. And Mr. Andrews was just seen going down to the engines." Penelope wrapped her arms around herself. Her father really must be half-asleep if he wasn't even commenting on how utterly dishevelled she looked.

Her father *hmm*ed. "We may have dropped a propeller. That can happen." He looked over her head, down the corridor. A moment later, his gaze returned to hers, and he smiled, softly rasping his knuckles against her cheek. "I'm sure it's nothing. Go back to your cabin and sleep. If it's anything we need to be made aware of, the stewards will let us know in due course."

Nodding, Penelope bade her father goodnight and made her way back to her room, where Ruby still stood on the threshold.

"Father says we should just head back inside and, if anything is amiss, the stewards will let us know," Penelope said in a small voice, trying her hardest to drown out the other passengers beside her who were still bickering. "What do you think?"

Ruby swallowed once, twice, before jerking her head sharply backwards. The gesture was enough for Penelope to understand, so she led Ruby back inside, closing the door and heaving a sigh when the voices cut off.

She sat on the small sofa, pulling Ruby down beside her. Penelope guided Ruby's head to her shoulder, bringing one arm around her as the other hand remained secured in hers. Her free hand started to stroke through Ruby's long, blonde hair.

Whilst the ship had slowed—in fact, Penelope was almost certain she had *stopped* now—that didn't mean anything. Perhaps that's all that had happened. Something had gone wrong with a boiler, maybe.

"Do you know one of the coal bins aboard had been aflame for nearly a fortnight?" Ruby said. "Captain Smith told His Grace, who told Daddy. They only *just* managed to get it put out today. And after all that trouble with *New York* at Southampton… I'm beginning to think this ship has a bit of bad luck." She snorted and then shook her head, sitting straighter. "If Mr. Andrews is going down below, it must mean there's something wrong with a boiler. If that's the case, there'll be an hour or two's delay."

"And do you think it is something with the boilers?" Penelope asked. "Would that explain the other things? Father said something about a dropped propeller…"

Ruby nodded slowly. "Oh, yes. Both would explain her slowing down and juddering so fiercely…" She drew another shaking breath in, and even as Penelope kept stroking her fingers through Ruby's hair, she knew that she needed to do more to take her lover's mind off the ship and what could possibly be going wrong.

She got up and walked over to their cases, finding Ruby's and pulling out the black book she had seen on the very first day of the voyage. She set it on Ruby's lap and sat down beside her. "I don't know a lot about stamps, beyond the ones I buy whenever I send letters…" She gently opened the book and pointed to the first one. "What's so special about that one?"

As Ruby informed Penelope of the history behind the stamps—one even being the very first stamp with Queen Victoria's profile against a black background—both of them seemed to calm. Penelope allowed Ruby's words to wash over her, and the distraction had the desired effect on Ruby, whose entire body relaxed.

After finishing an explanation of a stamp she had received from her relatives in America, she slumped against Penelope's side as her head drifted from shoulder to bosom.

"I think I'm more tired than anything," Ruby eventually said, after minutes had crawled by. She closed her stamp album and shuffled slightly before she lifted her head so that she could meet Penelope's gaze. "It all seems so silly now, to think of it being anything serious when so long has gone by and there's still nothing... I think, should it have happened during the day, I wouldn't even have noticed."

"You're probably right." Penelope covered the yawn that broke free. She grinned sheepishly before running her fingers through her hair, starting to braid it into something more acceptable for bed. Ruby followed suit a moment later.

"At this point, I'm considering whether we should get changed into our nightclothes and get back into bed..." Penelope pursed her lips, her head cocking to the side as she studied Ruby.

"Hmm. Perhaps we should give it a few more minutes, and if we still haven't heard anything, we can do that. It does seem rather foolish to sit about waiting for bad news that isn't going to come." Ruby finished braiding her hair, then stood and fished two ribbons out of her case, replacing the stamp album at the same time. She handed one ribbon to Penelope whilst she used the other to secure her own braid. She then flipped the long braid over her shoulder, placing her hands on her hips as she surveyed the room.

"It is strange, to stand here and not feel her move beneath me." Ruby's hands slid across her stomach until her arms were firmly around her midriff. "I have no idea what to think. One part of my brain is telling me it's nothing. And the other part is saying it's something so utterly serious that I can't even come up with a solution. One part is telling me to sleep and we'll laugh about this panic tomorrow, and the other is telling me to get to the Boat Deck because that's where we should be." Ruby wrenched her hands free and covered her face with them, pushing her fingertips into the hair that framed her face and giving it a solid tug.

It looked so forceful that Penelope jumped out of her seat and slowly, gently, disentangled Ruby's fingers from her hair.

"We. Are. Going. To. Be. Fine." Penelope spoke slowly, only grinding out another word when she was certain that the previous one had sunk into Ruby's heart and soul. Her fingers wound through Ruby's, and she lowered them to their sides. "I don't make promises lightly, but I'm going to promise you that, all right? We are going to be fine." Penelope took a deep breath in, squeezing Ruby's hand to encourage her to mirror it. She released it slowly, then took another deep breath.

After five or so rounds, when her own heart no longer felt as though it was going to burst through her chest, Penelope leaned forwards and pecked her lips against Ruby's. "We will laugh about this tomorrow. Just you wait."

Just as the words left her mouth, the door to their room burst open. They both screamed, and Penelope whirled around and pushed herself in front of Ruby.

The man standing on their threshold came into view, and Penelope realised he was a steward. She wanted to berate him for barging in like that, at such a time, but she couldn't form any words.

Not as her eyes were drawn to his hands, noticing what he held.

Two lifebelts.

"Sorry to frighten you, miss. But please put your lifebelt on and make your way to the Boat Deck." He threw the lifebelts onto the sofa and turned to leave.

"Wait!" Penelope called, finally finding her voice as she took a step forwards. She would bodily restrain this man if she had to in order to get answers.

He turned to her with a hint of impatience on his face, which served to fan the flames of panic in Penelope's gut. "Yes, miss?"

"What's going on?" Penelope asked. "Why do we need our lifebelts?"

The steward glanced over his shoulder. She noticed several other stewards walking up and down the corridor, all with lifebelts in their hands.

All the cabin doors she could see had been pushed open, and people were groggily coming to the thresholds.

When the steward turned to face her again, Penelope felt her entire body deflate. She swayed, feeling more like she was on a sailing ship than a sturdy steam cruiser.

"Miss, I assure you, this is just a precaution. We meant to run safety drills earlier, but we couldn't manage it." He stepped forwards with a smile, even as Penelope felt her own deepen into a frown. Surely they wouldn't wake everyone up in the middle of the night to run a *drill*? The First Class passengers would never stand for that. "We experienced a minor accident, so we decided to treat it like a real emergency since we were unable to run the drill earlier. I assure you that we'll be under way before long. But we must follow procedure."

Ruby swallowed audibly. "So... That's all this is? Just following procedure and giving your crew a taste of what it'd be like during a real emergency? There's...nothing to it?"

The steward's smile twitched a little. "Not at all. Don't forget, miss—our *Titanic* is unsinkable." Then the man retreated from their room and disappeared down the corridor.

"Did you believe a word he said?" Penelope asked after a moment, watching the other passengers and stewards bustling about.

"Not a word," Ruby replied, looking at the lifebelts still strewn haphazardly across the sofa.

Chapter Nineteen

Penelope was the first to move.

She strode forwards, and without much thought, slammed the door to their room shut.

She then turned to find Ruby staring at the lifebelts with wide eyes. Taking a deep breath, Penelope cupped Ruby's jaw with her fingers, watching as they trembled against the soft, pale skin.

Ruby finally shifted her gaze away from the sofa to Penelope, who smiled the second those soft blue eyes met her own.

"Hello," Penelope whispered, her thumbs rubbing gentle lines along Ruby's sharp cheekbone. "Come back to me. Don't get lost in there." She lifted one hand so that she could tap against Ruby's forehead.

The action brought a smile to Ruby's lips, a sight which caused Penelope's heart to soar. It usually did that anyway, whenever Ruby smiled at her—she had such a beautiful smile, after all. It was so easy, the kind that beckoned everyone around her to join in.

Penelope closed the space between them, pressing another petal-soft kiss to Ruby's lips. It seemed odd that the kisses they had been sharing mere minutes ago had been far fiercer and more passionate. This kiss was as soft as a breeze.

"I suppose we should head up to the deck," Ruby said when they parted. Her hands covered Penelope's, still framing her face. She threaded their fingers together. "Since that's what they want us to do..." Her eyes darted briefly to the lifebelts. "Do you... Do you want to go to your parents' room? To check on them?"

Penelope gnawed on her lower lip, considering Ruby's words, before she ultimately shook her head. "Father told me to wait and see if stewards came knocking. And ours did say to put the lifebelt on and go on deck. My parents are sticklers for rules, they'll follow the steward's orders, then look for me up there."

Ruby nodded, giving a low hum as she lowered their hands from her face. "Of course. My family will no doubt be the same. Victoria and Frank will look after Liam and Julia. And Daddy will be with His Grace." She nodded again, as if confirming her own assumptions.

Swallowing down the lump in her throat, Penelope moved over to their luggage, which had slowly merged over the four days they had spent together.

She fished out two scarves and two pairs of gloves. "It'll be cold, this far out in the Atlantic and so close to midnight," she explained as she handed one set to Ruby before tugging on her own.

Ruby frowned and regarded her wristwatch. "Eleven minutes past midnight, to be precise," she declared, that familiar twinkle in her eyes returning for just a moment before it faded as she looked at the lifebelts. "What about...?"

Penelope gathered up both belts, surprised at how light they were. She tucked them under one arm and grabbed

Ruby's hand.

"We'll take them with us to the deck and see what the situation is before we put them on." Penelope squeezed her hand, urging Ruby to take a step towards her. She then brought their joined hands up to her lips, pressing a kiss to the supple leather of Ruby's glove before heading towards the door.

They stepped over the threshold, and Penelope was surprised to see that their corridor wasn't utterly swamped with people hastily scrambling to the Boat Deck as instructed.

There were only a few people moving about. The majority of the doors remained shut, whether they had closed after leaving their room, or had shut them and were ignoring the stewards, Penelope couldn't say. The two men from earlier were still there, continuing to bicker about the severity of the situation but making no move to put on the lifebelts they held, or to head to the upper levels.

Penelope rolled her eyes, adjusting her hold on their own lifebelts as they made their way to the staircase, closing their door over a little but leaving it open, so those who passed by knew they had followed the order. It was no busier than during the day, and the people they did pass seemed to be hastily dressed or had just shoved coats over their nightclothes. None of the women wore their extravagant hats. It was such a surreal sight.

Penelope made sure to take in each face that they passed, certain that Ruby was so lost in her mind that she wouldn't notice if they passed their families.

As they made their way from E Deck towards the Boat Deck, climbing the stairs at a pace that made her calves burn and her chest heave, Penelope felt unsteady. And not just from the exhaustion taking over her body. There was something else to it that made her draw to a halt, causing Ruby to stumble into her back.

"Everything all right?" Ruby asked, her voice still a soft whisper.

Penelope cocked her head, stepping a little farther aside to give more space to the people who pushed past them. Part of her wanted to pretend she hadn't noticed it, but she didn't want to exclude Ruby from her thoughts just because she was worried about how she'd react.

"Does the ship feel...lopsided to you?" Penelope asked. Granted, she hadn't been on a ship before, so her experience was lacking, but there was definitely something...off...as they stood on the Second Class staircase that connected the Bridge Deck to A Deck.

She watched Ruby's thick brows tug down in confusion. Then she closed her eyes and rolled her shoulders a little, as if finding her centre of gravity. Then her eyes flew open, wide and alarmed. "She's listing," Ruby said breathlessly. "She's leaning to starboard. I..." Ruby shook her head as her gaze darted nervously around the stairwell.

Ruby's hand tightened around Penelope's to the point where their joints were grinding together and causing pain. She didn't care, opting to return the pressure, tugging Ruby that little bit closer so that she could feel her body against her own.

We're going to be fine. We're going to be fine. We're going to be fine. It was an endless mantra her mind started up as she took a deep breath to steel her nerves and turned back to the front. The ship was leaning to one side, but that didn't mean anything.

They would get to the Boat Deck and discover that this seemed worse than it actually was. They would get to the Boat Deck and the crew would tell them that it was all just a big misunderstanding and they could retreat to their room, and then they'd give them a free meal tomorrow for the inconvenience.

Penelope took off up the stairs, pulling Ruby along behind her, who seemed to be made of lead. Her feet caught on the steps and caused her to stumble several times. After what seemed like the hundredth time, Penelope stopped and turned, dropping their lifebelts at their feet for a moment as she gripped Ruby's upper arms.

"Darling, I adore you, but I am going to need you to *get a hold* of yourself." She gave Ruby a shake to ensure that she was paying attention.

Her glassy, distant eyes finally focused in on Penelope. She swallowed thickly and nodded, and Penelope moved her hands up to rest on her shoulders. "I *promised you* that we'd be all right. And I will keep that promise. But you need to help me here, Ruby. I can't do this on my own."

"I know, I'm trying, really." Ruby took a deep breath. "When I lost Mammy, I didn't see it coming. It was like one day she was fine, and then the next she was in her bed, struggling to breathe, and we weren't allowed near her. After that, I started to second-guess and question everything—every little cough or blemish. And yet, I didn't notice my father getting ill until it was too late. And now, things are looking up and *this* happens, and I know my luck, Penelope, I know nothing will be as *fine* as it seems." She scoffed, scrubbing tears away with her fingertips. "Perhaps it's not the ship that's cursed but myself."

Penelope tugged Ruby closer until their foreheads touched. She was glad that everyone around them was so distracted that no one looked twice at them. It broke her heart to hear the woman she had come to care for, whose carefree attitude inspired her so much, speak so darkly about herself.

"I know that noise made it seem scary, and the lifebelts don't help, but we don't even know what's happening yet. We'll get up to the deck, we'll find our families, and then we'll find someone who can give us answers." She gave Ruby a crooked smile that required far more effort and concentration than it used to. "And besides, Father has been constantly informing me that this ship is unsinkable. Just as the steward did. We have nothing to worry about, understand?" Her fingers continued to caress the back of Ruby's neck. "And trust me, my dear, you are many things, but *cursed* is not one of them. So hold your wheesht about that, all right?"

Ruby let loose a long sigh mixed with a hint of laughter, her shoulders slumping a little. She cupped the back of Penelope's neck, twining her fingers in the short, fine hair at the nape.

As they stood there, foreheads together, Penelope's eyes drifted shut. Despite the panic, the concern, the worry, they stood there, sharing the same breath, each inhale and exhale perfectly mirrored as if they were one.

When they pulled away, Penelope longed to press a kiss to Ruby's lips, but she knew that would be pushing it too far. Their interactions, if only glanced at, would appear sisterly or friendly. A kiss on the lips—the way Penelope wanted to kiss her, anyway—would be too obvious. She couldn't risk it.

Instead, she pretended there was something on Ruby's face, brushing her thumb softly along her lower lip before removing her hands from her completely. And to avoid any further temptation, she hastily gathered the lifebelts back into her arms.

Ruby reached for her hand, entwining their fingers, and with a final squeeze, they continued their ascent.

As soon as they stepped onto the deck, Penelope and Ruby drew to a halt.

It was so loud and there were so many people.

Penelope only noticed that she had gone numb from the shock when the lifebelts started slipping from her grasp. The Boat Deck was a rather small area, and from where they stood, Penelope could see so many people that she could hardly glimpse the ocean surrounding them. And she knew there were more coming.

"Including the crew, there're over two thousand people aboard." Ruby shook her head slowly. "If things get so bad that we need to abandon ship, where are we all going to go?"

Penelope swallowed. "I didn't even realise there were so many people aboard. You wouldn't have guessed with how thoroughly the different classes have been separated."

"None of that matters now, I suppose," Ruby said, and Penelope knew what she meant.

There were hundreds of people on the deck, every single one looking as confused and concerned as she felt. Mothers held children close to their bodies whilst fathers looked around, searching for answers to give their families.

Crew members were rushing around the deck. Some stood to the side, supervising and giving instructions with hand signals; others were assisting passengers, ordering them into their lifebelts, whilst the majority worked on the lifeboats, removing the covers and starting to wind the cranes that held them in place.

"Why are they readying the lifeboats?" Penelope asked, and as soon as the words were out, it was as though the world snapped back to her. Nothing was as overpowering as the whistling of the air that rushed from the funnels. It made it impossible to think.

"What did you say?" Ruby asked, shouting in Penelope's ear, and even then it sounded like a whisper. She wondered, briefly, if there'd be damage to her eardrums after this, but she banished that from her mind. She refused to think of anything going wrong.

Shaking her head, Penelope answered, "Nothing. Come on. Let's find our families."

Ruby's eyes narrowed for a moment and she pointed to

the lifebelts in Penelope's hand.

Gnawing on her lip, Penelope glanced around the deck. She noticed that not many people had their lifebelts on; they either held them or had set them nearby.

Taking a breath, Penelope moved the lifebelt to her free hand. "The ship still seems steady and those look terribly uncomfortable…" She laughed without humour. "Let's just… keep them in hand for now."

Ruby nodded.

Just as they stepped forwards, two stewards brushed past them.

"—get the passengers up and tell them to dress warmly. And to bring their blankets with them. That will be good for—" was all Penelope was able to hear as the stewards continued their walk and the funnel drowned out their words.

Penelope and Ruby shared a look of concern.

"Bringing our blankets would have been a good idea." Ruby offered with a fleeting smile, which then slipped from her face completely as she clawed at her coat. "My mother's shawl. And my stamps! I didn't think to—"

Just as Penelope opened her mouth to soothe Ruby, an awful screech filled the air. It was unlike anything she'd ever heard before. Even after it faded, she could still hear it ringing in her ears, a steady repeat that made her sway where she stood. The previous scream returned, filling the night with its ominous howl.

When she turned towards Ruby, she saw her blue eyes fixed on the funnels, watching as the steam gushed from them in a never-ending stream.

"What is it?" Penelope shouted.

"I always thought a banshee's screech was a tale," Ruby murmured, so quietly that Penelope had to press her ear next to her lips to hear. "It was just a story, meant to scare children, but that…" She blinked slowly and as she did, tears fell down her rosy cheeks. Penelope was so concerned about them turning to ice on her skin that she reached up and wiped them away with the cuff of her sleeve. "We're going to die out here, Penelope."

Penelope tucked her lifebelt under her arm so she could grip Ruby's arms. "No. What did I say?" She gave her a hard shake, no longer caring about being gentle or understanding. "I need you to stay *with me*. You don't get to panic, understand? Not yet." Her voice was like steel, strong and unyielding. And when Ruby didn't respond right away, she gave her another shake, prompting her to nod.

"Good." Penelope released her and turned, her eyes surveying the deck, desperately searching for a glimpse of her parents and Ruby's family. Someone older and wiser, who would be able to take over and allow her a moment's break.

But she saw no familiar faces.

Perhaps others would have heard "deck" and assumed that that meant either the Promenade Deck, or even the Bridge Deck. Not ready to give up, she pushed herself into motion.

She made her way past the crew members trying to organise the lifeboats until she got to the end of the deck, where the crowd had thinned.

Stepping up to the railing, she took only a second to consider her options before she pushed herself up onto it, using the metal as a step stool to lean over the side and get a view of the forwardsmost deck at the front of the ship.

A smile tugged at her lips as she saw people scattered about there.

She even saw men playing football with a large chunk of ice. It was that which drew her attention to the rest of the area, and she noticed several larger chunks of ice strewn all over the deck.

Her jaw locked and she started to lower herself back to

solid ground, but as she moved, her gaze was drawn to the body of the ship. Many portholes were illuminated, and they reflected in the water. It was enough to allow her to see the water level in relation to the ship.

And what she saw made her heart stop in her chest.

At the front, the water was brushing up against a line of portholes... But as her gaze followed that line along to the back, she saw that the water level lowered.

She felt the tilt to the side—that was obvious as the ship hung over the right side—but that uneven waterline wasn't just a result of that...

As her eyes landed on the back of the ship, she saw that the bright red line that marked the waterline was completely visible, as were the tops of the large, completely still propellers that normally pushed the ship through the water.

Penelope scrambled off the railing.

"Penelope...?" Ruby stepped forwards, reaching for Penelope's cheek.

Penelope eagerly covered Ruby's hand with her own. Not caring how it looked, she drew it to her lips and pressed a kiss to the palm. "Come. There're people down on the Bridge Deck. Our families may be there." She entwined their fingers and led Ruby towards the staircase that would take them back down to the Bridge Deck.

"Should we check A Deck? Just to be safe?" Ruby asked as they came upon the entrance to the Promenade Deck. She dug her heels in, causing both herself and Penelope to stumble to a halt. Penelope turned and glanced at the doors with a frown.

"That's... It's just for First Class passengers..." Penelope's words hung in the air around them as she stared at the doors, wondering what to do. She knew there was also a good chance that Ruby's father was there with the duke. But that would just be one father found. Penelope found herself worrying that, should they find Ruby's family first, Ruby wouldn't try and help Penelope find hers.

Penelope quickly banished that thought as she threw her shoulders back and marched towards the door. "We'll stick our heads in and see what kind of people are about... Though, when I hung over the railing, I couldn't see many people. The Bridge Deck was much more crowded," she explained.

As she pushed the door open, they were greeted not by panic or funnel noise—or even by many people.

A band of musicians played a cheerful beat, a ragtime tune that was so out of place that Penelope felt like she had fallen through the looking glass.

She blinked rapidly to gather her thoughts, clearing her throat as she surveyed the right side of the area whilst Ruby joined her.

The room had a roaring fire and was toasty warm, all its dark wood and gilded furniture adding to the homely feeling. It was rather similar to the waiting area she had seen when they had sneaked in to see the Grand Staircase. Multiple small chandeliers hung from the ceiling, and the furniture was all upholstered in a rich blue velvet. The entire room just radiated comfort.

"That's... That's His Grace!" Ruby shouted, and before Penelope could say a word, she had pulled the door open farther and dashed into the room.

The man that Ruby rushed up to was middle-aged, his hair greying and hastily combed. He had a silver moustache and the thick sideburns that were in fashion when Penelope was a child. He wore a fine, thick woollen coat, but below the hem, Penelope saw a glimpse of navy silk pyjamas.

"Your Grace!" Ruby cried out, her voice breathless as she dropped into a small curtsey.

"Why, Ruby! What brings you here?" He frowned at her, concern and confusion in his warm brown gaze. Then he glanced over Ruby's shoulder and met Penelope's eyes. His lips stretched into such an easy smile that it made her wonder whether he knew what was even happening outside of First Class. "Ah, this must be the Miss Fletcher I've heard so much about!"

Penelope bobbed into a clumsy curtsey, her legs shaking and refusing to cooperate completely. She was almost glad her mother and father hadn't been around to witness that.

"Do you know where my father is?" Ruby asked.

His thick brows furrowed and his gaze once more flitted over to Penelope before settling back on Ruby. "He isn't with you?"

Ruby's sharp intake of breath reverberated around the room.

"No, Your Grace," Penelope answered as she stepped forwards and took Ruby's hand in her own.

"He asked leave to find you and Victoria about...ten minutes ago, was it, Benjamin?" The duke turned briefly to a man nearby. Penelope recognised him as one of the men she had seen board from Cherbourg. "This is utter folly, but he is a father. He must ensure that his babes are safe, regardless. So I let him go. I'm afraid that, other than that, I know no more than you."

Ruby pressed her lips together and gave a slow, jerky nod.

Penelope offered both of the men a smile. "Thank you, Your Grace. Sir." She then turned and drew Ruby back to the stairs.

When they were once more in the confines of the stairwell, Penelope turned her attention back to Ruby. She found her with slumped shoulders and her chin fallen towards her chest.

"Don't," Penelope started, pressing two fingers under Ruby's chin and urging it upwards. "We'll find your father with your sister down on the Bridge Deck. He's probably staying there as long as he can so that he doesn't have to spend time around those toffs."

Her words startled a laugh from Ruby. It lasted only a second before it was smothered by a sob, but it was enough for Penelope. She brushed her thumb over Ruby's lip before they turned and continued their descent to the Bridge Deck.

Chapter Twenty

By the time they made it from the back to the front of the Bridge Deck, the number of people waiting for further instructions seemed to have doubled—or even tripled.

The funnels continued to howl at the stars, and the sound was a shock to Penelope's system as they stepped from the enclosed area back into the open air.

Penelope's eyes slammed shut, and her shoulders lifted to her ears in a futile attempt to lessen the sting.

The game of football was still going on, though Penelope supposed that they were playing with a new block of ice, since it seemed much larger than the other one. She pointed it out to Ruby. "That ice… That couldn't have anything to do with this, could it?"

"I did say we could have hit an iceberg…but I mostly meant growlers…tiny little things… If ice broke off and landed on this deck, it must have been a big one." Her brows tugged down, and she craned her head upwards. Her arms tightened further around her body. "Which then begs the question, why didn't they see that?"

Penelope wanted to curse herself for ever bringing it up. She watched Ruby's blue gaze unfocus as she stared up at the high mast which held the lookout area. She reached for Ruby's hand, peeling it away from her side and giving it a squeeze before starting to lead her around the deck in their search for their families.

They hugged the railing, doing a circuit of the deck by following the metal.

It seemed to take no time at all for them to work their way around the decking. They made sure to be obvious in their scrutiny of people so that, if their families were there, they would either notice them or hear about two strange girls closely examining every passenger they walked by.

All to no avail.

After maybe the fifth circuit—Penelope had been far too preoccupied to truly keep a tally—they drew to a halt.

Penelope scrubbed a hand over her face and switched the lifebelts to her other arm for what was probably the hundredth time. As she rolled her shoulder, she huffed and admitted defeat.

"Come here," she whispered, sliding one of the lifebelts from her grip so that she could guide it over Ruby's head. It wasn't a complicated contraption to put on—over the head, stick the arms through, then tie two pieces of tape in place, one around the chest and one around the waist.

Once it was secured, Penelope stepped back to regard Ruby. She let loose a low laugh. "You look like…" She shook her head, her laugh merging with a sob to produce the most bizarre sound. "…I don't even know. You just look so odd." A solitary tear fell down over Ruby's cheek, which Penelope brushed away with her finger. "No, you can't do that. If you do that, then so will I, and then we'll get nowhere." It felt like she was swallowing a ton of gravel as she lowered her hand from Ruby's face and then handed her the other lifebelt.

"Here, help me into mine."

With a sniffle, Ruby guided the lifebelt over Penelope's head and then secured the ties in place. It wasn't as uncomfortable as Penelope had initially thought it would be. The extra bulk made moving feel a little more cumbersome, but she was certain it was a sensation she would quickly get used to.

"Time to search the back?" Penelope asked, tugging at the bottom of the lifebelt to ensure it lay correctly. She waited until Ruby nodded before taking her hand and leading her back through the enclosed area of the ship, through corridors lined with First Class rooms and fancy restaurants, before coming out at the other side.

She hadn't noticed it much as they had made their way from the Boat Deck to the Bridge Deck, but now going from the front of the ship to the back, it was obvious just how much the ship was tilting. It felt like they were climbing up a long incline.

Her hand remained locked firmly in Ruby's, the two of them on equal footing, each keeping the other steady and moving.

When they made it out to the back, it was much like the previous areas—countless people, all of them scared and worried, unable to hear what they were saying due to the funnels.

They made their way to the railing, once again repeating their previous routine of making it as obvious as possible that they were looking for someone so as to help draw attention to themselves.

They started from the left side of the ship, slowly making their way around to the right and then back to the left once more. Ruby told Penelope the proper names for each area of the ship, but they went in one ear and out the other. Not that Ruby seemed to care—Penelope knew she was mostly doing it to keep herself calm rather than to share information with Penelope.

During the third lap, Ruby drew to a sudden halt, drawing Penelope with her.

Her gaze wasn't turned to the centre of the deck, scanning the faces to try and find their loved ones, but was instead facing the dark waters illuminated only by the portholes and the stars above.

"What is it?"

"They've launched a boat," Ruby answered, her voice so soft that it was nearly engulfed by the shrieking funnels. Penelope knew that that was a sound that would forever haunt her. No matter what happened or where she went, that howl would constantly be ringing in her ears.

She swallowed as they watched the lifeboat move away from the ship. Whether it was carried by the waves or the crew were rowing, Penelope couldn't tell. She couldn't even see how many people were aboard.

So it really is bad. They're putting us on lifeboats… She's going down. Penelope felt her stomach roil, and for the first time, she was thankful that it was after midnight. Her empty stomach meant she had nothing to bring up. Yet her body still tried, and she retched, her hands bracing herself on the railing as she heaved over it, her eyes watering as they focused on the black water that lapped against the metal of the body.

Ruby's hand rubbed soothing circles on her back, and she focused on that instead, losing herself to the sensation. It slipped under the lifebelt, and Penelope could feel the pressure of the fingertips through her coat, her blouse, and her corset.

Truthfully, she wanted nothing more than to feel the comforting touch of Ruby's skin against her own. She wanted to go back three hours to when she and Ruby had been tangled together in bed with nothing more to concern themselves with than each other's pleasure.

She closed her eyes. She wanted to wake up from this nightmare.

When she reopened her eyes, however, she was still on the deck, chest pressed up against cold metal and head tilted towards the sea. She swallowed down the bile that had risen in her throat, wincing before she straightened and wiped her hand across her mouth.

Ruby moved to her side, and they both stared at the lifeboat. Ruby slipped her arm through Penelope's and then held her hand.

"What if they're on that boat?" Ruby was quiet for several seconds before she continued, "Your mother and father...my sister, Frank, Julia, and Liam. Daddy..." She shook her head, then turned away from the retreating boat. "What if they're on that boat and we're still here, searching for them?"

Penelope knew that the chances of that were slim, but they weren't beyond the realms of possibility. And she had no idea what to say to Ruby to make her feel better. Until they actually *found* their families, there was no way of knowing whether they were on that boat or not.

"I... I..." She exhaled deeply, her shoulders slumping in defeat. "I suppose they could be. But that doesn't mean we should stop searching."

Ruby stared at her for a beat before she nodded. She pressed the heel of her palm against her eyes.

When she lowered her hand, Penelope offered her a tight smile and said, "We could try the Boat Deck again. They may have made it up there by now."

They set off to the stairs once more. It felt as though they had explored the ship more in the past thirty minutes than they had previously done in the entire voyage.

As they stepped onto the landing and regarded the two separate staircases—one that led up and the other down—

Ruby gripped Penelope's wrist. Her eyes were wide, locked firmly on the staircase which led down to the lower decks.

Decks which were no doubt consumed with water, if the ship's steadily increasing tilt was any indication. She had a panicked, stricken look on her face as her gaze shifted to Penelope. "What if they're still down there? What if they didn't think it was serious and stayed in their rooms?"

Immediately, Penelope felt dread wash over her.

The conversation she'd had with her father on the first day of the voyage came rushing back to the forefront of her mind. She had pointed out how few lifeboats there seemed to be, and he had replied *"This ship is* unsinkable. *The lifeboats are purely a precaution."*

"No." She shook her head as she narrowed in on the staircase. "No, they wouldn't be that foolish."

Ruby moved to her side, resting her hand on Penelope's shoulder. "No. No, you're right." She shook her head, guiding her hand along Penelope's jaw and turning her head to face her. "It was a ridiculous idea. Let's go and check the Boat Deck. They're probably waiting for us up there before they get into a lifeboat." The smile on her face was nothing but reassuring.

Penelope took in everything about Ruby in that moment—the way her blue eyes were lit up with false confidence to convince her; how her blonde hair was in utter disarray, falling out of its braid and framing her face in loose curls; how utterly bizarre she looked with odd layers of clothing and the lifebelt secured around her.

It was such a contrast to how she had looked on the very first day of the voyage, the first time Penelope had laid eyes on her. She had been so perfectly made-up, with a classic Gibson Girl hairstyle and the softest and most beautiful lace gown Penelope had ever seen. She'd truly looked like she belonged with the millionaires in First Class.

"These past few days have been the best of my life," Penelope said, because there was something in her mind telling her that she wouldn't get a chance again. That if she didn't say it now, she'd regret it.

"Oh no you don't." Ruby shook her head stubbornly. "What did you say to me earlier? You can't do that, because if you do that, so will I, and then we'll get nowhere. Well, that applies to you, to now. So don't."

Penelope gave a snort of humour as she dried her eyes, grinding her knuckles into her tear ducts with more force than necessary. But the sting of pain and the way it made her vision fuzzy for a second afterwards was just what she needed—something else to focus on so that she could ignore the voice in her head telling her she was doomed.

After a final deep breath, Penelope drew her shoulders back and lifted her chin. "Best not keep our families waiting then, eh?"

And with shared, almost emotionless smiles, Ruby and Penelope joined hands and took off up the stairs.

Chapter Twenty-One

As they stepped out onto the Boat Deck for the second time that night, there was no denying the panic and worry in the air anymore.

People crowded around the lifeboats that were being loaded. Many men ushered their wives and children to the boats, then seemed stricken when they were refused entry on the grounds that the men had to stay behind.

The deck was far too large and overwhelmingly busy to make another circuit around the railing. Instead, Ruby and Penelope merely stood there, among the crowds bustling around the deck, the screaming of the funnels, and the shouts of people trying to be heard.

Penelope had no idea where to start.

Just as she felt her shoulders slump, felt almost ready just to give up the search and hope they'd all make it through the night, she felt Ruby desperately patting her arm.

Even though Ruby's gaze was focused on the distance, her eyes were filled with relief and excitement.

Penelope's breath lodged in her throat as she whipped

her head around to follow Ruby's line of sight—and tried not to let her disappointment show when she saw only Ruby's family.

Victoria stood a few feet away, amongst the crowds of people waiting for the lifeboats. She had one hand on her stomach while the other held Julia's firmly. Julia's other hand was wrapped around Liam's. The three of them stood there looking around.

Ruby took off in their direction, dragging Penelope along behind her.

She hoped and prayed that her mother and father were around, too, and that she just couldn't see them. But as they finally reached Ruby's family, there was no sign of her own.

Penelope ground her teeth together, feeling shame rack her body at the feelings that coursed through her veins.

She *was* relieved that Victoria, Julia, and Liam were all right. She was pleased that Ruby didn't have to worry about her sister, brother, and niece anymore—but Penelope wouldn't know that joy until she saw her parents.

Ruby threw herself into her sister's arms with a squeal, gripping her as tightly as she possibly could, before she lowered herself to her knees so she could take Liam and Julia into her embrace, one arm for each child.

Tears fell freely down her face, and shame returned for Penelope.

How could she begrudge such a reunion?

Releasing Julia and Liam, Ruby pushed herself to her feet and wiped the back of her hand across her face to dry her tears. Her blue eyes met her sister's, and once more, Penelope was struck by how similar they looked—really the only difference was their hair colour.

Victoria's was just that little bit of a darker, muted blonde, whereas Ruby's was golden strands.

"Where's Frank? And Daddy?"

Victoria swallowed thickly as she placed one hand on Julia's shoulder and the other on Liam's, holding them closely in front of her, as if she were afraid they'd disappear if she didn't. "They went to the other side of the deck to see if there were any boats closer to being loaded there." Victoria's voice was weak, even as she shouted to be heard over the steam gushing from the funnels. "I don't think they'll be too long."

Ruby's shoulders visibly collapsed.

Penelope had never considered herself an envious woman before. She had always wanted change, but she had never once looked at someone else's life and thought *I want that.*

Until that moment.

She wanted that relief. She wanted freedom from the tension she carried in her neck, back, and shoulders. She just wanted to know where her mother and father were.

"Have you seen my parents?" Penelope asked, cutting through the conversation. She could feel guilt or embarrassment about her poor manners later. "Your room was near theirs, surely you must have seen them…" Penelope winced, hating how accusatory that sounded. She drew a deep breath, holding it for five seconds before she released it. She almost expected Victoria and Ruby to jump down her throat for the way she spoke, but instead she saw nothing but concern and worry and understanding on their faces.

It made her heart ache.

Victoria's blue gaze darted to Ruby for a moment before it landed on Penelope. "I…" She sighed, biting her lower lip as she looked around the deck. "Perhaps we should wait for Frank to—"

Penelope stepped forwards, her hand curling around Victoria's upper arm. "Victoria, *I implore you*, just tell me if you have seen them."

Victoria's gaze darted around for a moment longer before she sighed. Her eyes were heavy and laden with sadness as they fixed on Penelope's. "We—Frank, the children and I—put our lifebelts on and headed to the Boat Deck as soon as the stewards arrived and told us to. As we made our way from our room, Frank decided that it would be wise to check in on your parents."

Penelope sighed minutely. Mostly due to the relief that Ruby's family hadn't just disregarded hers. She had spent what felt like hours looking for Ruby's family, and there had been that voice whispering in her head that they wouldn't have returned the favour.

Now she knew that wasn't true.

"Did they join you on the Boat Deck? Are they already on a lifeboat?" Penelope ventured, because that was the solution that made sense. And she needed to have the answer be something that *wasn't* her fear from earlier—that her father's ridiculous belief in engineering and mathematics had caused him to turn away from the facts in his face.

But when Victoria shook her head, she knew that wasn't the case. "I'm afraid not, Penelope," she whispered in a broken voice. "Your father insisted that everything would be fine and that we were wasting our time going out in the cold…and your mother refused to leave his side. Frank tried to convince them, but—"

Penelope didn't hear what they had said to Mr. Cameron. She turned on her heel and bolted back towards the staircase that she had just left. Her legs ached, and her body lagged from the exhaustion, yet still she pushed on.

Her hand was fisted in her skirts so that the hem didn't get caught beneath her feet as she ran down the stairs.

She'd made it down a single step when she felt a hand on her elbow, drawing her to an abrupt halt with a force that nearly had her falling on her backside.

Even before she turned, she knew who it was.

"Let me go!" she demanded as she yanked her arm free.

She caught at the bannister to steady herself as Ruby's hand refused to budge. Her eyes found Ruby's vivid blue ones, and she chose to ignore the pleading and concern in them as she hissed, "Ruby, I mean it. Let. Me. Go."

"Penelope, stop and listen to me for a moment. Victoria and the others have been up on the deck for the *same amount of time* as us. Do you *really* believe your parents would stay below deck for that length of time when faced with the growing evidence that *Titanic* is in trouble?"

Scoffing, Penelope again tried to release herself from Ruby's hold. To no avail. "You don't know how stubborn my parents can be."

"If they're half as stubborn as you, then I think I can imagine!"

"Which is *why* I need to go down and see. I can't just take it on faith that they'd come to their senses. I need to go down to their room, Ruby!" Her voice grew in volume with each word until she was nearly shouting.

Just as she prepared herself for one more attempt to pull herself free from Ruby's grasp, a steward came running up the staircase carrying some bread and several blankets.

He shook his head at Ruby and Penelope. "I wouldn't go down there. Water's up to E Deck, coming along Scotland Road." He threw the words casually over his shoulder as he passed.

Ruby turned her head, watching him disappear out onto the Boat Deck, and it was just the distraction that Penelope needed to wrench her arm free. She took the steps two at a time, leaping down at a frantic pace that her mother would have reprimanded her for.

"Penelope!"

She heard Ruby take off after her, but she didn't slow. The tilt was much more noticeable the farther down she went, yet even that didn't stop her.

The exits for A, B, C, and D Decks all passed by in a blur, and when she finally reached the one for E Deck, her entire body shuddered to a halt, much like the ship had earlier that night.

When the steward had said the water was coming up to E Deck, she had pictured nothing more than a leak. Just some water flooding the floors; nothing that would even reach her ankles.

The water she was looking at now was easily several feet deep, and it was creeping up through the lower levels at a continuous rate.

It was deeper at one end, due to the way the ship tilted to the front and right, and Penelope was thankful that that wasn't the side her parents' cabin was on. As she glanced down the corridor, however, she realised that her and Ruby's cabin would be flooded.

Her heart stuttered as she thought of all the things she had left behind in her rush to leave—mostly the embroidery of Poppy she had been working on for her grandmother. And her sewing box, which had also been a gift from Granny. It was like losing the beloved dog all over again, like losing a tie to her home and her closest family member.

Her hand reached up for her locket, thankful that she still had that fastened securely around her neck. It was now he only thing she had that would remind her of her grandmother.

Penelope watched the water move towards her as she stood there. She regarded it with shock and trepidation, even as her thoughts reminded her of everything she had lost and would lose.

"Penelope, please come—" Ruby's voice trailed off with a startled gasp. "Our room...Mammy..." Ruby choked on a sob, and finally Penelope reopened her eyes. She turned on the spot and gathered Ruby into her embrace, taking a second to comfort her. Penelope had felt floored to lose reminders of memories with her grandmother, but at least she could always return to Scotland and be with her.

Ruby didn't have that. The shawl and the stamp collection were all she had had left of her mother, and now they were gone, the album no doubt ruined and the shawl drifting down to the depths since they had left their door open.

Hot tears fell against her neck, and even though she hated herself for doing so, Penelope pulled away. If she wanted to search her parents' room, she had to do it before the water spread even farther. Not only did she have to make it to their room, she then had to make it back to the stairs and get to the Boat Deck afterwards. She couldn't if the water—which was so fast that the sound was overwhelming her ears—took her under and swept her away.

"There's no way she can survive this." Ruby spoke in a whisper. She reached up and brushed her tears away with a trembling hand. "All that's been lost... She's doomed—*we're* doomed."

Penelope shook her head. She couldn't think about that right now.

She cupped Ruby's face between her own trembling hands. "I need to check my parents' room. And I need you to stay here and let me know when the water gets close to the staircase, so that I can make it back in time."

Ruby opened her mouth, no doubt to protest, so Penelope cut her off with a harsh press of her lips to hers. She eagerly swallowed whatever words Ruby had been preparing herself to say, losing herself in the touch and feel of her lips against Ruby's.

Before she could lose herself to it completely, Penelope pulled away. "Stay here. And watch that water." Then she turned, descending the final three steps in one leap and taking off towards her parents' room.

Chapter Twenty-Two

The water was freezing.

It was unlike anything Penelope had ever felt before. It covered her feet, the water chilling her through her boots. She suddenly wished that she had taken those extra few minutes to search for her woollen stockings.

But not even in her wildest nightmares would she have been able to conjure this. She'd thought the ship would be fine. That they'd be delayed a little, but that they'd be told to head back to their rooms.

Now that wasn't going to happen.

Now she wasn't even certain there was a way through all of this.

But that was a worry for later.

For now, she just had to get to her parents' room.

It was only a few more doors away, and although the water was steadily rising, it was still manageable. She hauled her skirts up around her calves and pushed through the water, trusting in Ruby to let her know when it got to a dangerous level.

As soon as she reached her parents' room, Penelope grabbed the handle and thrust the door open, throwing herself into the room. "Mother! Father!"

Her eyes darted around the room—the bunks, the dark wood furniture, the magnolia walls, and the rich, floral upholstery.

It was completely empty.

Her entire body started to shake, trembling so violently that it felt as though her bones were jittering beneath her skin. Her lungs ached with every ragged breath as she turned in a slow circle, even though there was nowhere for them to hide—the room was tiny. Everything was out in the open.

"No." The word was ripped from her throat with sharp claws. "No, no, no, no, no!"

She wanted to scream and tear her hair from her head. She wanted to destroy the room around her, to break things with her hands until she felt blood coat her skin. She wanted to collapse in a boneless heap and cry like a babe, hoping it would attract the attention of her mother.

She heaved, her breaths uneven and loud as tears fell freely down her face and her stomach roiled, causing her to wretch. She doubled over, arms wound tightly around her stomach, the pressure just enough to stop herself from bringing up bile.

Then new emotions coursed through her.

The first one she recognised was anger. Unadulterated rage at her parents for putting her through this—for even considering ignoring the warnings and remaining in their rooms until the last possible moment, even though her father had told her that if it were serious, the stewards would tell them.

Then there was worry, concern rushing through her veins, dousing the flames of anger as she realised that, at least if they had stayed in their room, she would have known where they were. She would be with them right now and would be able to shout at them, to convince them that the right thing to do was to get up onto the Boat Deck and into a lifeboat.

Now there was no way of knowing where they were. What they were doing. If they had even made it out safely, or if something had happened during their escape that had caused them harm.

"Penelope!"

And then the final emotion, the one that was causing her such difficulty breathing, was fear.

It wrapped long claws around her throat, squeezing the life from her as her mind conjured images of her mother and father lifeless, drenched, staring up at her with faces frozen in the panic that had consumed their last moments.

Her mind tried to reason—tried to tell her that she was *standing in their room*. The water hadn't reached that far, which most likely meant that her parents had made it to the upper decks before the water had stopped them.

She just couldn't shake the thought that her parents had done something utterly ridiculous, like head down to the cargo hold to try and get their luggage before the ship sank.

"PENELOPE!" The scream, so close to her ear, was enough to bring her out of her thoughts.

She bolted upright at the same time she felt a hand on her elbow, harshly pulling her towards the door.

Her senses came back to her.

The water had crept from the top of her feet to below her knees, seeping through her boots, skirts, and coat, and soaking her skin. It was colder than it had been to begin with, if such a thing were possible.

The parts of her legs that were submerged were utterly numb.

Ruby's hand moved from her elbow to her hands, entwining their fingers even though Penelope's struggled to bend. She was certain they were blue underneath her gloves.

"Three times!" Ruby hissed, tightening her grip as she dragged Penelope out of the room and into the corridor.

If it hadn't been for Ruby's hand on hers, constantly tugging her forwards, Penelope would have frozen at the sight in front of her.

The whole front of the ship was submerged, and the water was rushing in at an unbelievable pace. It had reached the staircase they had come down, and Penelope knew that, given a few more minutes, the water would be making its way up to start consuming D Deck above.

"Why ask me to stand and *watch the water* when you weren't going to listen to me anyway?" Ruby said, her free hand reaching for the railing that lined the walls mid-way from the floor. She used it to haul herself towards the stairs, fighting the current, all the while dragging Penelope behind her.

It wasn't until they had made it several feet that Penelope realised she had to help lessen the load. Her fingers ached as she forced them to wrap around the railing, and the pain only grew as she dragged herself forwards of her own accord.

"I didn't…mean to…" she ground out between clenched teeth, the tears still falling. Her lungs continued to struggle for breath, sucking in as much air as they could, but it never seemed to be enough. "Just because…you have your…family and can relax…" The words were out before she really registered what she had said, and she winced internally when Ruby dropped her hand and rounded on her.

"Is that what you think? That I don't care about your family? Because I have *news* for you, I do! But I refuse to let you kill yourself looking for them, just as I know you would refuse to let me put myself in danger if the situation were reversed. You won't be able to find them if you're drowning in the bottom of the ship, Penelope!" Ruby's shoulders heaved, her breath appearing in faint puffs of steam around them. Her cheeks were a bright pink and her blue eyes burned with an anger firmly at odds with the layer of unshed tears that covered them.

Penelope swallowed.

Before she could say anything to apologise, she felt a harsh force knock at her legs, a vicious lash of water that sent her stumbling. With a startled shriek, she clutched the railing to keep herself upright.

"Why don't we continue this argument somewhere where, as you pointed out, we don't risk *dying?*" Penelope offered as she hauled herself upright, every single inch of her trembling and convulsing from fear and cold and exhaustion. She honestly wondered how she was still functioning.

Ruby huffed and turned. With her back to Penelope, she gripped her hand, and they resumed their slow and tense journey along the corridor and back to the staircase.

When they finally burst free from the water, hurling themselves onto the dry stairs, they took a long second, kneeling on the steps, to catch their breath. Their hands remained entwined, the only thing anchoring them to that moment.

The icy water, however, took no such break.

As they lay there, Penelope could feel it creeping up her legs, climbing from toes to ankles. They had to get up and get back to the Boat Deck. And then they had to get into a lifeboat, because, for all the talk of her being unsinkable, RMS *Titanic* was going down.

Chapter Twenty-Three

There were three lifeboats drifting away from the ship when Penelope and Ruby emerged from the stairwell back onto the Boat Deck.

Despite three boats already being gone and many more still loading, even more people than before crowded the small deck. Given how far *Titanic* had already sunk, no one could pretend that she would survive now.

Rather than plead with people to get into the lifeboats, the stewards were having to push people back, reminding those who approached that it was women and children first.

Penelope stood to the side, watching the commotion with dull eyes.

If she believed herself to have been cold before, it was nothing compared to what she felt now, with the cold air hitting her soaked clothes. The convulsions that racked her body caused her teeth to chatter and her bones to ache, and no matter how much she huddled in on herself, nothing helped.

"We need to find my family..." Ruby started, but

Penelope shook her head, arms wound tightly around herself. "Penelope, I'm not saying that means stopping looking for yours, but if we get their help…"

Again, Penelope shook her head. She finally found the strength to explain. "I'm not saying that. Go and find them. I'll wait here."

Ruby moved to stand in front of her, her gloved hands cupping her face, but Penelope couldn't even feel it. Everything was numb, from her body to her mind. "We promised not to separate. I'm not leaving—"

"Ruby…find your family. And bring them here. I just… I need to… I can't stop…" Her teeth chattered so much that it made talking difficult. She trailed off with an aggravated grunt, trying to wrap her arms farther around herself.

"If you're sure." Ruby's eyes narrowed into a glare. "Do not move from this spot, do you understand? Move and I will find you just to kill you."

Despite the amount of effort it took her, Penelope tugged her lips into a grin. "I understand." She looked around and found a bench nearby. Then she forced herself to take the five or so steps needed to make it there. "I won't move from here. I promise."

Ruby stared at her for a moment longer, as if ensuring she was telling the truth, then she nodded and took off. Penelope watched her go until she disappeared among the crowd.

With nothing else to do but wait, Penelope focused on the people around her.

The sight of mothers cradling children to their chests wrenched at her heart. The poor babies had no idea what was happening or why they were wide awake so far past their bedtime. And their mothers were putting on brave faces even as they waved goodbye to husbands and fathers, not knowing whether they'd make it into a lifeboat of their own.

"No! I refuse!"

Blinking, Penelope turned her attention to an elderly woman with greying hair hastily combed and pinned up.

Her face was soft, kind, the sort of face that despite being lined with age, still displayed the beauty she'd had in youth. She had a lifebelt secured over her chest, and, much like everyone else, was dressed rather improperly for such a public place, her modesty only saved by the coat she wore.

"I have been by your side for forty-years. Do not ask me to leave you now." She was addressing an elderly man whom Penelope could only assume was her husband. He was balding and had a thick beard and a pair of glasses perched on his nose. "We either both get in that boat, or we both stay here."

The man shook his head. "I cannot, in good conscience, get into a lifeboat when there are still women and children to be saved."

His wife smiled at him, nothing but love and adoration in her gaze. She reached for his hands and gripped them both tightly in her own. "Then we stay here. Where you go, I go." Her eyes narrowed in a playful glare, "And you know that arguing gets you nowhere, Isidor."

Huffing a laugh, Isidor brought his wife's hands to his lips and pressed a fierce kiss to her fingers. "Then come, and let us not crowd the area for those still loading." He guided his wife's hand into the crook of his elbow, and they headed towards the back of the ship.

As Penelope watched them go, she removed one hand from around her midriff to wipe at the tears that had fallen from her eyes.

They were so utterly devoted to each other that, even after forty years, they refused to leave each other's side.

Penelope had never believed she would ever find a love like that. She knew she would never find it with a man, and the chances of finding a woman who would love her in such a devoted way were slim when it was something they couldn't be public about.

And yet, now, as she sat there thinking about Isidor and his wife, she thought of Ruby.

She couldn't say she loved her—she barely even knew her—but they had been through so much in such a short time that she felt as though her soul was tied to her.

Ruby had been there when she'd felt like she would never find another girl who felt the same way she did. Ruby had taught her what it was like to laugh and be daring for a change. Ruby had shown her that being adventurous was just as important as everything else she had been raised to be, and Ruby was there now, as they navigated their way through a disaster neither of them could have ever imagined.

How could she not think that the woman was tied to her?

Who was to say that this wasn't her chance to know devotion, no matter how brief? Even if it lasted only for a few more hours before she knew nothing more of the world, she could at least depart knowing she had felt that.

With a deep sigh, Penelope returned her arms to around her stomach. Those were thoughts for later—if there was a later, of course—and she couldn't be distracted by them now.

"Penelope! Penelope!"

Ruby rushed to her side, and before Penelope could say a thing, Ruby dragged her into a standing position. "Daddy has a space for us on a boat! Victoria and the children are boarding right now, we have to go!" Ruby gripped her hand tightly and started to drag her through the crowds and towards the other side of the ship.

"Wait, Ruby!" She yanked her hand free, tucking it under her armpit so Ruby couldn't reach it again. She shook her head fiercely. "What do you mean, there's a boat?"

"A *lifeboat*. Daddy managed to find one for us. One that knows we're coming, so..." Ruby stretched out her hand towards her.

"I... I thought the plan was to find your family so they could help me find mine?" She glanced briefly over Ruby's shoulder, finding a lifeboat being loaded with women and children, as were most of the others. More men seemed to be standing around this side of the ship.

"That was the plan. Victoria and Frank even agreed with me—"

Penelope cut her off, voice sharp. "Then why are *we* going into a boat?"

Ruby let out a long breath. "Because Daddy arrived, and he refused. He wouldn't let us go down with the ship. But I mentioned you and he told me I could come and get you! I promised I wouldn't leave you, Penelope!" Ruby approached her, taking Penelope's face in both hands.

Her words caused Penelope to frown, surprised at their resemblance to the words Isidor's wife had said to him.

With a deep inhale, Penelope wondered if things would have been different for the elderly couple if they had been younger. Would he have insisted his wife board because she had her life ahead of her? Would she have gone because she hadn't had decades of marriage to point at and declare it enough?

Exhaling, Penelope covered Ruby's hands with her own. "Let's go to the boat."

Ruby's answering smile was breathtaking. It reminded Penelope of the very first *true* smile she had seen from her when she had volunteered to help watch the children with her. How open it had been, how it had totally transformed and lit up her face, morphing her from beautiful to ethereal.

Ruby turned and led Penelope through the crowds, a flurry of apologies breaking free from her mouth as she pushed and nudged people in a most unbecoming manner.

There was a group of people around the lifeboat when

they finally reached it, and Penelope spotted Victoria, Frank, Liam, and Julia, along with Ruby's father.

All their eyes landed on her when they finally reached them. She had no doubt that she looked a state, still shivering intermittently, and still utterly drenched, though she could no longer feel that much.

"Miss Fletcher," Ruby's father said by way of greeting, tugging at his forelock in lieu of his absent hat. She smiled at him, unable to make her mouth cooperate with words. "I'm sorry our second meeting must be under such circumstances."

As am I, she wanted to say, but no sound came.

She wondered if she'd ever be able to speak again. She wanted to say a lot of things—to apologise that he was ill and to promise to look after his daughter, to care for her. She wanted to thank him for raising Ruby so well, to praise him for bringing her up to be a bright star in the darkest of nights.

But all she could manage was a shaky smile that faded almost as soon as it had flickered onto her lips.

He turned away to the lifeboat, and as the crowd around the area started to thin, he waved his arm to bid his family to move.

He reached for his son first, kneeling to his level and whispering something in his ear.

Then he embraced him tightly, a tear falling down over his lined cheek which he brushed away on Liam's lifebelt.

When he pulled away, he gently stroked Liam's jaw with his knuckles before hoisting him into his arms. The seaman in the lifeboat took him from his father, settling him between two women who wrapped their arms around his shoulders, comforting him as he seemed to understand what was happening and started to cry.

Penelope watched Mr. Cole swallow hard before he turned away, reaching for Victoria's hand. He gave her the same treatment, whispering in her ear and giving her a final embrace before guiding her into the boat. After that followed Julia, who, safely positioned between her mother and her uncle, turned to the front and asked, "Why isn't Daddy coming with us?"

Penelope's heart leapt to her throat and she had to turn away. She knew that, should she look much longer, her expression would give away the severity of the situation, which was no doubt the last thing Victoria and Frank wanted.

After saying something to the officer in charge of loading, Frank stepped up to the boat, but he didn't board. "Daddy's going to get on another boat, darling. This one is just for women and children. But Daddy will meet you later." He swallowed heavily, reaching for her hand and pressing a fierce kiss to her knuckles. "I promise."

Tears were streaming freely down Victoria's face when Penelope finally found the strength to face them again. She watched as Victoria buried her face in her daughter's hair, trying to mask her crying so that Julia didn't notice. Penelope was thankful that it seemed to work.

Frank then stepped away from the boat, thanking the officer and rubbing at his eyes. He took a few steps away, watching from a distance, but out of sight of his wife and child.

Ruby's father then beckoned Ruby forwards. She turned to Penelope, offering her a dazzling smile, and gave her hand a squeeze. It was the sort of squeeze that made it seem that, in five seconds' time, they'd be holding hands again and it would be like they had never parted.

Once more Penelope watched the ritual as father embraced daughter, watched them whispering goodbyes into each other's ears, speaking of their love in a way that was possible only for people facing their own mortality.

It made her heart ache.

Not just because it didn't seem fair for a father to have to say a final farewell to his daughter in such a rushed manner, trying to fit a lifetime's worth of love into a few seconds.

But also because she wouldn't get to do that.

Her relationship with her parents may never have been as steady or as solid as the one Ruby shared with hers, but that didn't mean anything.

In that moment, all Penelope wanted to do was let her parents know that, despite it all, she loved them. She needed them to know that she *understood* their feelings for her; that emotions were complicated. Penelope's own mind had warped and twisted things to make them seem worse, and now she just wanted to let them know that she loved them.

Ruby was assisted into the boat by her father and the officer, and she settled herself on the other side of Liam, thanking the woman who had been comforting him before taking over.

She tucked her brother against her side, bringing his head to her chest as she ran her fingers through his hair.

Ruby then raised her head and met Penelope's gaze. Her smile was a soft, gentle thing, beckoning Penelope closer. "Come, my dear, they want to start lowering the boat."

Mr. Cole reached his hand out to Penelope, who stared blankly at it for a long moment before she finally got her mouth to work. She cleared her throat and asked, "Which boat is this? I… I understand they're all numbered…?"

Mr. Cole turned to the officer and repeated the question, who answered, "Lifeboat sixteen," before he turned and started to shout orders for it to be lowered. He focused his attention back on Penelope. "Hurry, Penelope, there's no time to waste."

"Penelope?" Ruby called out. She sat upright, her brother still resting on her chest, his eyes now closed. She looked so earnest. Her brows were furrowed, but she had a welcoming smile on her lips, as if she were trying to assuage Penelope's fears.

Everything was still, quiet, floating away until all Penelope could think of and see was Ruby. All she heard were memories of her laughter, her voice, her moans.

"Penelope?"

Blinking, Penelope took one step backwards. "I'm sorry," she whispered, unsure if Ruby would even be able to hear her. Then she took off into the crowd with Ruby's cry of her name haunting her mind.

Chapter Twenty-Four

"Mother! Father!"

Her throat burned. The only thing she was truly able to *feel* was the sting in her vocal cords, the rasp with each syllable as she pushed her way through the crowds, clawing at the backs of strangers who had similar features to her parents and turning them around only to be disappointed when they weren't them.

She gathered looks from everyone she passed, a mix of concern, confusion and embarrassment, but she didn't care. She had to find them now. She had to find them, because if she didn't, then she had left Ruby alone on that lifeboat for no reason.

A part of her—in fact, it sounded more like Ruby in her head than herself—tried to say that there was a good chance her parents, or at least her mother, were already in a lifeboat.

But she couldn't accept that. Not just because that would, once again, mean that she had given up her one chance of getting off the ship safely for nothing. But because it would mean that her parents had left her. Without trying to look for her.

And Penelope couldn't accept that. For all she had resented their constant nagging, it was really their bizarre way of showing they cared. They didn't want her to be shunned in society for the way she acted or dressed or spoke. They wanted her settled with a good husband, which wouldn't happen if she hadn't learnt proper manners.

She refused to accept that they had just *left* her.

"Mother!" she tried again, her voice hoarse. "Father!"

Just as she started to descend to the Promenade Deck to once again search her way through the different levels, a hand caught her arm. She turned, a gasp lodging in her throat. For a brief second, she worried that Ruby had followed her off the boat and caught up with her.

But those fears were allayed when she was greeted by the face of a stranger. He had kind eyes and a thick, black moustache. His pyjamas showed under the coat he wore. He didn't have a lifebelt on, a fact which filled Penelope with curiosity.

"Dear girl, what are you doing? All the women and children are supposed to be on lifeboats." His grip was sure and strong, unyielding but still gentle. He started to lead her back the way she had come, but Penelope ground her heels into the deck, throwing all her weight into the action and stopping them both short.

"No."

The man raised his brows in astonishment. "No?" He leaned down to her level so that he could look her dead in the eye. "What's your name?" When she told him, he continued, "Penelope. I'm Mr. Ismay. Though, I suppose, given the circumstances, you can call me Bruce." He smiled warmly at her. "No one is more devastated than I am about this, but there is no way *Titanic* can survive. She is going down, and I refuse to allow a young woman such as yourself to be a victim. There are still plenty of lifeboats waiting and—"

"I don't want to go down with her," Penelope cut him off,

sounding breathless. "Believe me. But my parents... I don't know where they are, and I can't leave them. And you can't make me."

He sighed heavily before he straightened. "No. No, I cannot. There are another thirteen or so boats left, Penelope. And they're being launched rather quickly. I implore you, if you can't find your parents in the next twenty minutes, give up." His eyes were solemn. "I assure you that your parents would not be happy about you dying for them."

Hearing those words—*dying for them*—caused Penelope to shiver. Her teeth chattered, and her arms wrapped subconsciously around her waist. It was the first physical sensation she had felt in what seemed like hours. She wasn't even certain how long had passed since that screeching had filled the silence of the night and the juddering from the ship striking the iceberg that had nearly knocked her and Ruby from their bed.

"I can promise that much," she agreed in a small voice.

Then, with a heavy sigh, Mr. Ismay nodded and beckoned her to leave.

Penelope took off without another thought, not wanting him to change his mind.

She had only taken two steps when she heard three loud bangs in quick succession. A scream tore its way from her throat, adding to the cacophony of others.

She whirled around on the spot, her eyes wide and darting frantically as she searched for the cause. She worried that something inside the ship had snapped due to the strain of being so far submerged.

As she followed the gazes of those around her, she found the source of the bangs.

One of the officers helping to load the lifeboats held a revolver above his head, pointing it towards the sky. Penelope could only assume that he had fired it.

Had he just wanted to get people to listen to him so that they wouldn't overwhelm the boats, or had he been aiming at someone?

She couldn't see anyone lying wounded, so perhaps it was the former.

As if this isn't hard enough, she thought, taking a deep breath to try and calm herself.

She scrubbed the back of her hand across her face, trying to ignore how utterly weary she felt. All she really wanted to do was lie down and sleep. She wanted her old bed, back in Scotland, with its thick blankets, and her hot water bottle to keep her warm in the cold winter nights. She wanted the comfort of her own trappings.

Steeling herself, Penelope released the breath she had been holding and continued her journey to A Deck. It felt silly, going down to an area reserved for First Class passengers, but she doubted that mattered much now. And her cries on the Boat Deck had gotten her nowhere, so she was willing to try anything.

As she rushed into the exclusive promenade, making her way down the Grand Staircase that she and Ruby had been so eager to see, she thought of her lover out in the boat.

She knew that she had been kept there—if she had managed to break free, she would be at Penelope's side right now. She hoped that she wasn't beating herself up too much. Penelope hadn't meant to hurt her; in fact, she had even planned to follow her into the boat.

But seeing the families say farewell had struck something inside her. She needed to find her own family before she could try to get to safety. She wouldn't be one of those people who saved themselves without a care for the ones she loved.

Penelope burst into the First Class smoking room, surprised to find it occupied by several men, all in white tie. None of them wore lifebelts. They lounged about in their chairs, cigars and cigarettes in their hands.

All their heads turned towards her when she entered, and she could see the concern on their faces. As they rose from their seats as was the custom, she wondered if they would try to persuade her onto a lifeboat.

"My lady, why aren't—"

Penelope burst out laughing, unable to help herself.

She knew she sounded close to hysterics, yet no matter how hard she tried, she couldn't control it. She shook her head. "I'm not a lady. I'm…" The laughter gave way to sobs, and she raised her trembling hand to her lips in an attempt to stifle them. "My mother and father. I don't know where they are. I can't leave them here. I can't, but I don't know where they are, and I need to find them before the last boat goes. But I've searched everywhere. And the only options left are that they're dead on one of the decks below or they're off on a lifeboat, and I don't know what's worse. Them being dead or them abandoning me without a care."

One of the men, a large fellow with a round face and gentle eyes, approached her. Penelope recognised him as the man who had been with the duke when she and Ruby had been looking for Ruby's father earlier. His Grace had called him Benjamin. He didn't seem to recognise Penelope, however; not that she could blame him. She was in such disarray that she probably looked like a completely different person.

He offered her his glass, which was full of a dark-brown liquid. She had no idea what it was, only that it must be alcoholic, so she took it from him, gulping it down in one go.

It burned her throat, adding to the pain from all her screaming and crying, but it reminded her that she was alive. Everything seemed to come alive for a brief moment, sensation returning to her body as the fire spread down her gullet to her stomach.

"There, there," the man soothed as he took the glass from

her and handed it off to another man. She looked around, briefly wondering what had become of the duke, but was distracted as the man said, "Now, I don't think your parents would take off without you. Granted, I don't know them, but no good parent would willingly leave whilst their daughter is still aboard. And if they would... Well, you'd be better off without them anyway, my girl."

He gave her a smile, one that Penelope wished to return, but her mind was still running wild. She hated the thought of her parents out in a lifeboat, not giving a damn about her. She knew this gentleman spoke the truth. If that was indeed the case, and they really had left her, she would never speak to them again.

Of course, that was assuming she'd *survive* to do so.

"If it is any consolation, however, this is no longer the deck for the richest of the rich—this is the deck for those who have...accepted their fate." His eyes became sad and solemn. "It may be worthwhile trying the promenade out by the stern, where the masts for the antennae and such are hung up. Your parents may be under the illusion that you got off safely and are content with that."

The second man appeared with the glass, refilled with the same brown liquid. He handed it to Benjamin, who pressed it into Penelope's grasp. He smiled. "For luck. And then you must go."

"Thank you," she replied, her voice no louder than a whisper. She raised the glass to her lips, chugging down the liquid, relishing the burn this time around as it glided down her throat and settled in the pit of her stomach.

The taste was more pleasant than the beer she had tried at the Third Class party, but she still preferred the wine she was allowed to drink at dinner to anything else.

Handing the glass back, Penelope reiterated her gratitude before leaving the room and setting off for the promenade.

Chapter Twenty-Five

This time, Penelope walked slowly across the deck towards the promenade instead of rushing and looking frantically around her.

She did so mostly because her energy was failing and her legs were threatening to collapse underneath her, but also because she was terrified of what she would—or rather *wouldn't*—find when she reached her destination.

In order to distract herself, Penelope focused only on her surroundings. She realised that the ship had straightened out as the front had lowered farther into the water. Whilst the deck felt as steep as the trek up to Arthur's Seat, Penelope no longer felt like she was on some bizarre attraction at a village fair.

When she stepped onto the exterior promenade deck, the first thing she saw was the mast, covered in the rigging and cables that the man in the smoking room had talked about. The White Star flag—the white star of its name displayed on a vivid red pennant—usually flew proudly there, but it was always lowered at sunset and tied away until the next morning. Which was where it sat now, resting at the bottom of the mast, never to be raised again.

She blinked up at it, feeling a strange fluttering in her stomach. The poor ship was going to go down without her flag flying.

Her gaze moved slightly to the left, finding the cables that led to the Boat Deck. She had seen them around her town enough to know that they were the antennae for the Marconi telegraph room. She wondered if they were still working, desperately trying to let other ships know that *Titanic* was doomed.

Penelope returned her gaze to the deck, staring numbly at the few people there. None of them seemed too concerned. Most were looking at the horizon, their grips tight on the railing as the ship's back rose from the water and the front continued to be pulled down.

Everyone had their backs to her, and Penelope had no energy left to be discreet or to make a lap of the small area. She took a deep breath and called out, "Mother? Father?"

Every head turned to face her. Her hands wound themselves tightly in the fabric of her skirt. It felt as though it was freezing rather than drying. She glanced at every face before they turned away from her, realising that they didn't know her.

Before she had fully examined them all, she heard her name.

She turned towards the source, and when she saw her mother and father, both of them dressed but without lifebelts, she choked back a sob and took off towards them.

She threw herself into their arms. She was thankful that they caught her, for she felt as though she could no longer hold herself upright. Their hands clawed at her back, pulling her closer, holding her so tightly she felt pain lance through her body.

Not that she cared. She relished the touch. It was yet another reminder that, despite how everything was going, she wasn't dead yet. And she still had enough strength and fight in her to get out of this.

She felt lips against the top of her head, pressing never-ending kisses to her hair, before she pulled back. Her face was drenched with tears, but the emotion was mirrored in her mother's and father's faces, their tears glistening in the light from the deck.

Her mother cupped her face. She wore leather gloves, and even though Penelope was certain they were icy to the touch, she couldn't feel them against her skin. She reached up, pressing her mother's hand more firmly against her cheek so she could *feel* it.

"My darling Penelope." Her mother sniffled as she wiped the tears that had fallen to her chin on the fur collar of her coat. "What are you doing here? You're supposed to be on a *boat*!"

"You're supposed to be *clever*, my girl," her father chimed in, pressing his hand against her face, over her own and her mother's. "Why aren't you on a boat?"

Penelope sniffed back her tears. "Why aren't you?" she demanded. She wanted to pull away from their touch, but no matter how angry she was at them, she knew she couldn't. She had longed for this moment since she'd realised the ship was going down.

"They were only letting women and children on the boats," her father replied easily, giving her a gentle smile.

"And I refuse to leave your father's side."

Penelope immediately thought of the elderly couple on the Boat Deck.

She had thought it sweet, the devotion they had shown to each other and their marriage vows. But now, as she was faced with losing her own parents, she felt only anger at their ridiculousness. "The ship is going down! The front is nearly *completely* submerged. This is life and death—you understand that, don't you? Chances are, if you go into that water, you are not coming out."

No matter how much she loved them or wanted their final moments to be soft, sweet, and gentle, Penelope couldn't stand their touch any longer. She pulled her head back, and all their hands landed limp at their sides.

A sad look washed over her mother's face, and she looked at her husband before returning her eyes to Penelope. She opened her mouth to speak, but Penelope didn't want to hear it.

"And what of me? Did you even *try* to look for me after you told me to do what the stewards said? Even though you had no intention of doing such a thing yourself? I saw Mr. Cameron, and he said that, when the stewards were waking everyone up and telling them to get to the Boat Deck, you refused to move." Penelope shook her head. It was easier this way. Easier to pick a fight than to realise that she was losing her mother and father. "Did you not even care enough to look for me? Do you really *resent me* so much that you were happy to die just *assuming* that I'd got into a lifeboat because I'm supposed to be *clever*?" Her chest was heaving by the time she'd finished speaking. Her hands were tightening into fists and then loosening, a constant movement that grounded her, even though her fingers were far too stiff to curl all the way into her palms.

Her parents stared at her for a long moment, their gazes darting between her and each other.

Her mother was the first to speak. Her voice was small as she asked, "Resent you?" She frowned, a thing so deep and full of concern that, if Penelope's blood had still been running in her veins as liquid rather than ice, it would have made her flush in embarrassment.

She was beginning to regret her words, but there was no way to take them back.

"Why on *earth* do you think we resent you?" her father questioned, reaching for her shoulder. He gripped it tightly, placing his hand so that he touched her rather than the lifebelt. "Penelope, we *love* you. When we realised the severity of the situation, we rushed to your room. It was empty, with no sign of you or Miss Cole. We know you're clever, and we just assumed that you had got into a lifeboat as soon as you were able. If we had expected you to stay to search for us, we never would have stopped searching for you."

Now it was Penelope's turn to be confused. Her gaze darted between her mother and father. In each of them, she could see herself.

She had her mother's eyes, brown irises with flecks of green, but she had her father's hair; dark chestnut brown, thick but fine. She was also there in the way her mother smiled and had dimples in her cheeks, and the way her father held himself tall and sure, despite the chaos and devastation around them.

"Why wouldn't you think I would search for you?"

Once more, her parents shared a look before her mother turned back to Penelope and said, with a voice laden with regret, "We know you didn't want to move. You fought us right up until the final week. You were determined to stay with your grandmother in Scotland." Her mother's shoulders slumped. "We worried if…perhaps you would blame us for this. And so you might just have left…"

Penelope had no words.

She hadn't known that her actions, her protests about moving, had weighed so heavily on their minds. Weighed so heavily that they had truly believed she would have *blamed* them for this. She wasn't even certain there was *anyone* to blame, except perhaps God.

Unable to think of something to say to help alleviate their worries, Penelope threw herself into their arms, wrapping both of them in her embrace. She buried her face between their shoulders, relieved when their arms circled around her back again.

"I'm so sorry," she whispered, because it was really the only thing she could think of. And when she started saying it, she couldn't seem to stop. Even when she felt her mother and father stroking her hair, trying to calm to her down, she couldn't stop.

I'm sorry.

For her mother and father, for doubting their love and making them doubt her own. And for not even realising how foolish she had been until it was too late.

I'm sorry.

For her grandmother back in Scotland, who would be told that not only had she lost her daughter, but her son-in-law and granddaughter as well. All at once. And what the grief would do to her.

I'm sorry.

Even for Caroline. She wasn't sure she would ever forgive the way she had treated her and for stealing away her sense of wonder, but Penelope still believed that, when the news reached her, back at home with her husband, she would still feel saddened. Deep down, Penelope knew that Caroline had loved her in her own way.

I'm sorry.

And for Millicent, Deborah, and Emma. Whom she hadn't spoken to in an appallingly long time because of Caroline, but whom she still adored. Who would have to hear the news and know that there would be no more joyful walks and mindless gossip shared between them.

I'm sorry.

And lastly, for Ruby. For leaving her behind without a second glance.

For making her believe that she would join her in that

boat. For betraying that squeeze of her hand that had said she'd be holding it again in five seconds. For making her drift off in cold, icy waters and watch as the ship went down, knowing that Penelope was still aboard. And that she could do nothing to help her.

I'm sorry for it all.

Her mother drew back and cupped her cheeks. Her heart-shaped face was drenched with tears. And her skin looked paler than usual, mottled red painting her nose and cheeks. "Dear, you have *nothing* to apologise for." Her thumbs brushed away Penelope's own tears. "Your father and I love you *so much*."

"But now you have to do something for us, Penelope," her father said as he gave her a smile. "One last promise to your parents before we depart."

Penelope choked back a sob as she nodded. "Of course. Anything."

"Live." It was a simple word. So simple that it took Penelope a minute before she fully understood what they were asking of her.

The second it sank in, her eyes widened. She started to shake her head, but her mother held it tight in her hands.

"My girl, we made peace because we believed you were safe. You are *so young*. You deserve to experience everything life has to offer—fall in love, become a mother, get married." Her mother's lips quirked when she noticed the way Penelope's lips turned down. "Or go to those colleges you spoke of. Get an education, be tied to no one. I just want you to *live* and be *happy*. For so long I've watched you hide inside yourself, afraid that people would turn away when they got to know you. And I am sorry that it took me until now to speak of it." There was a twinkle in her mother's eyes that added an extra layer to her words. She wasn't just talking about her personality being a little bit different from everyone else's.

Penelope's heart hammered out a rhythm against her

chest. At some point, her mother had noticed that she and Caroline had been something more than friends; that perhaps she and Ruby had been as well. And she hadn't once tried to talk her out of it or make her change who she was—she had just quietly let Penelope live her life.

And even though Penelope slightly resented the fact that all this time she had been hiding herself from her mother who had *known* all along, she was mostly just glad that, despite everything, her mother still loved her and accepted her.

She didn't know whether her father knew or would respond the same way, so she said nothing in reply to her mother, hoping that the thankfulness was as apparent in her eyes as the love and acceptance was in her mother's.

"My proudest achievement has been watching you turn into a clever, beautiful, strong-minded young woman, Penelope," her father began, after allowing the moment between mother and daughter. He didn't seem to realise the gravity those words held for Penelope as he continued without pause, "so I beg you not to throw that away. I beg of you: *live*."

It was painful. How difficult it was to get her mouth to work. Her throat was dry, and as raw as her emotions seemed to be.

Tears fell in an endless stream down her face as she blubbered in front of her mother and father, trying to put everything she was feeling into words.

"We know." Her mother moved forwards and pressed a fierce kiss to her forehead. Then she released Penelope and allowed her father to give her the same treatment.

They both stepped backwards, no longer touching. Then they looped their arms together and her father gave Penelope a watery smile. "Go, darling. Before time runs out."

"I love you both," was all she was able to get out before she turned and walked away, leaving her parents behind.

Chapter Twenty-Six

As Penelope stepped onto the Boat Deck, she was overwhelmed by the ship's position.

She had been so preoccupied with her mother and father that she hadn't really focused on the way the ship had started to tilt again, this time to the left side rather than the right.

But what blew her away more than anything was how submerged the front of the ship was.

The Bridge Deck had been one of her favourite places to go.

She had loved standing by that railing, watching the sea pass by and feeling the wind in her hair. Only yesterday, only a matter of hours ago, she had stood on that deck, now slowly disappearing into the water, and had leaned over the edge, trying to see if any whales were following the ship to help her mother prove a point to her father.

She had asked her father about the mechanism behind the anchors and the cranes. She had sat on the benches after a short walk around the perimeter, and she had enjoyed the deckchairs with Ruby on more than one occasion.

So many good memories had been made on this ship.

And now they were all tainted.

"Penelope!" a breathless voice called out before she could begin to move again.

Her promise to her parents still bounced around in her head, and she had no intention of letting them down. But God above, it was hard to find the will and strength to move when faced with the devastation before her.

"Penelope!"

This time Penelope looked up and finally saw who was calling her. Shame washed over her as she saw Mr. Frank Cameron rushing to her side. He stopped in front of her, eyes wide as he asked, "What are you doing here? I thought you were getting into the boat with Victoria and the others?"

She swallowed hard, wondering if he'd had to walk away after saying farewell to his daughter and wife for what was probably the last time, and so had missed Penelope running away like some lemming, desperate to throw herself off a cliff. "I... I had to find my parents. I couldn't leave without knowing what happened to them..."

"Did you find them?" he asked, his voice soft and full of concern. Her heart thudded in her chest. It was unfair that such a sweet man should be parted from his family. He didn't know her. He didn't need to be this kind or caring, and yet here he was.

She nodded, trying to hold back her emotions. He had enough to deal with without Penelope adding to his burden. "I did. They're... They didn't wish to take up space on the boats when..." She tried to force a smile, but it came out more as a grimace.

"That is...noble of them." He sighed and shook his head. "Forgive me."

"No, I understand completely. There's no need to apologise."

"I had rather hoped you would have been there with Ruby and Victoria. They both appear as if nothing concerns them, but it is more of an act than anyone knows. When things start to go wrong, their bravado disappears. I had felt relief knowing that you would have been there to comfort them. They will inevitably start to panic when they watch the ship go down, knowing that myself and their father are aboard." He pinched the bridge of his nose. "God above, I dread to think how they must feel right now."

Penelope's chest constricted, and she almost tore her lifebelt off, desperate to lose the pressure that it added around her, the extra bulk that made her feel like she was being held in an unwanted embrace.

Everything around her swayed, and her hand darted out to grip at the railing, using it to steady herself and stay upright.

"What did I do?" Her voice was a grating whisper to her ears as she turned to face the water. She bowed her head, unable to see the way the surface was fast approaching or look at the lifeboats that had launched, knowing that one of them had Ruby in it. "Oh *God*, what did I do? Why did I leave? My one shot at happiness—and I threw it away." She shook her head and squeezed her eyes shut.

She'd thrown it away for her parents. Her parents, who, in the end, had just wanted her to be safe and happy. As she would have been if she had got into that boat with Ruby.

Why hadn't she got into the boat?

She felt Frank's hand on her back. It was inappropriately low, but with the lifebelt on, she wouldn't have been able to feel his touch if he had placed it higher.

"I'm sure it's not too late." He stepped around her and reached for her hand, gently prising her fingers off the metal railing. "Come on. Let's see if we can find you a lifeboat. It's going to be okay, Penelope."

As they slowly turned, another familiar face appeared before them. "Miss Fletcher! You did a foolish thing, if I may say so," Mr. Cole said.

"Yes, Lewis, I don't think she needs to hear that now!" Frank hissed, giving her hand a squeeze.

Mr. Cole ducked his head, his shoulders reaching his ears as he sheepishly scratched the back of his neck. "Forgive me. I just meant…" He trailed off with a heavy sigh. "Never mind what I meant."

"We'll see you aboard a boat," Frank repeated, as Penelope continued to stare blankly ahead, still trying to get her breathing under control. She focused on the thudding of her heart, the beats reverberating in her ears.

She felt Mr. Cole take her other hand, and together they walked her like some poor, injured animal down the right side of the Boat Deck. Her eyes took in the cranes that held the lifeboats, noticing with growing panic that they were empty.

This was confirmed when they reached the one farthest away and the officer in charge announced, "All the lifeboats from the side have been launched. We're working on getting the collapsible ones erected now." His eyes flickered over Penelope. "Try the port side. I know they were still launching there the last time I heard."

With a solemn nod, the three of them took off. It was growing more and more difficult to keep their footing, especially now that they had to make their way to the side the ship was leaning towards. The tilt towards the front made it feel like climbing a hill with two left feet.

Penelope's grip on both Frank and Mr. Cole was tight, to the point she was certain she was spraining their fingers, but they didn't seem to care. Perhaps they, too, had lost all sensation in their limbs and were just going through the motions, appearing alive when they really felt like dead men walking.

They started from the edge closest to the front, stopping at each area where a lifeboat should have been, only to find it empty. When they glanced over the edge, they saw the boats either just reaching the water or too far down for Penelope to get to them.

When they reached the final one, at the back of the ship, Penelope could guess the words that came out of the officer's mouth before he even had a chance to speak.

"Sorry, miss, you just missed it." He smiled sadly at her. "We're going to launch the collapsible ones now. You're welcome to a spot on one of those."

Penelope felt her legs tremble, and she let Frank and Mr. Cole lead her over to a nearby bench. She buried her face in her hands, bending over as she tried to calm herself and keep her breathing even.

"I can't move," she declared when she felt the men trying to persuade her back to her feet. She lowered her hands and looked wearily up at them. "I know the boat on the other side will be ready first. But I...I don't have the energy to do another circuit. I cannot."

Frank and Mr. Cole shared a look before they slowly nodded their heads. "Then, I suppose we shall wait until the one on this side is ready," Mr. Cole said.

"It won't be long, I gather." Frank sat down beside Penelope as Mr. Cole continued to stand.

His eyes kept flickering to the nearby loading area. Penelope watched him curiously—he was always pacing, always turning this way and that.

"He can't keep still, can he?" Frank joked quietly, causing Penelope to offer him a vague smile. It was all she could muster. "He fought in the Boers. I think that's where it comes from, that feeling of always needing something to do. Feeling as if he has to be constantly on the lookout. It annoyed me to no end when I started courting Victoria..." At the mention of his wife, the smile on his lips froze, and his gaze grew distant. Penelope didn't want to disturb him, so she remained quiet, instead turning her attention back to Ruby's father.

Mr. Cole's thick brows were pulled into a frown. He kept his back straight and his arms clasped behind his back, looking more like he should be in a sitting room than on a sinking ship. Penelope once again wondered where the duke was—if he had been in the smoking room with Mr. Benjamin and they just hadn't noticed each other, or if he had retreated to his room.

She wanted to ask Mr. Cole but couldn't find the strength.

"Dear God," he whispered, his eyes growing wide.

"What is it?"

"They're loading one of the davits near the bow." He turned to Penelope and reached for her, hauling her to her feet. "We must get you there now before they start to lower it."

But as soon as he released Penelope's hand, she fell to the ground as pain shot through her legs. She landed with a thud, just catching herself with her hands and stopping her head from cracking against the hard wood of the deck.

"The water has reached the Promenade Deck. It'll only take them a couple of minutes to get the boat lowered into the water, and they'll start rowing as soon as they do. We must hurry," Mr. Cole said as he knelt beside Penelope, trying to ease her back to her feet.

"I can't."

"You can. Just stand, and Frank and I will carry you."

"I can't," she tried again.

Everything was aching.

She wished for before, when she had been so numb she couldn't even feel her own body.

Anything was better than feeling the pressure in her legs, the pain from the cold water she had waded through that had since dried in the cold air. The fabric of her clothes was still icy to the touch, doing nothing to lessen the sting.

It was as if she was made of the most delicate porcelain. She had been dropped, and now she was cracked into a million tiny pieces, and there was no way she'd be put back together in time to reach the lifeboat.

Strong hands gripped her under her arms and lifted her to her feet. She stumbled forwards and only stopped herself from falling by gripping the railing. She nearly went over headfirst, and her breath was knocked from her lungs as the hard, cold metal rammed into her stomach.

The ship juddered again, making Penelope realise what had happened.

The water was flooding the body faster and causing the ship to tilt farther, both sideways and front-wise.

Her hands ached as they gripped the railing as tightly as she could, turning to see where Frank and Mr. Cole were. They had managed to get their footing a couple of feet away from her right-hand side and were also leaning against the railing. Just as she'd begun to think that perhaps the sudden movements had settled, however, the ship lurched once more.

Penelope watched in horror as Mr. Cole lost his footing, his knees buckling and sending him towards the railing. He wasn't able to get a grip of the protective rail in time. He went careening over the railing and disappeared into the water.

Chapter Twenty-Seven

"Lewis!" Frank scrambled to the railing, leaning as far over as he could.

Penelope's gaze was stuck on the place where Mr. Cole had gone overboard, as if she expected him to crawl up at any moment, having caught himself in some bizarre miracle.

Yet the longer she stared, the more she realised that wasn't going to happen. No doubt the sudden shock of the cold water had stopped his already weak heart.

He's gone, her mind whispered as her gaze flicked over to Frank, who was sobbing over the railing, staring down at the vast sea.

Penelope knew she should try to help him search, to cling to that hope that he was still alive and they could save him, but she couldn't. *He's gone,* her mind whispered once again, and she felt her heart shatter into a million tiny pieces.

No matter how hard she tried to convince herself that she needed to go and help Frank, she could only grip the railing as tightly as possible and remain where she was. As still as a statue, refusing to share Mr. Cole's fate.

Frank continued to scream his father-in-law's name. He was begging Penelope to help, begging God for him to be okay.

Each prayer went unanswered.

As Penelope opened her mouth to try and coax Frank away from the railing, another thought entered her mind. One that asked her how she was supposed to tell Ruby that she had stood by and watched as her father had died, and that she had done nothing to help him.

How she had chosen, instead, just to stand and watch as Frank had broken down in front of her.

Bang. Bang.

The shots had the exact same effect on Penelope as the earlier ones. She let out a startled scream and her grip loosened, causing her to stumble a little, sending her sliding towards the submerged front of the ship.

Her gaze darted around the deck. She wanted to see what had happened this time, whether it had just been the same reason as before—yet she couldn't see any sort of commotion, leading her to believe that the altercation had occurred on the other side of the ship.

Just as her nerves started to settle, and she was preparing herself to turn and finally give some comfort to Frank, another loud bang filled the silence of the night.

This one was unlike anything she had ever heard before. It was much louder than a gunshot, and it seemed to shake the entire ship. She felt the vibrations beneath her feet and through the metal of the railing.

"The boilers," Frank said. "It's...the boilers exploding." He sounded so lost. So dejected.

All Penelope wanted to do was let him know how sorry she was; how awful it was that this was something he had to go through. As if saying farewell to his wife and child hadn't been hard enough, he had just watched his wife's father die.

In another life, in a different time, I could have been his sister-in-law. The thought rose unbidden in her mind. She tried to banish it, as it came with images of her and Ruby, happy and content, living together, married for all intents and purposes, even if the law and the rest of the world would never see it as such.

As she tried to expel those thoughts from her mind, a loud explosion tore another scream from her throat.

She gripped the railing as tightly as she possibly could, closing her eyes to steel herself for any further explosions so that she wouldn't startle and go flying down towards the water which had now fully covered the open area of the Bridge Deck. Only the large mast remained to remind her that, at one point, this had been a ship.

When the explosions seemed to stop, Penelope opened her eyes. She found herself in total darkness.

Without the boilers, there was nothing to give the ship power. Everything was dark.

The only illumination came from the countless stars in the sky above. Not even the moon was there to witness the devastation.

She watched as the water crept upwards. As the ship's incline started to increase. As the remaining passengers came rushing up towards the back of the ship, hoping to outrun the water. She watched as several people decided to take their chances with the sea, jumping overboard instead of going down with the ship.

Should I do that? she wondered briefly before her thoughts were captured by the chilling sound of metal grating and groaning. She had no idea what it meant, and as the passengers—God, there were *so many* of them—started to get closer and closer, she realised that she didn't want to find out.

"We need to move farther towards the back," she said to

Frank, who nodded numbly and turned.

The two moved away from the railing, using whatever they could touch to stabilise themselves as they made their way to the stairs that would take them off the Boat Deck. Thankfully, their position meant that they didn't have to walk far before they reached them.

Penelope's hands immediately latched onto the bannister and she refused to let go until they reached the Bridge Deck.

The stairs had taken them directly to the area where the last rooms gave way to open decking, making it easier for them to get outside and start the journey to the Poop Deck at the very back of the ship. The area was familiar to her, as it was where she had spent most of her time when not in her room with Ruby or down in the lower decks, helping her watch over the children.

Navigating the deck was going to be the hardest part, she knew, because of how steep the incline had become. It seemed that the back of the ship rose to an even more unbelievable angle with every step she took. She knew that should she misstep once or allow her grip on the railing to loosen, she would be a goner. And that was the last thing she wanted.

What she wanted was that image that her mind had painted. A life with Ruby.

Of course, such a thing coming true now was damn near impossible, but she wanted to at least *try*. She had already broken her promise to Ruby by leaving her side. She had, in a way, also broken her promise to her mother and father because they had wanted her to live, and how could she manage that now?

At the very least, though, she could fight.

So she kept her hands on the railing, even though the leather of her gloves caused her grip to slide; even though her arms ached and the ship kept trying to pull her into the water below. She kept pulling, one arm in front of the other, hauling herself along the deck until they reached the back.

Once she'd reached the very back of the Poop Deck, the groaning sound of metal came again, covering the passengers' screams as the boat continued to pull them and their loved ones into the water.

She saw the funnel closest to the back sway where it stood. Her eyes widened as her body began to tremble. There was no way that the funnel would break. It didn't seem possible.

Yet it did.

The large yellow and black funnel swayed and then fell backwards, thankfully in the direction of the front, away from Penelope. The crack as it snapped free from its foundation caused her ears to ring.

She knew that, should she survive, she'd never have the same hearing again, what with the funnels shrieking, the gunshots, the boilers exploding, and now the funnels collapsing. Everything was reverberating in her skull, a constant echo that spoke of lasting damage and constant hauntings.

As the funnel crashed into the sea, a huge wave rippled outwards, and Penelope watched as it sank, dragging the ship down farther as the extra weight from the funnel hit the front decks.

She saw those who had decided to risk the sea get sucked under with it, and she grimaced, turning her face away.

She shared a panicked look with Frank, who was to her left, as they noticed just how quickly the water was moving now.

It was no longer creeping towards them. Instead, it rushed. Every time she blinked, another section of the ship had disappeared below the waterline. And as it did, the incline grew steeper, until it was almost impossible for her to keep her footing.

Several people around her lost their grip and went sliding

down the deck. They collided with the walls that divided the external areas from the internal structure, or with the countless other objects that littered the area, such as the electric cranes or the benches or even the very funnels that were dragging them faster towards the water.

It took only a matter of seconds before the water reached the second funnel and the same groaning sound filled the air. Penelope clenched her jaw and tightened her hold on the railing, knowing that eventually, gravity would get the better of her.

"Penelope!" Another explosion came, but Penelope was able to ignore it as she turned and found Frank. He was no longer holding on beside her. Instead, he had pulled himself over the railing and lodged his feet between the metal bars. Rather than fight against gravity, he was making it work for him.

He reached out and gripped one of Penelope's hands. She took a deep breath as she pushed herself upwards, helping Frank as best as she could as she scrambled over the railing and took up a perch beside him.

"Clever," was all she was able to say, her hands once more gripping the metal. She knew that she was less likely to slip and fall this way, but she didn't want to take any chances.

She turned her attention back to the front. She saw that the second funnel had fallen, just as she had suspected. And just as before, the additional weight was now pressing down on the part of *Titanic* already underneath the water, speeding up the sinking process.

Before the water reached the third funnel, however, the sound of grating metal came back.

This time it was louder, resonating through the entire ship until it vibrated to where she and Frank stood. They had been joined by several others who had seen the logic in their position and seemed to feel the shuddering as well.

Tightening her hold, Penelope took a deep breath, knowing deep in her gut that the noise heralded something big. There was no way it was just the third funnel preparing to snap.

Her heart lodged in her throat. As did her stomach and lungs.

Everything was so utterly overwhelming.

She couldn't breathe, even though she was choking down so much air that she was probably filling her lungs past their capacity. Her stomach heaved, making her feel like she was going to vomit, although there was nothing in her stomach. And her muscles—every single one of them trembled and shook so much that it was a surprise that they hadn't given up yet.

The back of the ship continued to rise out of the water, an incline of nearly 90 degrees, and as she looked down past her feet, the sight of the ocean's surface far below made her vision sway. She could see the propellers that had powered the ship from Southampton to Cherbourg to Queenstown and then across the Atlantic, destined for America.

They were huge, utterly still, and so terrifyingly far above the water.

As she turned her gaze back to the front, the groaning and grinding of the metal reached a crescendo, and a huge bang filled the night. The entire ship juddered and jolted.

Penelope's grip tightened on the railing, and she no longer felt like they were sinking. There was no sure, steady decline into the water. Rather, it felt like something was pulling them down. As if the titans the ship had been named after had wrapped their hands around her and were drawing her deep into the depths of the ocean.

Cries filled the darkness, and it took Penelope a long time to notice that she was one of those screaming. No matter how hard she tried, she couldn't stop herself.

The ship was tugged unevenly underwater, at a greater speed than it had moved previously. The remaining two funnels collapsed, making it even more unstable than it already was. The back of the ship that she was clinging to for dear life started to twist, no longer smoothly entering the water, but spinning and turning as it rose out of the water until it stood nearly vertically.

Seeing it move like that made Penelope realise that the ship had split in two—maybe not all the way through, for the weight of the front half was still there, dragging them down—but for the most part, the mighty ship had broken down the centre.

Between the angle, the weight of the front half tugging the backside down, and the way the ship rotated, it was near impossible for most of those on the deck to keep their hold on the railing. Penelope watched as many of them went plummeting into the water, screaming as they went, until they disappeared under the surface as the suction dragged them down.

Others chose to jump instead. And then there were those like Frank and Penelope, who could only hold on for dear life, watching as they approached the water, having no way of stopping it.

"Take a breath!" a voice cried out. It was one unknown to Penelope, but her brain had the good sense to listen. She forced herself to stop screaming and drew in a huge lungful of air just in time. The ship disappeared into the water, taking her with it.

Chapter Twenty-Eight

Penelope believed that, since she'd grown up in Scotland, she knew what cold meant.

She was used to chilly breezes and icy rain. She spent her winters wearing twenty layers of wool and fur because the snow was several feet deep.

She had spent her lifetime wishing for somewhere warmer and drier. It was the one upside she'd been able to hold onto when she'd finally given in to the idea of moving to America.

But now, she realised, she had no idea of the meaning.

As soon as she entered the water, it was as if she had been stabbed by a thousand knives made of ice.

Sensation came rushing back to her body, but only to fill her with a burning pain. It seemed so odd to think of cold as burning, but that was what it was like. It felt like her skin was being sliced from her body and she was powerless to do anything to stop it.

Her entire body was submerged, and, for a split second, she seized up and refused to let go of the railing. It was only when her lungs started to ache, demanding air, that her brain took over and her body relaxed.

The ship disappeared into the darkness of the night and Penelope kicked her legs as hard as she could. She could only hope and pray that she was heading in the right direction, because she couldn't really tell the difference between up and down. Every direction was pitch black, and none seemed to promise safety.

Just as she was about to give up hope, she broke the surface and her reflexes took over, shovelling down lungfuls of air as she continued to tread the water. She was suddenly thankful for that summer when she had sneaked away to the nearby loch with Millicent, Deborah, and Emma. It had been a warm, sunny day, and they had spent the entire afternoon frolicking in the water. Millicent had taught her how to swim, and Deborah had shown off holding her breath under water. Emma had stayed on the shore, refusing to get her hair wet.

It was one of the happiest memories of her three friends, but the main achievement of the outing was that, at the end of it, she had learnt how to remain afloat. Which was all that mattered to her now.

As soon as her brain was certain that she was able to breathe, everything else came crashing in around her. And the first thing she noticed were the screams.

They came from every angle, varying in pitch as men, women, and children all let loose the most bloodcurdling screams they were capable of. Some were wordless cries, whilst others were pleas for help. Some even called out to God, begging for His aid.

Penelope fell into the first category. Her screams just seemed to be an automatic reaction to everything she had gone through. The knowledge that the ship was going down, the sinking itself, and now dealing with the freezing water cutting through her skin and seeping into her bones.

No matter how many times she told herself to just *stop*

screaming, she couldn't.

The pain continued to spread until it started to disappear entirely. It began with her feet and her legs, so that even as she continued to kick them in a desperate attempt to keep herself floating, she couldn't actually *feel* them move. Her throat was utterly raw, as if someone was ramming a red-hot poker down it and still expecting her to speak.

It occurred to her a moment later that she didn't actually have to keep paddling, as her lifebelt was designed to keep her afloat. Still, there was a voice whispering in her ear, telling her that keeping moving was the best thing she could do.

The voice came to her again, and it sounded so much like her father's that she looked around, almost expecting to find him at her side. Instead, she was greeted only by strangers. It was then that she realised that Frank was nowhere to be found.

Her gaze swept frantically left and right around her. She tried to cry out his name, desperate to draw his attention, but she couldn't. All she could do was scream, adding to the crescendo around her.

She choked on a sob as she surveyed the area and saw so many bodies in the water, most of them just bobbing idly, thanks to their lifebelts. Some of them clutched at furniture, some to wood that had broken from the ship, anything to keep them afloat. And it was the sight of them that kept her screaming—so many were face-up, showing glassy eyes and frozen faces.

She had never seen a dead body before—had been too young to attend the wake of her grandparents—but now, countless bodies drifted by her, searing their faces into her mind, never to be forgotten.

And yet none of them were the man she was looking for, for which she was just a little bit thankful. She had already lost her parents, had watched Mr. Cole fall to his death, and had pushed Ruby away onto a lifeboat which, no doubt, still floated several hundred feet away.

She couldn't lose Frank as well.

She couldn't be the reason Victoria had lost both her father and her husband.

And until she saw his body, there was still the chance of him being alive.

Get out of the water, her father's voice said, urgent and desperate, cutting through her worry as she tried to call for Frank.

Penelope looked around again. One last attempt to find Frank, to bring him to safety as well. She could barely see what was in front of her, and she found it almost impossible to believe that the ship had once sat there, proudly.

What had Ruby and her father said? She weighed forty-six thousand tons—and now she was just...gone. The ocean had claimed her, and all that was left were the screaming passengers who had once sailed on her and some random pieces of furniture.

And all because of an iceberg?

She almost wanted to laugh at how utterly ironic it sounded. Such a huge, mighty ship, named after the titans of Greek mythology—and it had been taken down, utterly destroyed, by a piece of ice?

Before the hysteria could start to sink in, her father's voice whispered in her mind once more. *Penelope. Get out of the water.*

No matter how hard she looked, she couldn't find Frank.

"I'm...sorry..." she whispered as she finally focused on her father's words. She needed to find something she could pull herself onto so that she would no longer be bathed in ice. She considered clinging to one of the deckchairs, but all the ones nearby were already be used by other passengers. And she couldn't see anything else large enough to hold her.

Motion caught her attention from the corners of her eyes, and she saw several people move towards something in the distance. Her eyes narrowed, desperately trying to see what they were aiming for...and her heart leapt when she finally noticed it.

A lifeboat.

She blinked. One, twice, twenty times, rubbing the saltwater from her eyes to ensure that she wasn't seeing things.

But no. That was most definitely a lifeboat. It didn't appear to be the right way up, but that didn't matter. It was something she could climb onto to get out of the water.

She focused on swimming. It was a lot stranger with the lifebelt on, as though she was competing against it. It impeded the motion of her arms, and being unable to feel her legs meant that she just had to trust that they were still there and still working.

She moved slowly through the water, past people who screamed at her and cried out to God for help. Penelope wanted to assist; she wanted to be able to find *some way* of helping the hundreds, if not thousands of people in the water.

But she couldn't think of anything. The lifeboat wouldn't hold them all. She could only focus on her father's voice in her head and the promise she had made to him and her mother.

Suddenly she jolted to a halt, unable to move no matter how hard she tried.

Letting out a startled scream, Penelope turned. She saw a figure in the darkness, a hand wrapped around her ankle, holding her still. As she pushed herself closer to the man, demanding that he release her, she realised she *knew* him.

"Mr. Wright?" she asked, no longer struggling but continuing to tread water. At the sound of his name, he released her ankle, allowing Penelope to turn and fully face him. He was utterly drenched, his blond hair and moustache slicked to his face. His blue eyes were glassy, staring but not seeing.

"My Betsy," he choked out, in between shivers and convulsions. "Betsy…"

Penelope recalled the redheaded beauty he had danced with at the parties. They had plans to get married as soon as they landed in New York—her entire face had lit up whenever she spoke of the life they would have when they reached American soil.

Now it was all gone.

"No, it's Penelope. Penelope Fletcher, remember?" That party seemed like a whole lifetime ago.

"Betsy," he called out again, and rather than fight it, Penelope went along with it. She swallowed hard, her eyes darting back over to the lifeboat she had been swimming towards. Several men had already reached it, and she knew she had to keep going because there wouldn't be an infinite amount of space aboard.

"Come on, we need to go…"

At the loch with her friends, they had swum together. It was how Millicent had taught her to swim, acting as if they were one person with two arms and four legs. Now she tried to manoeuvre herself and Mr. Wright into a similar position. Only he was much larger than Millicent in every sense; taller, heavier, wider… The second she slung his arm around her, she felt like she was being dragged beneath the water.

She closed her eyes for a beat. "Albert. Albert, I need you to…swim. We need to make…over there." Talking was proving more and more difficult, so she gave up and tried just swimming again, hoping that her words had got through.

She made it only a couple of strokes, however, before his weight started to feel overbearing. It was slowing her down and pulling her under, countering her lifebelt.

She drew to a halt, looking around herself, hoping

someone could come and help—that the lifeboats that had been launched at the beginning would make their way back to them. To no avail.

"Betsy…" Albert Wright called out again, his voice sounding softer, weaker. "'M sorry, Betsy. Love…you…"

Penelope wasn't certain if tears fell; she had no sensation in her face to be sure. But her heart stuttered and stammered at his words. She gave him a shake. "No. Albert. Stay—" Her words lodged in her throat, unable to break free.

Once more she tried to move them forwards, but when her chin struggled to stay above the water, she knew what had to be done. She sobbed, turning to face Albert, finding his face pale and his eyes shut. His chest remained still, and she felt her voice once more join the heart-wrenching sounds that filled the air.

I'm sorry, she thought to herself, brushing fingertips over his face for just a moment before disentangling herself from him. Penelope almost wished he didn't have his lifebelt on as he remained afloat, face down in the water, drifting away from her in the soft ripples.

She couldn't allow herself another moment to think. She knew that if she did, the guilt would claw at her until it consumed her. And she needed to survive. She had promises to keep.

The sounds were overwhelming as she continued her journey towards the lifeboat. The most painful of emotions all rolled into one endless plea. Anger, fear, agony, utter despair—she could name every dark emotion being wrenched from the lips of those in the water with her.

She knew that the lifeboats would come back. All the women in the boats would want to rush back to find their loved ones, now that they no longer ran the risk of being pulled under with the ship.

It was that which allowed her to keep swimming.

Until she passed another dead body. Her screaming started again as she drew to an abrupt halt. She stared at the man, at his pale skin and the dread that was frozen on his face.

His face morphed between those she knew—Frank, Mr. Cole, Albert, Father...all of them in an endless cycle as she bobbed in the water.

And even when the body started to drift away from her, she kept screaming, remained frozen.

I can't do this.

Her chest heaved and her heart thudded an erratic, uneven beat against her ribs.

Get out of the water. Her father's voice came back to her, more urgent this time. It wasn't just a coaxing encouragement, but a demand. He was ordering her to keep moving, to keep swimming towards that lifeboat.

It was a tone he had used a lot before—one that held no room for negotiation. One that Penelope had always obeyed.

Maybe she would die anyway. Maybe the cold would get to her and stop her heart, but she would die knowing that she had *tried*. She had to try.

And she did.

Just as she was ready to believe that it would be too much, that her body would give out and her heart would stop just ten yards or so from the boat, she heard someone call out, "There's a young girl there!"

It was enough to renew her, to give her body one last push to close the distance, where the men already aboard helped her onto the boat.

Coming out of the water, being greeted with the cold chill of the air, made her feel even colder, and for just a second, she missed the water. But then she looked around and saw the forty or so men who were already there, still alive, and knew that she now had a *chance*.

"Women were supposed...lifeboats! How were... missed?" one questioned, his words jumbled from the shock and cold, even as he guided her towards one side of the boat. She had a brief moment to take him in, to notice his square jaw, large nose and thin lips. She clung to the body of the lifeboat, refusing to slip back into the water even as the convulsions that racked her body threatened to do so.

"P-parents," she answered shortly, wrapping her arms around her waist to try and protect her organs. As long as her chest remained warm enough to keep her heart pumping, she knew she had a chance of making it through this.

He frowned at her, no doubt wondering just what she meant, but he said nothing more. His eyes were kind, faintly framed with what Penelope's grandmother had called joy lines.

He wore an officer's coat, but she didn't know enough to be able to tell what his position was. She almost turned to ask Ruby, until she remembered that Ruby wasn't there... She was safe in one of the lifeboats, and Penelope was thankful for that. She wouldn't want Ruby to experience any of this.

As she sat on the upturned body of the lifeboat, watching as a few more men approached and were helped up beside her and the others, all Penelope could focus on was the pain.

Her entire body ached in a way she had never known possible. Her bones seemed to be made out of ice, and every time she moved—even to shuffle a little—it was as if she was breaking them. She couldn't feel her feet, or her hands, or even her face. The only thing she was acutely aware of was her heartbeat.

That was the one thing she focused on, over the screams and the cries for help, the pleas for the lifeboats to come back.

Every thud meant she was still alive.

And at that moment, that was all that mattered.

Chapter Twenty-Nine

Penelope had never been good at keeping track of time.

Often, five minutes could seem like five hours, and a whole night could pass in the blink of an eye. But she *knew* that it didn't take long for the screams to dwindle.

One by one, they turned into shouts, into moans, into silence. Until Penelope was almost certain that the quiet was even worse.

She knew that the cries would always stay with her.

She would forever close her eyes, should she survive, and she would hear them.

She knew, from talking to one of the men who had helped load the other lifeboats, that they weren't all filled to capacity. Nearly all of the twenty lifeboats floating out there would each have been able to bring a good forty or so people aboard—he even said that one had left with only twelve people aboard when it could have held forty.

Now, with the silence, and still trapped on the upturned lifeboat with around fifty other people, Penelope knew that no one had thought to return and save the lives of those who hadn't been lucky enough to enter a lifeboat.

Every person who had entered the water, who had started that haunting crescendo, was now dead. Floating in the water. And their loved ones sat close enough to help but were unwilling to do anything about it.

She thought of Ruby. Had she tried to convince people to come and search for Penelope and her family? Or had she resigned herself to the idea that no one would have survived the sinking?

She couldn't make her gaze move away from her knees. She had brought them up to her chest and wrapped her arms around them not long after being brought aboard the lifeboat and realised she wouldn't be moving any time soon.

She didn't want to see the faces of dead strangers drifting nearby—of husbands and fathers who would never make it back to their families. She didn't want to see the faces of those she knew—to see Mother and Father, Frank and Mr. Cole.

She didn't want to see that kind gentleman in the smoking room who had helped her find her parents. Or Mr. Ismay, who had told her to get to a boat because her parents wouldn't want her to die. She didn't want to see Isidor and his wife. Or even the eccentric Duke who would never see his many animals again.

So she kept her gaze locked on her knees and concentrated on the thudding of her heart.

Those on the boat around her remained quiet.

She had no idea how long she sat there in utter silence, lost in her thoughts, memories cropping up just when she didn't want them to. She remembered the look on Ruby's face as she'd realised Penelope wasn't getting into the boat.

She remembered her parents' surprise at her still being aboard and promising them that she would live.

She remembered the days before, when her greatest worry had been sneaking into First Class and not getting caught.

It seemed so small. So utterly insignificant now.

It was even more ridiculous that she had thought that was fear.

The girl she had been before knew nothing of cold, knew nothing of fear.

"What was that?" someone asked, causing Penelope to blink herself back into the present.

The man in front, the one who had brought her aboard, said, "The lifeboat's losing air underneath." A beat passed before he added, "It's sinking."

Penelope cringed at that word, feeling utterly helpless as she finally raised her head to look at him. Her eyes automatically darted out to the sea, wincing as she saw the bodies lifelessly bobbing alongside them.

Panic gripped her throat as she realised that, should the lifeboat also sink, there'd be no way for them to survive. She'd end up dead, just like all those bodies out there. And she refused to let that happen.

"Is there…" It was so difficult to make her mouth work. She had screamed and then been quiet for so long. "…anything we can do, sir?"

A small, gentle smile appeared on his lips, highlighting the joy lines that surrounded his kind eyes. "Second Officer Charles Lightoller, at your service, miss."

"Penelope Fletcher." It was so strange to be making such formal introductions. She shook her head. "You…didn't answer my question."

"The ocean will get up soon." He paused for a moment, swallowing with difficulty. "The tide will cause the air underneath to be lost."

"So what do we do?" another man questioned.

"We need to…keep her even," Lightoller announced as the lifeboat moved a little in the swell that was starting to build around them. "She's losing air… If we keep her steady…" His sentences were incomplete, but Penelope was just glad that an actual sailor was with them, helping them through this.

"How?" one of the men asked.

"We need…stand…two lines…keep her stable."

Penelope nodded and shuffled as Lightoller started to organise the men with short, curt orders, showing them where and when to stand.

As the men around her started to rise, however, she realised that he wasn't addressing her. He was actively choosing to ignore her. "Lightoller," she called out, her voice soft due to the pain in her lungs. He didn't hear, so she drew a deep breath in and tried again, this time with a sharp, "Charles!"

He stopped and turned to Penelope.

"Where…want me?"

He shook his head. His own legs trembled, Penelope could see that much from where she sat, but from the way he held himself, no one would have been able to tell. "Young woman, such as yourself…" He shook his head again and started to return to give further orders to the other men, but Penelope gritted her teeth.

Slowly, surely, she pushed herself to her feet, thankful that her frozen limbs didn't lock up and send her over the edge into the water. She pushed her shoulders back as far as they would go and fixed her stare on Charles Lightoller again. "Where. D'you. Want me?"

Lightoller sighed and pointed to a spot to the right. Penelope hesitantly stepped over to it and turned back to him, watching as he demonstrated how to bend their knees and shift their weight, following the waves so that they remained stable.

She gritted her teeth, determined to concentrate and copy his movements perfectly.

She had made it this far. She wasn't going to stop fighting now.

Chapter Thirty

The tears had long since frozen on Penelope's face.

Even if she had seen someone she knew among the lifeless bodies surrounding them, she couldn't have summoned the energy to cry for them.

The lifebelts on the dead ensured that they remained afloat. Those without had drifted to the bottom of the ocean, but it was still a sea of corpses as far as the eye could see. The only thing that was more overbearing than the dead bodies was the debris—so much broken and splintered wood floated alongside them, along with deckchairs and personal belongings that hadn't yet sunk.

It was utter carnage.

As if that wasn't bad enough, the strength of the men with her on the lifeboat had started to dwindle.

For some, the effort of being upright and having to focus on their movements proved too much. Their hearts gave out, and without warning, they would just collapse into the water.

That would rock the boat, sometimes sending others back into the sea. There was nothing they could do. The shock of a second plunge was just too much for their bodies to handle.

She hated that voice in her head that told her that fewer bodies meant there was less weight pushing on the boat, which meant that it now had a greater chance of remaining afloat. She tried to banish the thought, but every time one of them fell into the water and never made it back out, it would creep back in.

Still, the boat slowly sank. Like Charles Lightoller had said it would.

First, the water brushed over their feet.

Though Penelope didn't really feel that. She couldn't feel her feet at all. If she hadn't still been standing, she'd be concerned her legs were no longer attached to them. And she dreaded to think of the damage she'd have to deal with if—*when*—they were rescued.

"Do you think...they'll come back?" someone asked, and he didn't need to clarify who he meant. The lifeboats. Penelope had initially believed that they would—how could they not? So many of them had loved ones who were in the water; surely they would want to come and help as soon as possible?

But now that the screams had stopped and the only thing most people would need were coffins, she couldn't stop herself from scoffing. "No," she hissed out, uncaring if she had killed everyone's hopes.

She felt their gazes land on her for a second, but before she could snap at them, another man piped up. He had worked in the Marconi telegraph room, sending messages right up until Captain Smith had allowed him to abandon his station, and even after that. He rattled off a long list of the ships that had heard *Titanic's* distress call and had agreed to come to help. He was adamant that it wouldn't be long before they were rescued, even if their own lifeboats refused to come to their aid.

"Just keep an eye on that horizon, Penelope," he said. He was a young man, no older than herself. He had introduced himself simply as Jack. His eyes were steady, sure, even as his lip trembled.

Penelope clung to that hope, even as the boat sunk farther and the water reached the top of her boots and started to fill them. The ice-cold water brought back a hint of sensation in her toes, which made her smile for just a second before it disappeared.

As the boat continued to sink farther, it meant that there was less surface for them to stand on. Every time they had to shuffle upwards, another man would lose his footing and go tumbling into the water.

And every time Penelope whispered a prayer and remained focused on the roll of the boat beneath her feet, desperate not to follow him.

"Tell me their names again, Jack," Penelope whispered into the cold air, just in an attempt to stay awake—stay alive.

His voice was a little weak as he replied, "*Carpathia. Frankfurt. Olympic. Cali—*" A particularly strong wave came, cutting Jack off as he started to give the name of the fourth ship that he had been able to contact before the ship had gone down.

Penelope braced herself, loosening her knees so she could follow the rise and fall of the boat and stop herself from falling into the water.

"Jack!" another voice called, and Penelope turned as Jack started to lose his balance. His arms flailed about, trying to keep him upright. He knocked the shoulder of the man to his left, and Penelope watched in horror as they both slid from the lifeboat.

"Brace!" Lightoller snapped, reminding them to keep steady or they'd risk losing more people. Penelope's breath was lodged in her throat as she stared at the darkness, wishing that the two would rise from the water.

It was becoming too familiar a feeling—watching someone descend into the water, praying that they would resurface and feeling the heart-wrenching grief when they didn't.

A sob broke free from her lips. She scrubbed both of her hands into her eyes, relishing the pain that it brought. It was another reminder she was alive.

She remained that way, refusing to look up at anyone else, lest they befall a similar fate. Every time she got close to someone on this damned ship, she was doomed to watch them leave. The lifeboat had started with fifty, a number that had dwindled down to just over thirty. And just as the fifteen or so men who had fallen in had proven, if they entered the water, they weren't coming back out.

On more than one occasion, she even considered jumping in, just to end it on her terms.

"Is there anyone out there?" someone shouted.

Penelope looked up, and her breath left her in a ragged gasp as everyone turned to see who was calling out to them. The movement caused the boat to shuffle.

"Stay still! For the love of *God*!" Lightoller snapped as he fished about his person. He drew a whistle from his pocket and, after taking a deep, shaky breath, he blew into it, filling the night with a screech.

A torch beam flew their way, and Lightoller raised his hands above his head, waving his arms to gather their attention.

"It's a lifeboat." There was nothing but disbelief in the man's voice.

It seemed ironic that, just as Penelope had dashed everyone's hopes of a lifeboat ever coming for them, one showed up.

The boat had a sail, which confused Penelope to no end.

She had no idea that the lifeboats were even capable of such a thing.

But regardless, she was thankful for the man who had made use of it. It pulled up aside their capsized boat in no time at all, thanks to its oars and the small breeze that was filling the early morning air.

"Is that you, Charles?" The torch cast him in an eerie light, but Penelope could see he had a long face, very thin lips and, much like Charles, he, too, wore an officer's overcoat. His tone fluctuated in the manner distinctive to a Welshman.

Lightoller laughed. "Thank God for you, Harold." He then turned back to the crowd, shooting them all a glare as the men started to shuffle forwards, eager to get into the new lifeboat. "Ladies first."

He held out his hand to Penelope who, after only a split second of disbelief that this was *actually* happening, placed her own in his. Her legs wobbled and threatened to collapse, and she could barely feel her hand as it was passed from Charles to the man he had called Harold.

"You're safe now, miss," Harold whispered as he placed an arm around her waist and lifted her into the lifeboat. His features seemed almost stern, yet his eyes sparkled, and his lips spoke of kindness.

She wanted to weep at those words, but she found that nothing would come. She allowed Harold to guide her into a seat beside some other men. She had no idea whether they had chosen to come to help retrieve survivors or if they had been in the water themselves.

All she was aware of was a blanket being draped over her shoulders before she felt her energy start to ebb.

"Check her pulse!" was the last thing she heard before she closed her eyes.

Chapter Thirty-One

Penelope was acutely aware of a hand on her wrist, fingers pushing against the underside with a steady pressure.

She blinked and raised her head from where it was slumped against her chest.

"You gave us a fright, miss," Charles Lightoller's voice seeped into her mind.

As she fully opened her eyes and took in her surroundings, she found herself still aboard the new lifeboat. Several men were rowing, pushing them gently through the field of corpses and away from the wreck site.

Which meant she couldn't have been out for long.

"Sorry." She pinched at the bridge of her nose as she straightened herself. "I…have no idea…"

"Probably just shock."

Penelope offered him a smile, knowing that he probably spoke the truth.

She was just glad that she was awake. And that she was in a lifeboat that wasn't sinking, with two officers who knew what they were doing.

After that, it turned into a waiting game.

When someone finally pointed out the lights on the horizon, Penelope felt as though her heart was going to burst with relief, even though it seemed to take the ship forever before it got anywhere close enough to them.

The rising of the sun brought a new and unwelcome clarity to the scene.

The sight of the bodies in the water at night had been bad, but it was nothing compared to the full view in daylight. Amongst them floated huge blocks of ice, and it amazed Penelope that anyone had survived the night partially submerged in such cold water. And littered across the surface was wreckage from *Titanic* herself, large chunks of wood making up most of the carnage.

Their lifeboats bobbed through all of this as the ship steered closer. Lightoller called up to the sailors on board, informing them that his passengers were in no state to climb up and would need aid.

Her name was *Carpathia*, if Penelope was able to make out her nameplate correctly. Her colouring was similar to *Titanic*'s—a black body, a red waterline, the same faint trim of white around the deck area. She only had one small funnel that was red and black, but four large masts spaced in a similar fashion to *Titanic*'s masts.

Penelope wanted to take in everything she could about the ship, because it was her *survival*. If it weren't for the ship before her, she'd be dead, regardless of the fact that she was now in an upright lifeboat. If *Carpathia* hadn't shown up when she did, the cold would have stopped Penelope's heart before much longer.

A sling was lowered down the side of the ship, and, once more, Lightoller insisted that Penelope go first. She was happy about that, even if it seemed wrong. But she couldn't help it as she settled into the fabric and began the slow haul up the side of the ship and over onto the deck.

She immediately froze, however, as she straightened and saw the large number of people who were milling around the deck.

"Miss, we need to get the others up," one of *Carpathia*'s sailors said.

Penelope nodded numbly and stepped away from the edge, pulling the blanket she wore tighter around her frame. It had long since gotten wet as it had soaked up the water from her body and clothes and was now stiff to the touch, thanks to the cold air.

Penelope stumbled forwards towards the crowds that had already gathered, somehow knowing just by the amount of people that hers had been the last boat to be picked up.

It almost made her want to laugh, to think that she had been left until the very last moment. Just as she had been on *Titanic* until its very last moments.

As she moved forwards, someone approached her and asked her name. He was wearing a jacket with an unfamiliar logo embroidered into the breast, so Penelope could only assume he was from *Carpathia*.

"Penelope Fletcher."

"And which class were you sailing with?"

She swallowed. "Second. Room E-56." He started to scan the piece of paper that he held, so she said, "My parents didn't make it. They won't be…" She felt horrible for saying such a thing, but she couldn't cling to any hope that they had survived. How could she, remembering all those bodies they had had to row through, and the men who had fallen from their shared lifeboat to their deaths? One look at all the wreckage had made Penelope certain that, hard as it was to admit, her parents were gone.

He shrugged, giving her an apologetic look. "I am sorry for your loss. There is a physician in the Second Class dining room who will be able to look you over."

Nodding, Penelope offered him a smile, praying that he'd leave without another word, and feeling thankful when he did. All she wanted was to sleep, to rest without the fear that she would die if she did.

At the reminder of her parents, however, her heart felt heavy, and without realising, she reached up to grab her grandmother's locket.

Only for her fingers to touch skin.

Frowning down at her chest, Penelope saw no sign of the delicate chain around her neck, nor of the beautiful silver locket, engraved and set with sapphire stones. Her heart picked up in pace, thudding against her chest, and her hand flew to her throat, hoping to be greeted by the sensation of linked metal.

But it wasn't there.

It was the final straw, taking that last glimmer of hope away from her. Penelope buried her face in her hands, feeling the tears flow and flow, unable to staunch them. She had felt the pain when she had seen her and Ruby's room engulfed by water and known that her sewing kit and her thread-painting of Poppy were gone.

But she had always had her grandmother's locket with her, holding a piece of Scotland inside.

And now it was gone, surely lost to the bottom of the ocean.

Along with everything else she knew and loved.

When the tears finally stopped, Penelope removed her hands from her face.

Wiping her tears on the back of her hand, Penelope straightened herself to the best of her abilities and followed the crowds that were heading down to the lower decks. The new ship was much smaller, which made it easier for her to find her way, joining the steady stream of people towards the

Second Class dining room, which had been turned over to the survivors hauled from the water.

Every time the ship gave a shudder, something that she had easily become accustomed to on *Titanic* before the sinking, her heart leapt to her throat, stressed that something else had gone wrong. She couldn't get the thought out of her mind that some other tragedy would befall her.

She stared numbly ahead as the physician gave her a once-over, warning her that she would need to get to a hospital as soon as they docked in New York, because of her toes. Penelope was pretty certain she could have worked that out for herself, since several were an alarming shade of blue-purple.

After that, a bowl of hot soup was handed to her. She ate one spoonful of it and then felt as though she would bring it back up if she ate any more. She pushed it away, giving it to a young mother who was feeding her two children with one bowl.

Everything after that passed in a blur. She could do no more than focus on her hands cradled in her lap, occasionally watching as people moved around her. All her hope had long since died—claimed by the depths, just like her locket.

She couldn't hope that those who had gone into the water with her—Frank, Mr. Cole, her mother and father—had survived. Not after losing some of those who had been on the lifeboat with her, like Jack, and Mr. Wright as well.

And whilst she knew that there was a good chance of Ruby being aboard, she was certain that she would want nothing to do with Penelope.

Not after how she had left.

So she sat there, staring down at her hands, listening to the screams that haunted her, made afresh by people realising that loved ones hadn't made it off the ship—that they had boarded *Titanic* with loving families and now were widows and orphans. It didn't help that the one action she usually performed to ground and comfort herself—tug at her locket—was gone. Her neck felt dreadfully bare and too light, which made her entire body feel off.

It was overwhelming. So, when the opportunity came to sleep, she no longer fought it.

Instead, Penelope lowered herself to the floor, a blanket draped around her and many other bodies beside her, and allowed herself to succumb.

Chapter Thirty-Two

She didn't have a peaceful sleep.

All she saw were the ghostly figures of those she had known—Mother, Father, Frank, and Mr. Cole. Of those who had helped her when she had been stuck on board *Titanic* and the final lifeboat had left. Even Mr. Wright came back to haunt her.

They stared at her with accusing eyes, saying not a word. Instead, every time their mouths opened, seawater dripped from them and started to fill the room she was locked in. She tried to claw the door open, but it wouldn't budge. And the water just continued to rise until she couldn't breathe and it forced its way down her lungs.

Penelope awoke with a start, heart thudding against her ribs. She wasn't surprised that the people around her weren't sleeping peacefully either. Several of them twitched and groaned, some of them lay still, as if dead, whilst other were still awake, not even willing to risk it.

It felt like no time had passed at all, even though she knew she *had* slept. And when she pushed herself upwards into a sitting position to look around, she noticed that there were still people milling about, completely awake and recounting the experience.

She frowned and turned away from them.

She didn't want to think about it. And she didn't want to talk to anyone.

All she wanted to do was try and get some more sleep before the medicine the doctor had given her wore off and she felt the pain of her body starting to thaw. She reached for her locket and sighed when her fingers were greeted only with skin.

Just as she closed her eyes, however, she heard it.

"Penelope!" The sound was the sweetest thing Penelope had ever heard. It was enough to drown out the screams that seemed to haunt her whenever she let her mind drift for too long. It banished them like some holy light.

She blinked blearily up from the place where she lay, craning her head over her shoulder as she followed the source of the voice. She felt her lips spread into a smile as she was greeted by what she could only assume was an angel, even though her eyes were red-rimmed and puffy and her hair was in utter disarray, knotted and standing in every direction. Ruby looked a little pale, her red-rimmed eyes framed by dark shadows and a flush mottling her cheeks and reddening the tip of her nose.

But she was still the most beautiful sight Penelope had ever seen.

"Oh, thank the Lord!" Penelope whispered, the words breaking through her lips like a prayer.

It seemed almost too good to be true. Not just because Ruby was several feet away from her, surrounded by Victoria's, Liam's, and Julia's sleeping forms, but because it meant she was *alive* and she was seeking Penelope out. Just being able to look at her, to take in the golden hair and blue eyes and that relieved smile that spoke of nothing but joy.

Before Penelope could say a word, to begin to apologise or explain, Ruby extracted herself from her family and stepped across the other bodies sleeping between them. She threw herself onto her knees by Penelope's side and wrapped her arms around her shoulders in a fierce embrace.

An involuntary gasp of pain broke from Penelope's lips. She felt Ruby begin to pull away, so she weakly raised her arm and returned the embrace.

Ruby buried her face in the crook of Penelope's neck, allowing her to feel the wet drops of tears against her skin. She could also feel her own tears falling over her face and onto Ruby's shoulder. Ruby was in her arms. Willingly in her arms, the thud of her heartbeat a reminder that they were both alive. And for some bizarre reason...Ruby was *holding* her. She wasn't screaming or clawing at her face for leaving her.

"Don't ever do that again, do you hear me?" Ruby warned, her voice low and barely above a whisper. Her grip tightened a little, and this time, Penelope was able to swallow her gasp of pain. "I swear to *God*, Penelope Fletcher, if you ever try to do anything like that to me ever again, I will personally hunt you down just so I can strangle you with my bare hands."

Ruby pulled away and cupped Penelope's face in her hands. Her smile was watery, her tears a never-ending stream down her face, but she was still as beautiful and dazzling as the first time she'd laid eyes on her. Penelope's hands trembled and *ached*, but cradling Ruby's face in her own hands was still the sweetest sensation.

All Penelope wanted to do in that moment was kiss her. She wanted to kiss her until both of them were breathless and had put everything behind them, until they no longer felt as though a dark cloud had covered them and would never move again.

"I promise."

Ruby snorted. "I've heard that before."

Penelope smiled weakly at her. "Well, I shall just have to spend the rest of my life getting you to trust in my promises again." Her eyes lowered to her lap, and she only raised them when she heard Ruby's breath catch in her throat.

She half expected to see horror and rejection, but instead she was greeted with that smile she loved so much growing wider and more tears falling from her blue eyes.

Ruby's thumbs brushed along Penelope's cheekbones, drying the tears there, before one briefly flitted over her lower lip. She then leaned in and embraced her once more, whispering in her ear, "I wish I could kiss you right now."

It made Penelope smile that she wasn't the only one who wanted to reclaim this moment of horror with something beautiful. But they couldn't do that, no matter how much they wished they could.

"Just hold me," Penelope whispered as she turned towards her. She felt Ruby shuffle a little until she, too, was lying down. She had squeezed herself into the small gap between Penelope and another survivor, who was thankfully sound asleep.

Ruby lay on her back and opened her arms, allowing Penelope to roll forwards, resting her head on Ruby's shoulder before shifting lower until it rested on her chest. She then wrapped her arm around Ruby's waist, fingers gripping at the fabric so hard that she was pretty certain her hold made it through to skin.

"Just hold me like you never want to let go," Penelope said. She felt tears sting her eyes, but she forced them to stay at bay. She didn't want to ruin this wonderful moment by crying over their lost ones. That would be for later.

Right now, all she wanted was to celebrate that they were both still alive.

That they were together.

"I never want to let go." Ruby pushed herself that little bit closer. Penelope felt her lips against her forehead, so she returned the kiss by pressing one to Ruby's collarbone. It was risky, but, with the way her head was buried against Ruby's chest, no one would have even seen it.

"Neither do I." Penelope's eyes fell shut as it grew more difficult to stay awake, but she had enough energy left to say, "I'm so glad I made it back to you."

She heard Ruby gently shush her as her hand started to rub soothing circles on her waist.

It was the thud of Ruby's heart beating a rhythm in perfect sync with her own that brought the realisation to Penelope's mind. *I'm alive.*

She'd fulfilled her promise to her mother and father. She'd survived. And now she was able to live. She was going to take however long she got with Ruby, to see how far they could go. She was going to relish every moment and *live.*

"I'm glad you survived, Penelope," Ruby whispered into her hair. "All those hours on that lifeboat, watching the ship go down, all I could do was pray for you. And I am so thankful that God answered my prayers."

Penelope frowned. Just a little line between her brows was all she could manage as she asked, "What of your father?" She hadn't wanted to mention him, in fear that Ruby would start to ask questions that Penelope knew she wouldn't be able to answer yet. One day, when they were both ready, they would talk about *Titanic*'s final moments and what they had meant for the men in Ruby's life.

"Daddy sacrificed himself for me. It was difficult. I'll never forget him. But we said our goodbyes. You... You just took off without a word, and I had no idea what had happened to you." Another press of lips against her forehead. "So I spent every second praying that you'd make it through the wreck; that you'd find what you were looking for and return to me. I feel like we're fated to be together, Penelope." The combing of Ruby's fingers through her hair was lulling her further to sleep, so much so that Penelope was surprised she was still able to hear what Ruby was saying to her in soft, whispered tones.

Ruby paused for a long moment, then asked in a whisper so soft it could have been blown away by a breath, "*Did* you find what you were looking for?"

Penelope swallowed thickly, allowing the constant thump of Ruby's heart to soothe her. Tears welled in her eyes, but she refused to let them fall. "I did. They... They thought I blamed them, for making me go on the ship when I didn't want to move, and then for the crash. They thought I was on a lifeboat, and they were content to die together believing I was safe." She turned her face into Ruby's chest, drying the tears as they broke free, her willpower no longer strong enough to keep them from falling. "We said our goodbyes, cleared the air, and they made me promise that I would *live*. And when I vowed to do so, all I could see was you and the life we could have together."

Ruby remained silent. Her hand didn't stop in its constant brushing of Penelope's hair. Her breath hitched beneath Penelope's head, and Penelope knew that Ruby was holding back tears of her own. "I'm glad you found them, Penelope. And I'm sorry it didn't go as you planned. But I am also so glad that you're alive; that you made that promise. I'm glad you're here in my arms. I'm glad you've promised to never leave again." Her arms tightened around Penelope's waist. "And I'm glad you want me to hold you."

Penelope wanted to say something. She wanted to mirror those sentiments, to let her know that, through it all, Ruby had been her source of hope.

But Ruby's fingers were stroking her scalp, and her

touch was so soft as it rubbed gentle circles on her waist. Her warmth was so overwhelming that Penelope couldn't fight it.

So she didn't bother trying.

She drew a breath and allowed herself to finally surrender to sleep. Despite the trauma they had endured, she was alive.

Ruby was alive.

And that was all that mattered.

Epilogue

Penelope curled her body closer towards the fire.

She shuffled forwards so that her toes grazed the grating that protected the burning coal, until her hands could reach out and caress the flames should she wish. They were, however, occupied with the small hoop that she was working on. The piece that she was only ever able to work on in the wee hours of the morning, after the nightmares had woken her up.

Her back ached. She had no idea how long she had sat there working on her embroidery with her Golden Retriever, Kaidan, resting his head on her thigh.

A soft hand curled around her shoulder, yet Penelope didn't flinch. There was only one person it could be, and Penelope could never be startled by her.

"Bad dream?" Ruby whispered as her other hand came to rest on Penelope's other shoulder. Kaidan's tail beat a steady rhythm at her voice. Ruby's hands slid down Penelope's arms as she came to crouch behind her.

Penelope took Ruby's hands in her own, entwining their fingers and pulling her further around her body so that she was wrapped up fully in Ruby's embrace. "Is there any other kind?" Penelope whispered, continuing to stare at the fire.

Ruby gave a thoughtful *hmm*. "Well, there's that dream we had of returning to Scotland and buying a little cottage. That was a good dream."

That dream had sprung up not long after they had arrived in New York ten years ago. They had stayed with Ruby's family as the inquests were held. They had refused to be parted—and had both been adamant about returning to Britain, even if that meant boarding another ship.

A smile finally tugged at Penelope's lips as she turned her gaze to the side, finding her lover's head resting on her shoulder.

She didn't look much different from the way she had ten years ago; she still had the plumpest lips, the brightest of eyes, and the prettiest of faces... Of course, they were adorned with a few faint lines, but those were memories—reminders that they were alive.

"*Was* being the key word there, my dear, since we made it come true." Penelope turned her gaze back towards the fire and gave Ruby's hand a solid squeeze. "It is no longer a dream but a reality."

It hadn't been a simple process, not just because of the trauma, but because of Ruby's family, who'd tried to put up a fight against their leaving. But after having lost so much, both Penelope and Ruby had realised that life was too short not to live it the way they wished.

So they had stayed in New York long enough for the inquest, and then had returned to Scotland and lived with Penelope's grandmother until the compensation money had allowed them to buy a cottage of their own.

And they'd been there ever since.

The softest, most fleeting of sighs escaped Ruby's lips—so quiet Penelope was certain she wasn't meant to have heard it, and so she said nothing, watching as the flames continued to dance.

She wiggled her toes, pleased that she was able to do so. She took care not to look at them—it was still too painful to see the reminders on her body. Especially after the nightmares. She tried so hard to pretend that she was all right, and that wasn't so easy when she looked down and saw the gap instead of the three toes she'd lost due to her time in the water.

Kaidan shuffled and she lowered her hand to stroke through his fur. He was always good at knowing when her thoughts led her down dark paths. He had been Ruby's idea—somehow, she had known that having his companionship would help both of them.

"Do you want to talk about it?" Ruby eventually asked, pulling one hand free from Penelope's so that she could brush it through the strands of hair that had fallen loose from her braid. She gently pushed them back behind her ear, then wound her arm around Penelope's chest. "In all these years, you never have…not to me. I know you have talked to Victoria. Not that I blame you if you don't want to tell me…" She stopped talking when Penelope gave her hands another gentle squeeze.

The nightmares had started not long after they had been rescued, and they had continued to haunt her throughout the years. Sometimes she was lucky, and months passed without one. Other times, it was continuous, every night ending the same way.

And when it came close to the anniversary…there was never any stopping them.

Yet, despite it all, she had suffered in silence, never

wanting to worry Ruby with *dreams*.

She had lived it as well—what had Penelope seen that Ruby hadn't? The fact that Ruby didn't have nightmares didn't mean she felt it any less.

Penelope sighed and let her head fall back against Ruby's shoulder. She felt her shuffle a little, and her legs ended up framing Penelope's hips. She had never felt as safe as she did then.

It was at that moment she realised that Ruby wore her navy embroidered shawl. It had fallen from her shoulders and pooled in the crooks of her arms, allowing Penelope to reach out and trace the delicate floral embroidery that she herself had done. It had taken a long time and a lot of secret conversations with Victoria in order to recreate it, but she had managed to do so to the best of her ability.

Perhaps it wasn't the same as the shawl that Ruby had lost ten years ago, and nothing would ever replace the memories that had come with that one, but Penelope had wanted to give Ruby *something* that would remind her of her family, something that wasn't tainted by so much darkness.

And judging from the way her lover never seemed to take the shawl off, it had worked rather well.

With a sigh, Penelope started to speak. "I only spoke to Victoria because she asked. And after everything, it didn't seem right to deny her that." Penelope took a deep breath as her eyes flickered towards the ceiling, illuminated only by the orange of the fire. She almost wanted to close her eyes, but she was worried that would make the memories *too* vivid. "The nightmares are always the same. I'm on the deck and *Titanic* is sinking, the funnels are falling, and I'm holding on to the railing, but I'm not strong enough and so I fall into the water. And everything is cold and dark. I hear everyone screaming until they can't anymore."

Ruby began to rub soothing circles on the backs of her

hands with her thumbs. Penelope focused on that sensation, watching the movement, as well as on the softness of Kaidan's fur against her leg.

"I see people swimming towards a lifeboat that hasn't been properly launched, and they pull me aboard. We all sit, shivering, praying, sobbing...hoping that all those other lifeboats will come and pull the rest from the water, since there's no more space in our boat for them. But no one comes." Penelope saw Ruby frown from the corner of her eye.

Ruby raised her head and turned towards Penelope, pressing a soft kiss to her cheek. "But they did come. I'm holding you in my arms, my love, so someone definitely picked you up."

Giving a soft shrug of her shoulder, Penelope huffed. "I can't explain it. It always gets twisted at the end. We watch as *Carpathia* arrives, as she starts to pull everyone else to safety, but they don't seem to know we're here. The men start to row, paddling with their hands, desperate to get to the ship. But I can't move...still too cold, too frozen, too sore, too numb. And they notice this and tell me that, if I'm not helping, there's no point in keeping me. And so they throw me overboard.

"I'm back in the water. Surrounded by so many dead bodies, all of them floating thanks to their lifebelts. I see my mother and father. I try to swim after the boat, but it's going too fast and I'm still too tired. And then I feel something grabbing at me—and I turn, and it's Mr. Wright, do you remember him? He was the one who invited us to the party. I met him in the water, asking after his fiancée... He died in my arms. It's always him who grabs my ankle, just like he did that night, and he pulls me under, down, down, telling me about this great party on *Titanic*..." Drawing a shuddering breath in, Penelope reached up and swiped at the tears that had spilled over. Ruby's hold around her tightened almost painfully, but it was a pain she relished.

It was a pain that reminded her that it was just a *dream*, that she had made it away from the wreck alive, and that she still had plenty left to live for.

Kaidan whined and licked her fingers.

"My love…" Ruby sighed, one hand rising to start smoothing her hair.

"That's always when I wake up. And I'm always so *cold*, as if I'm back in the ocean and nothing will ever warm me up."

Ruby's lips quirked up at the corners in that grin that Penelope loved so much. "I suppose that explains why I always find you at the fire, burning through all our coal as if our money is limitless."

A laugh was startled from Penelope's lips, easing just a little bit of the tension that the nightmare had caused her. She noticed that the fire was starting to dwindle, so she grabbed the poker, reaching through the gaps in the grating to stoke it.

Between their combined compensation from White Star, and the inheritance Granny had left Penelope, the two of them had been able to live rather comfortably. Whenever they needed a little extra, Penelope would create needlework to sell, and Ruby would sell jams and cakes at the weekly market.

Ruby pressed a kiss to Penelope's bare shoulder, uncovered due to the thin straps of her nightgown and the fallen sleeve of her dressing gown. It was the thicker one that she normally kept tucked away for the cooler winter months, but she had dug it out to help ease the feeling that she was back in those icy waters.

"It still haunts me too," Ruby whispered after a minute had passed, her lips still pressed against Penelope's skin. "Every little sound I hear, I fear that it's something going terribly wrong and we just don't know. And my nightmares…"

Penelope's head shot up, her brows raised in surprise. "You never told me you got nightmares."

The light from the fire danced over Ruby's soft face, casting shadows that made it look more sunken. She sighed and lifted her head. "They're not like yours. You know I didn't go through the sinking like that. You made sure that I didn't." Ruby's eyes narrowed a little. "That's what my dream is. I see you shove me away, and I'm held down in the boat, prevented from climbing back out to you, and I wait, in that tiny dinghy, wondering what's become of you. And when *Carpathia* arrives, you're not aboard. No one saw you, or even knew who you were... It was like I had conjured you up from thin air. And I always wake up just as I'm screaming for you, begging for you, before you get to answer me..." A sob lodged in Ruby's throat.

Penelope turned in Ruby's embrace so that she was on her knees in front of her lover, her wife, and she reached up with hands that still felt too cold to cup her face.

Tears trailed down over Ruby's soft cheeks in a steady stream, and Penelope brushed them away, first with her fingers, then with her lips.

Ruby launched herself into Penelope's arms, her grip like iron, bundling the fabric of Penelope's dressing gown in her fists to haul her closer and closer. Her tears continued to fall against Penelope's skin, causing chills that Penelope shoved away, focusing only on the woman in her arms.

Her fingers entangled in Ruby's blonde hair, letting the texture of the strands ground her as she rubbed them between her fingertips.

"I knew there was a chance I wouldn't find my parents in time, that there wouldn't be a lifeboat waiting for me, and I refused to let you go down with me..." Penelope felt her own tears begin to fall and dried them in Ruby's soft curls. "But that doesn't make it right...pushing you away as I did..."

Penelope lifted her head and moved her hands to Ruby's shoulders to gently coax her away.

Once again, she dried Ruby's tears with her fingers and then cupped her face. Her heart ached as she stared at her, wondering how something so good and pure could have come out of something so awful.

Their feelings had been so young, so fleeting, back when they met on *Titanic*, so brief that Penelope had felt certain they would be forgotten the second they docked in New York... and yet the wreck had ensured that they were bonded in a way that they couldn't break. And between Ruby's extended family thinking they knew best and society's demands on them to be married off to men, to suffer in silence, that bond had been tested and strengthened tenfold.

"I came back though, didn't I?" Penelope said. Ruby nodded at her question. "I will always come back to you, my love. As long as such a decision is in my power—and even if it isn't, I'll try my hardest to outmanoeuvre God Himself."

Her words brought a smile to Ruby's lips. She looked at her for a moment more before surging forwards and sealing her lips over Penelope's. Penelope gasped in surprise, and Ruby slid her tongue into her mouth as her fingers curled further around Penelope's dressing gown.

Penelope returned the kiss, eagerly pawing at Ruby's head, her fingers combing through the long strands of hair and tugging her closer.

They were both breathless when they parted. Penelope felt like she was on fire, every inch of her burning from the passion that Ruby ignited in her. She sometimes wondered why she ever bothered slipping from bed to come to the fire whenever she had had a nightmare—Ruby had the ability to send her blood pumping with the merest of looks.

"Come back to bed," Ruby whispered, resting her forehead against Penelope's, whose eyes drifted shut. "And know that I'm always going to be here for you—I'm never going to turn you away after your dreams have tried to claw at you."

With a gentle nod, Ruby stood and aided Penelope into a standing position. And then, hand in hand, with Kaidan leading the way, they moved from the fireplace back to the comfort of their bed.

Acknowledgments

This is another book where the first acknowledgment needs to be for my wonderful editor, Jen. Mostly because this book wouldn't exist if it hadn't been for them bursting into my messages with the simple request of "u + gay romance set on the titanic". From that one message, we got here. And I can't wait for more.

To my family: Mum & Dad, Gran & Papa, Greg & Jenna, Jack & Tammy. I know you'll never read this, but it still wouldn't be possible without your support, so at the very least, you get to open the book, flip to the end, and say "Hey, that's me". And because I can't forget the pets even though the only thing they think books are for is to chew, I love you: Smudge, Izzy, Clyde, Ollie, and Rico.

My niblings: Emily, Jack, and Rosie. You're my everything. One day you'll get to look at this page and know just how much I owe to your existence. But for now, I'll keep telling you I love you every chance I get.

For my best friend, my rock, my person, my platonic soulmate, Tiana. Stumbling upon your fanfic and leaving a review for it was quite possibly the best thing I ever did. I miss you, I adore you, and I wish nothing but the best for you.

Kristina and Amber. I never thought I would meet two people who I would understand and know so well. Especially at a crappy college writing course. Here's to all those night outs, and the many more to come (when we're able and not suffering from all the work we do).

To all the friends I've made through the book community, know that I adore you and I wouldn't have made it this far without your support.

And to you, the very person who made it all the way to the end of the book to read these acknowledgments. I am so happy you picked up my book and chose to support me. I hope you enjoyed Penelope and Ruby's story—thank you for taking a chance on me and my little sapphic heart.

About the Author

Charlotte Anne Hamilton is a blue-haired mermaid-wannabe who lives in Ayrshire, Scotland with her two fur-children, Izzy (chocolate lab) and Smudge (queen cat). She is currently studying Astronomy and Planetary Science and in her spare time she enjoys reading and gaming, as well as dabbling in all forms of art and her craft as an eclectic witch. Her main source of inspiration in writing and in life is the popular phrase: "but make it gay".

Also by Charlotte Anne Hamilton...

OF TRUST AND HEART

Discover more New Adult titles from Entangled Embrace…

AN UNEXPECTED KIND OF LOVE
a novel by Hayden Stone

Bookstore owner Aubrey Barnes likes his quiet London life exactly how it is, thank you very much. His orderly world is thrown into chaos when a film company leases his shop and he crashes into distractingly hot American actor Blake Sinclair. And keeps crashing into him. Aubrey isn't cut out for the high-profile life of dating a celebrity, especially one who's not out yet. Good thing their tryst is absolutely not going anywhere…

MOST ARDENTLY
a novel by Susan Mesler-Evans

From the moment they meet, Elisa and Darcy are at each other's throats—which is a bit unfortunate, since Darcy's best friend is dating Elisa's sister. It quickly becomes clear that fate intends to throw the two of them together, whether they like it or not. As hers and Darcy's lives become more and more entwined, Elisa's once-dull world quickly spirals into chaos in this story of pride, prejudice, and finding love with the people you least expect.

FULL MEASURES
a Flight & Glory novel by Rebecca Yarros

She knew. That's why Mom hadn't opened the door. She knew Dad was dead. Twenty years as an army brat and Ember Howard knew, too. Her dad would never be coming home. Then Josh Walker enters her life. Hockey star, her new next-door neighbor…and endowed with the most delicious hands that have a way of erasing her pain with a single touch. But just when Ember lets him in, Josh's secret shatters their world. And she must decide if he's worth the risk that comes with loving a man who could strip her world bare.

Printed in Great Britain
by Amazon